Butterfly 3

Butterfly

3

ASHLEY ANTOINETTE

ST. MARTIN'S
GRIFFIN

First published in the United States by St. Martin's Griffin, an imprint of St. Martin's Publishing Group

www.stmartins.com

Designed by Omar Chapa

Library of Congress Cataloging-in-Publication Data

Names: Ashley Antoinette, 1985– author.
Title: Butterfly 3 / Ashley Antoinette.
Identifiers: LCCN 2020028397 | ISBN 9781250136404 (trade paperback) | ISBN 9781250136411 (ebook)
Classification: LCC PS3601.S543 B885 2020 | DDC 813/.6—dc23
LC record available at https://lccn.loc.gov/2020028397

Our books may be purchased in bulk for promotional, educational, or business use. Please contact your local bookseller or the Macmillan Corporate and Premium Sales Department at 1-800-221-7945, extension 5442, or by email at MacmillanSpecialMarkets@macmillan.com.

First Edition: 2020

10 9 8 7 6 5 4 3 2 1

To Ash Army. Wow. What a ride we've been on. It's been two years since we submerged ourselves in Ethicland. Thank you for loving these characters to life. Without you, this journey would simply be fiction, but because of your connection to these pages, you have added a pulse to the ink. To the Morgans out there, follow your heart. It will never lead you astray, even if you encounter bumps along the way.

-xoxo-

Ashley Antoinette

For the official playlist, join the Ashley & JaQuavis Reading Club on Facebook!

Butterfly 3

1

"I don't give a fuck who in that bitch. Air that mu'fucka out."

Isa leaned against the grille of his BMW as he looked at the house in front of him. He gripped the black 9 mm in his hand, resting it at his side as he looked at the gang of shooters who trailed him. Eight motorcycles lined the block, and the sound of engines roaring filled the air as a custom Slingshot came speeding down the street. It pulled recklessly in front of Isa's car.

"Lil' Henny, my nigga, I ain't hit yo' line," Isa said.

"You know I ain't missing no action. When it's time to put in work, I punch that clock, big homie," Hendrix said.

"You got the heater on you?" Isa asked.

"Come on now," Hendrix answered, lifting his shirt slightly, revealing he was strapped.

Hendrix was bred by the best. He had been running product and packs for the Crew since he was a little boy, but Isa was his big homie. Isa had groomed him. Isa had made him a killer. He may have been the youngest on the team, but he wasn't last place. Hendrix had more heart than grown men . . . more respect than most too.

Isa had no idea who had taken Aria. All he knew was when he had returned, his home revealed a struggle, and the cameras showed she had been snatched. Niggas were about to bleed. Even when he got her back, the city would still run red because now he felt like killing shit. They should have never flipped his switch.

He folded his arms and leaned against the driver's side of his car.

"How you know she in there?" Henny asked.

"I don't," Isa answered. "I'm getting at every nigga that I got a problem with. Spray that bitch."

Rat-tat-tat-tat-tat-tat-tat-tat-tat-tat!

The house in front of him was obliterated. So many bullets rattled off the aluminum siding of the house. The AK-47 one of Isa's hitters used dropped shells against the concrete, playing keys in A minor like a pianist. Isa was unmoved by the screams in the air. He didn't care that it was the middle of the day and that witnesses were everywhere. Niggas knew enough to know nothing whenever the Crew came through to handle business. He had no idea who was inside the house. Probably a couple of kids. Probably somebody's mother. Somebody's girlfriend or wife. Fuck them all. Aria was missing, and every victim that came as a result of that was necessary.

Isa pulled a blunt from the pocket of his blue-and-black button-down shirt as the gunfire drummed in the air. He lit it and then pinched it between two fingers, sitting on the hood of his car before lifting a hand in the air. The signal stopped the gunmen instantly.

"Yo! Isa! Man! We don't want no problems!"

The voice came from inside the bullet-riddled house. He

recognized it. Dario Morrow. An east-side nigga who had been talking reckless against the Crew. The beef between Isa and the Hispanic gang ran long. He wasn't sure if they were behind Aria's disappearance, but he didn't need to be. Everybody was liable, everybody would be held responsible until she was returned to him, and if a hair was out of place, God help them all.

Isa motioned for the man beside him and took the AK-47 from his hands. He positioned the blunt between his lips, folding his lips down over it to hold it in place as he used both hands to hoist up the gun.

"Isa! We got kids in here—"

Isa lifted the AK and sprayed anyway. He walked up the lawn toward the front door, firing without regret or regard.

He spit so many rounds the screen door came off the hinges as he walked inside. He found Dario cowering over a young boy.

"Fuck is this about, man? Fuck you want?" Dario screamed, laying his entire body over his son as Isa bent down.

"Where's my bitch?" Isa asked.

Isa put the gun to the kid's head. The boy couldn't have been a day older than ten.

"Please, man! *Es mijo!*" Dario shouted.

"You gon' bury your motherfucking *mijo* if you don't start talking," Isa said. "Where's my bitch?"

"I don't know nothing about your girl being snatched, man. That wasn't my call! Word is it was out-of-town plates, man! Nobody's making moves on Crew territory, man! It wasn't me."

"What kind of plates?" Isa asked, changing his aim from son to father. Dario seemed to find some relief in that.

"D.C. plates. It wasn't nobody from the city. That's all I know. I swear on my kid," Dario pleaded.

Isa heard the sniveling kid and nodded to Dario.

"Getcho ass up," he ordered. "I heard you been flexing, steady with my name in your mouth, talking real big. Let's see if you 'bout that shit you been spitting. Cuz me? I'll blow yo' fucking head off in front of your kid, no problems." He tapped the barrel of the gun against the tip of the man's nose condescendingly.

Isa was the type of monster that terrified grown men.

"It wasn't like that, man. Just corner shit, just jokes, man! I don't got no issues, man. Please, man. Please, Isa!" Dario begged.

"Get up, man," Isa stated. He was in a foul mood. "I believe you. Let's go for a ride so you can tell me what you know about these D.C. plates."

Dario stood and pressed his son to his body, covering his ears as the young boy clenched his eyes closed. "Go down the street to Pepe's, *mijo*. Stay there until I get back," he instructed. "I love you. Go now. Run, *mijo*."

The little boy ran full speed up the block as Isa tapped his chest lightheartedly. "Relax, man, let's ride. Ayo', Snoop, let me take your whip," Isa ordered to one of his henchmen. The six-foot killer handed over the keys, and as he did, Isa stepped in close. "Turn the lights out on the kid," he whispered. Isa didn't leave loose ends. That same little boy would grow up with hate in his heart one day, and Isa eliminated all possibilities of a threat, both large and small.

It was the price for being the seed of a bitch-ass nigga who couldn't reinforce the threats he made, and the result of Aria's disappearance. Until he found her, nobody was safe.

"Isa, man, please," Dario pleaded.

"Nigga, I said quit fucking groveling. You're good. I just need information. Spin the block with me for a minute."

Dario reluctantly entered the car, and Isa climbed behind the wheel, then pulled off.

"We ain't never been stingy with these blocks. Always gave a fair price and let every nigga occupy they own, you know?" Isa asked as he hit the blunt that still burned between his fingertips. He passed it to Dario, who shook his head.

"Y'all been fair, man. Y'all been more than fair," Dario admitted.

"So why the uprising? Why the talk of takeovers and shit?" Isa asked. "See, talk like that is dangerous. When shit happens, when shit goes wrong, I immediately think it's you behind it. You been talking greasy, my bitch go missing, and you see what happens? I think it's you. Ya' mouth done wrote a big check, homie. Better hope that bitch cash."

"I swear to God, man, some nigga from D.C. made that move. I don't want no problems. It was just me acting hard in front of my boys, man, talking shit," Dario explained. "You know how it goes."

"Yeah," Isa scoffed. "Just kicking the shit. I know how that go." He was calm, and Dario seemed to breathe a sigh of relief. Isa's mind was spinning as he thought of the out-of-town plates Dario spoke of.

It's her fucking brother, Isa thought. *Got to be.*

Isa had looked Nahvid up after their first encounter. He knew Nahvid had to be the only nigga crazy enough to test him, because Dario was shaking in his boots.

"I just want to be square with you. We're good, right?" Dario asked.

"Yeah, nigga, we good." Isa pointed out the window. "Aye, you see that house over there?"

Dario's eyes followed the direction of Isa's finger. "Yeah, I see—"

Bang!

As soon as Dario's eyes turned away, Isa pulled the trigger.

"For talking shit, nigga," Isa sneered. He reached across Dario's body to open the passenger door, and he pushed him out, leaving him in the middle of the empty street.

He didn't care that Dario wasn't behind it. He didn't take threats lightly, and nobody was given a pass when it came to his respect.

"Fuck, man!" he shouted in frustration. He needed his girl back, and he needed her back soon or his ill temper was going to leave more bodies in his wake.

"Where are you taking me?" Aria shouted as the man pushed her through the empty warehouse. She resisted the entire way, refusing to walk, but she was overpowered. "Stop fucking touching me!"

Aria's head throbbed. She could barely see straight she had hit her head so hard.

"Nobody's going to hurt you. Just keep walking, please. Damn," one of the men said in exasperation.

Aria's feet stopped when the men opened a door that led down into the basement.

"I'm not going down there. I'm not, no," she said, dragging her feet and attempting to turn around, fighting against the huge men who kept her trapped.

"Yo, this bitch is difficult," the other man said.

"Yo' mama's a bitch," Aria spat.

The chuckle that came from one of her captors threw her off, and before she could protest, he was picking her up and carrying her over his shoulder as he descended the steps.

"Put me the fuck down!" she screamed.

The man did as he was told, and when she turned to view the room, she saw red.

"Nahvid!" she screamed. Her brother sat behind a desk, calm and collected, like nothing at all was wrong.

"What the fuck happened to her head, yo?" he asked.

"She fucking slipped, man. She's gave us hell trying to get her here," one of the men protested.

"You sent these niggas to my boyfriend's house to snatch me?" Aria shouted. "Nah!"

"You weren't supposed to get hurt. Just brought to me. To show you that nigga ain't capable of keeping you safe," Nahvid answered, standing before rounding his desk to look at the damage that was done to her sweet face.

Aria pulled away from him.

"Didn't I fucking tell you not to hurt her?" Nahvid asked. His gun was drawn before the man could answer.

Crack. Crack. Crack.

The man's teeth were demolished under the steel of the gun and the weight behind Nahvid's blows as he pistol-whipped his worker. "Get your incompetent ass out of here before I blow your shit off, man. Look at her fucking face!" He was seething, and Aria folded her arms across her chest.

"You should have never sent him!" she argued.

"You should have never been there!" Nahvid bit back.

Siblings at war.

"Get this nigga out of here, bleeding all over my shit," Nahvid ordered the second goon.

When the room was cleared, Nahvid reached for her face. Aria slapped his hand away.

"I can't believe you had me kidnapped!"

"Quit being dramatic. I sent for you because you're coming

home. Might as well call this Michigan shit a wrap," Nahvid said. "We leave tomorrow."

"Nahvid, I have a life here. Friends. Isa!" she said.

"You're not safe with him. I said no. We're family. I've always taken care of you. You don't go against family. Do you know how many enemies that man has? I know you don't, but I do. Do you see how easy it was for me to have you grabbed up? You're coming home. End of story. You stay here, and I'm done with you, Aria. What's it gon' be?"

Aria saw red, but she didn't protest. They had never chosen anyone over each other. It had always been their promise. Their family creed. Blood over everything.

"What about graduation, Nah? I worked hard for this! You're going to make me leave without walking?" she asked.

"You can come back for commencement. This is the fucking murder capital, and you got me out here inheriting beef over you. Niggas around this bitch don't have a code. They wolves out here, Aria, and you laid up with one like I didn't teach you better," Nahvid scolded.

"I can't just leave without telling him." Aria's feelings were so hurt she could barely manage the words. A goodbye? To her man? She had just let him in. Now, Nahvid was pushing him out of her life, and she regretted playing hard to get at all. She had wasted time, and now she was out of it. They were ending against her will.

"So tell him," Nahvid said. "Take the driver out front. Go pack your shit. We're out of here first thing in the morning."

2

Morgan stood in front of the full-length mirror. Her chest filled with so many things. Pride. Sadness. Disbelief.

"I did it."

"You did it, Mo," Ethic confirmed. His voice came from the doorway, and she lifted her eyes, meeting his gaze through the reflection. He was so proud. She could feel it. She wondered if he would be proud if he knew that Bash's family had helped accelerate her way through college. If he knew they had changed her grades, cheated for her on exams, elevated her GPA. He leaned against the frame and she turned to him, the long hunter-green gown hanging so long it touched the floor. Graduation. She had made it to commencement. It felt like a hard-earned win.

Ethic was silent, and he bit into his bottom lip, then pinched the bridge of his nose.

"You look so much like her." His voice held nostalgia, and Morgan's heart dipped. "But you're not like her, Mo. You made it. It was important to me that you make it."

She nodded. "I did, didn't I?" she asked. There were so many times she thought she wouldn't. So many obstacles had stood between her and the finish line, but she had endured. She had struggled through a suicide attempt, through loss, through heartbreak, through sleepless nights, and through raising twins to make it to this point. Even with help, finishing school had seemed impossible some days. Morgan had fought for this.

He gave one nod. "A man is proud of his daughter many times in a lifetime. I've never felt this, though, Mo. This type of pride is just for this moment with you. You've given me a feeling that no one else has before. I love you, Mo. I'm a fucking proud man today."

Morgan crossed the room and rushed into his strong arms. Ethic. Her Ethic. She loved no one like she loved him. How she had put him at risk she didn't even know. She had been so stupid. Her jealousy of Alani and the attention Ethic gave her had made Morgan slip and share a secret no one should have ever known. But Bash knew, and now he was using it to hold her hostage. Morgan squeezed Ethic so tightly as they stood there. She wanted to tell him. Wanted to ask for help because he had the power to free her, but to get his help, she'd have to admit to the ways she had exposed him. She would have to look him in the eyes and tell him she had betrayed him. She wasn't that girl anymore. The jealous, selfish girl who didn't want him to find love. She loved Alani now. They were her family. Nothing had changed after he'd married Alani. In fact, things had gotten better. She'd gained a confidante in Alani. Their family had grown and was continuing to grow, and they included Mo every step of the way. Now Ethic was at risk because she had been stupid.

"I'm so sorry if I ever hurt you, Ethic," she said.

Ethic pulled back to stare in her eyes. Morgan diverted

her gaze because he could pull the truth out of the most skilled liar, and she wasn't even that great at mistruths.

"You never have, Mo. You've been the light in a lot of dark days, and that hasn't always been fair to you. I gave you my very best, and I'm glad it was enough to get you here," he said.

"It was everything," she said, smiling as she laughed a little while he cleared her tears. The forehead kiss he delivered felt glorious. Nobody loved like Ethic.

"You think Alani can fix this for me? It's kind of long," Mo said, glancing down and pulling at the fabric of her graduation gown.

"I'm sure she'll be happy to, Mo," Ethic said. Mo removed her cap, and Ethic took it from her hands. She smiled with half her heart as she watched him take in the decorations she had covered the top with. A collage of pictures. Her family. Raven. Her father. Her mother. Ethic. Eazy. Bella. The twins and . . .

"You put Alani on here," he said. Not much surprised Ethic, but this gesture certainly did. Mo's history with Alani was rocky. It had been a challenge for Mo to even accept her, so the move was unexpected.

"I was wrong about her," Morgan said. "I wasn't easy on her, and she never gave up on me or this family. I'm really glad to have her." Mo paused. "I'm glad you have her."

"I'm a lucky man," he said. "I know you said you're fine, Mo, but I'd be a whole lot more comfortable if you spent a little more time around here. At least until I find out who was behind it."

"I'm okay, Ethic," she assured. She wanted to do exactly what he was proposing. Retreat to him, to the safety he guaranteed, but she knew it might ruffle Bash's feathers, and she couldn't rock the boat right now. "I just want to be at home. If I feel unsafe, I'll come to you. I promise." She lied right to his face, and it made her feel horrible because if no one else deserved her honesty, he did.

Ethic pulled Morgan in for another hug before they joined the rest of the family in the living room.

"Mo, I can try to fix that hemline if you want. I should remember enough of what Nannie taught me to do that," Alani said as soon as Mo walked into the room. It was just like her to see a need and attempt to fulfill it. The people she loved hardly ever had to ask. Alani sat on the couch holding Messari to her chest as he fought the sandman with all his might. His little eyes closed every few seconds only to pop back open, then droop again. Morgan warmed at the sight of the two of them. Alani really filled a huge void in all their lives. Her children called her their La La. Morgan loved the way Alani loved on them.

"Thanks, Alani. That would be perfect," she answered. "I can take him."

"He's fine right here, Mo. I love holding him," Alani said, closing her eyes for a few seconds as her hand rubbed circles against Messari's back three times, and then she gave three pats. A pattern that lulled him to sleep. "He's getting so big. I have to do this while I can. They grow up so fast." Alani opened her eyes and changed the subject. "How do you feel about a graduation dinner?"

Morgan frowned as uncertainty crept up her spine. "Hmmm. I don't know. The last party in my honor was a disaster," she said.

"Doesn't have to be a big deal. Just family. You worked really hard. You deserve to celebrate with the people you love," Alani said.

"I guess something small couldn't hurt. Maybe just dinner

at a restaurant or something," Mo answered. "Where's Bella and Eazy?"

"Eazy's out back with Yolly. We're about to plant some things in the garden. Bella's with Hendrix," Alani answered.

Morgan lifted stunned brows to Ethic. "By herself?"

"I got eyes nearby," he said. "The illusion of freedom."

Morgan snickered. "Is that what you did with me?" she asked.

"Nah, I held on too tight with you, Mo. I'm trying to do things differently with Bella. Extend some trust. You taught me a lot."

"B's a good girl," Alani said.

"It ain't Bella I'm worried about," Ethic stated.

The chime that interrupted commanded their attention to the front door.

Morgan walked down the corridor toward the foyer. "Where did they go anyway?" she yelled.

She pulled open the door, and her heart stalled. Ethic was speaking behind her, but she couldn't hear him. She couldn't hear shit.

The scowl that drew wrinkles into his forehead eased some when he saw her face. Surprise. He was shocked to see her there. Gratefulness. She saw the thought manifest in his mind. He was happy to see her. Messiah. Motherfucking Messiah. Morgan's chest automatically caved around him. It was like he had taken a knife and carved out her heart every time he was in her space. She hated he had that power. She hated that she would always feel him, be affected by him, love him. Stupid ass.

"Shorty," he greeted.

Morgan gripped the wood of the door as her entire body tensed. She hated that her eyes misted.

His eyes took her in. "Damn, shorty. You graduating? I missed a lot."

"You missed everything," she whispered. He took two steps and was crossing the emotional fence she had put up. Fuck the fence. He was in her yard, fucking up her grass, trampling all on her flower bed as he trapped her against the wall. Just like Messiah to fuck shit up to get to her. Morgan's breath hitched, and her lashes fluttered. Stupid-ass nigga. She both adored this feeling and despised it. He just controlled her. Like there was a remote control to her emotions and he was pressing every damn button like a badass kid.

"I don't want to miss shit else, Mo," he said.

Morgan tried to ease by him, but he placed a hand to the wall, stopping her. She went the other way. Another hand. She blew out a breath and rolled her eyes up to him. Niggas and the traps they captured her in. Trap niggas. Hood niggas. Why the hell did she have to be attracted to that type?

"Hear me, shorty. We gon' get this wrong until we get it right, cuz I ain't come back for nothing else but you. I'm not accepting nothing less than you."

"And I'm not accepting nothing less than loyalty. Can you look me in the face and tell me you're done hurting me? That there are no more secrets? Nothing else I don't know? That I'm safe with you?"

Messiah bit into his bottom lip and turned his head as thoughts of Bleu ran through his mind. Thoughts of other things too.

Morgan scoffed. She could see the secrets he was keeping. She didn't know what they were, but she felt them. She had learned to listen to her intuition. He had taught her to trust it with his deception. She had ignored them before when it came to him. She would never do that again. Ahmeek didn't make her feel this. Like she had to protect herself. He didn't scare her at all. A huge part of her was fearful of Messiah. Like she was alert, on the ready, bracing for emotional impact because he was going to deliver another blow that would devastate her.

"Same Messiah, different day," Morgan said. She lifted his arm and walked away.

She couldn't get away from him fast enough. The fact that she was practically running away from the man she used to desperately pray she could run to bothered her. The change between them unearthed raw emotion.

"How are you okay with him being here?" she asked as soon as Ethic came back into view. Messiah trailed her slowly, coolly. He knew now was not the time to give chase.

"He's trying to make amends, Mo. It's not my place to stop a man from attempting to right his wrongs," Ethic said. "You two have a lot to talk about."

"We have nothing to talk about," Morgan answered. She was adamant in her disdain. Stubborn. Too hurt to let the present heal the wounds of the past.

"Mo, you have every reason to hear him out," Alani reminded as she stood to her feet while carrying Messari. Ethic moved to help her. "I've got him, Ezra." She turned back to Mo. "You've got damn good reason, Mo."

"I don't owe him anything."

"Shorty's right. She ain't the one with debts to settle. This is her crib. Y'all her people. I'ma get out of here and make it easier on everybody."

Messiah backpedaled. He wasn't trying to upset her. It was like a jab to the chin that his presence upset her so much, but he was willing to baby-step his way back into her life.

"You can stay. I was leaving anyway," Mo said.

"You might as well stay and wait for me to hem this gown,

Mo. Cut it out," Alani said. She struggled to her feet with Messari in her arms. "Messiah, you don't have to leave either. I actually really need your help. Well, Ezra does. He's building me a greenhouse." Alani pointed at Messiah. "Might want to take off that fly-ass jacket, playa, because you're helping him."

Messiah licked his bottom lip and debated if he wanted to follow directions. Alani somehow gave them out like a schoolteacher. No questions. All statements. Messiah didn't particularly like it. He didn't particularly dislike it either. Something about her felt like he was supposed to listen. Like she was the core of everyone in the room, and they were to protect her at all costs. It was an odd feeling. He had never felt that before for anyone. Motherly. It was almost motherly. He nodded and then peeled out of the jacket.

The room felt small to Morgan. She and Messiah in the same space. The tension. The things floating around in their heads but trapped by sealed lips. Morgan heard her heart racing. She was uncomfortable. Being around him didn't feel the same. He used to fill her with so much confidence. Now all she felt was the insecurity of unfamiliarity eating her alive. Distance and dishonesty had done a number on them. The thought of how much of a stranger he was to her made her sad.

"Let me put Ssari in the hammock outside. Mo, you can come out when you're ready," Alani said. "Grab the sewing kit from upstairs in the closet in the master."

Morgan felt Messiah's eyes robbing her of her courage. Damn outlaw. He stayed stealing shit. She huffed and retreated upstairs, leaving him with Ethic and Alani. Morgan quickly located Alani's sewing kit, and then she made her way to her old room. It overlooked the backyard. She watched Yara play in the wading pool with Eazy, and she smiled as he signed to her. Her eyes drifted to Messiah. Unease filled her, but she couldn't deny her relief. Just to lay eyes on him again was a gift, no matter how angry she was with him. Morgan felt as if she were staring at a force. Messiah was energy, and Morgan could feel his pull.

Her heart clenched when she saw Messiah walk over to the pool where Yara played. She sucked in air, forgetting to release it as he squatted. Eye to eye, he lingered in front of Yara, the daughter he didn't even know he had, and Morgan froze. Yara retreated, crying as she ran toward Eazy. She didn't know him, and her deaf daughter was an empath. She sensed the wickedness in this gangster. Yara had no idea that the devil inside Messiah would burn an entire city to the ground for her. If he only knew that she was of his loins. Blood of his blood. The combination of what their passion had made. Morgan wasn't sure if it was love anymore. She wasn't sure of anything. What she felt for Ahmeek was different from what she felt for Messiah, and she was sure that she loved Meek. Messiah's connection felt like ownership. Like he had purchased her outright and paid in full, all big bills, and he was refusing to sign away the title.

Morgan felt exposed when Messiah lifted his attention to the window.

"Let me get that, shorty."

It would have been crass had he spoken the words. It was fucking charming as hell, however, because he had signed them. Signed them better than ever. Morgan felt her face heat as her fair skin turned scarlet. The arrogant smirk that pulled at the corners of his lips pissed Morgan off so badly she closed the blinds, blocking his view of her.

She wanted to sit in her room, barricade herself inside, but she refused to give Messiah that power. She had cried many tears between these four walls over him. She had prayed to God to bring him back all those years ago. Her prayers had never come true, and Morgan had fallen down a rabbit hole of dysfunction. Morgan was just beginning to feel like herself after losing him, and as if he had an alarm that warned him that she was about to move on, he had popped back into her life. It was so overwhelming that Morgan hadn't even taken the time to process his resurrection. She took a deep breath and headed toward the backyard. This was her family. She had every right to be here. Messiah could only make her feel uncomfortable if she let him. She walked downstairs and headed toward the back, but as she entered the kitchen, Messiah came waltzing through the sliding doors. Her breath hitched, and she stopped walking. Messiah stood before her. Fresh fade, white T-shirt, and hoop shorts with fresh J's.

"You good, shorty?" he asked.

"I'm fine."

She didn't even know how she answered him, because she was stuck. Stuck in the past, stuck in that kitchen pantry he had devoured her in all those years ago. Stuck between the four walls of her bedroom, where she used to grease his scalp. Her memories were like quicksand, and although she was standing there calmly, she was screaming on the inside.

"After the shooting, I mean. I know how you are with shit like that. You good good?" he asked.

Morgan shrugged and looked down at her feet.

"You're so fucking pretty, man."

Her eyes shot to his, then teared. *Stupid-ass nigga.*

"Nah, Mo. No more tears. Not over me. I don't even deserve 'em," Messiah said.

"What do you want, Messiah? Why are you here?" Morgan asked. "This is *my* family."

"They're mine too, Mo. I ain't got you. Ethic's all I got."

Morgan felt a bit of guilt because it was true. Messiah had

no one. Morgan would have to share her world because, for so long, he had been a huge part of it too.

"What do you want?" she asked.

"You," he answered. He had never been one to hold punches. No point in lying. They both knew why he had returned.

"We happened a long time ago, Messiah. It was like living in the clouds back then. You dropped me so hard. You don't make me feel like I'm flying anymore. I sink with you. I just can't let you fill my head with air this time. I've got to keep my feet on the ground."

"Fuck gravity. I want to be high, Mo," Messiah said. He leaned against the wall and lifted one foot as his eyes penetrated hers. She didn't know what to say. She couldn't join him this time. She couldn't let him take her to outer space. There was no oxygen there. She would die this time.

"Mommyyyyy!"

The interruption of her screaming toddler felt like relief as Messari banged on the sliding glass door. Messiah opened it, and Messari came rushing inside. He was moving so fast he tripped over his own feet. The dramatic wail that followed the fall turned Morgan to putty. She hated to hear her children cry. Before she could act, Messiah bent to pick him up.

"Yo, that's a lot of tears, lil' G. We ain't about all that. You a'ight," Messiah coached.

Morgan felt her soul stir. So many days she had wondered what Messiah would be like as a father. Watching him with Messari in his arms both worried and endeared her.

"Slow down, shortstop. You ain't rounding no bases, homie. Got to keep it, playa. No running."

Messari leaned his head back curiously as he inspected Messiah. Morgan got goose bumps. Messari had her entire face, but that demeanor was all Messiah. His little brow bent. Messiah's forehead filled with wrinkles. Lion and cub, Messiah and Messari squared off.

"You ain't tough, G. What you looking at?" Messiah asked. The corner of his lip curved into a smirk.

"Mommy, who is him?" Messari asked, turning his head to Morgan.

"You a man. Ask me," Messiah said as he sat Messari on the island in the center of the room. He placed his arms around Messari, leaning against the island as he stared the toddler in the eyes. Messiah's heart ached.

"We used to dream about bad little niggas just like him, shorty. Damn, you really had another nigga's kids. You wanted to touch a nigga where it hurt, didn't you?" Messiah asked, voice dripping in angst as he stared Messari down.

Messari's hands and eyes went to the chain around Messiah's neck instantly. Anything shiny was like a magnet to Messari. He just had to touch it. Messiah didn't seem to mind. Messari was yanking on the chain like it came out of a Cracker Jack box, and Morgan cringed.

"What's you name?" Messari asked, head cocked to the side curiously. Messari pressed his forehead against Messiah's and growled at him. The laugh that erupted from Messiah was one Morgan had never heard. It was free. Like he didn't think twice about his amusement.

"Messiah, kid. My name's Messiah," he said.

Messari's face lit up. "Mommy! Him name is like mine!"

"What's your name, kid?" Messiah asked, smirking.

"Messari Benji Atkins."

Morgan's soul left her body. Messiah turned to stone. His back stiffened as he stood up straight and turned eyes of disbelief to Morgan.

She hurried to Messari, squeezing between him and Messiah, grabbing her son up and heading outside.

"Yo, Mo, what the fuck type of shit you on, shorty?" Messiah asked as he followed her.

Morgan ignored him as she headed over to the kiddie pool. "Yara, let's go, baby," Morgan signed urgently. She reached down and practically pulled off her baby's arm as she dragged her across the lawn.

"Mo! What's wrong?" Alani asked as she stood from the table.

Ethic looked up but didn't stand as Morgan bypassed them. Messiah was on her ass.

"Shorty got some fucking explaining to do with her slick ass! That's what's wrong! Why the little nigga got my name, Mo?" he asked.

"Aren't you going to do something?" Alani asked, turning to Ethic.

"Nope," Ethic answered.

Messiah pulled at Mo's arm. She snatched it away.

"Stop touching me!" she shouted.

Yara felt the tension between them. Her little legs could barely keep up with Mo's pace as Morgan dragged her along.

"The nigga got my name, Mo!"

"He don't got your name! He got his own name! Move, Messiah!" Morgan shouted as she pushed past him. She stormed back into the house, struggling with two babies as she retrieved her keys and then exited out the front door. She pulled open the back door to her car. Messiah pushed it closed.

"How old are they, Mo?" Messiah asked.

He was pulling at her, desperate for information. His stomach was empty, sick, twisting in torment at the possibility that these could be his whiny, snotty-nosed little motherfuckers. The ones they had dreamed of all those years ago. He tried to search their faces for similarities, but he found none. All he saw was Morgan Atkins.

"Get off me!" she shouted.

Messiah pointed a finger in her face, tilting her forehead back. "Answer the fucking question, Mo!"

Messari was in her arms, and the tone of Messiah's voice flipped a switch inside his little body. At just two years old, his instincts kicked in.

Bop!

The tiniest fist connected with Messiah's eye. The stun behind the punch brought Messiah to an abrupt halt.

"Ssari!" Morgan shouted.

Messiah pulled Messari from Morgan's arms and held him by both shoulders, extending his arms up above his head as he stared the little boy in his eyes.

"Hey! Put me down!" Messari shouted. He swung and kicked as he dangled at Messiah's mercy. It took everything in Messiah not to laugh.

"Badass." He smirked. "Keep protecting ya' mama, kid. That's exactly what you do if a nigga run up talking crazy. Remind a nigga when he doing too much, and touch him where it hurt if he don't stop." He pulled Messari into his body and looked down at Yara, who was hiding behind Mo. He pinched Morgan's chin between two fingers. "We gon' talk, shorty. Stop crying and get your kids home safe."

He kissed her lips like he had a right to. Nothing major. A peck on the mouth like he had been doing it for years. He placed Messari on his feet, then turned to walk back into the house. Morgan thought about yelling after him. The twins were his children. They were their children. But then she thought of who he was and what he had done. Messiah was toxic. If she had learned anything at all from him, it was to not trust words but actions. His actions had made him her enemy, and it would take a lot more than charm and aggression to get her to trust him with her babies. Morgan wouldn't ever put them in jeopardy. She couldn't gamble with their safety, and Messiah was full of uncertainty. Until she was sure he was safe, he couldn't know. She tucked her kids into their car seats and drove away. Distance was needed, because being around Messiah brought on a familiar ache inside her. One she never wanted to feel again.

3

Ahmeek watched in silence as the medical examiner pulled back the sheet. He felt a bit of pride over the fact that Morgan had been the one to deliver them here.

She really laid these niggas down, he thought.

Little Morgan wasn't as fragile as she pretended to be. The thought of her trapped inside the dance studio did things to Meek. The thought of the twins being there with her infuriated him more. He tried his best not to abuse his position in the streets. He tried to collect his paper quietly, building strong alliances along the way, only taking what was needed and never more, and respecting the worth of other men. It wasn't often that Ahmeek encountered static, because the love the streets held was overwhelming. Any beef he had was usually drummed up by Messiah or Isa, and he came off the bench every time, but this time, somebody had gotten disrespectful. Now it was time for him to remind niggas why he had gotten the name Murder Meek. The Crew had been young terrorists in the city from the ages of fourteen. Meek had never been shy about laying anybody to rest, but after an altercation on the hoop court left a body on the blacktop when he was sixteen, Meek learned to control himself. He went away for five years for manslaughter. The only thing that had saved him was the fact that he was a minor and the video that surfaced proved he had been provoked. He only had to be locked up one time to know that he never wanted to go back, so instead of moving recklessly, he moved smartly. He listened more than he spoke, but sometimes his temper flared . . . times like these it felt uncontrollable. He hadn't realized how far he had swum out in Mo's waters until this very moment. She had drowned him because she had joined the very short list of names that he'd die behind. He looked down at the dead bodies and nodded as he handed the Indian man an envelope. Five thousand dollars was the going rate for an unauthorized viewing of the bodies, but it was worth every penny. Just one glance, and he knew who had sent them. There was no denying the affiliation of these men. The tattooed markings on their necks told the story. These were Beans's men. Ahmeek's blood boiled. There was no need to call anyone. No time to rally shooters. His temper had him flying through the city, headed straight to the source of the problem.

It was Sunday. Family day. There was no slinging on the Lord's day. Niggas took a personal day on the Sabbath, so Meek knew not to take it to the block with this. Ahmeek pulled up to Beans's home where his girlfriend, Tammy, lived with their two kids. He didn't give a fuck. Beans had taken it to Mo's safe place, so Meek was reciprocating. Couldn't be the bigger person with a shooter like Beans. Keep that same energy as fuck. He pulled into the driveway and hopped out.

"Yo, Meek! What's up? Can I wash your wheels, man? You only got to pay me five bucks! I'll give you a discount!"

Meek smirked as he slapped hands with Beans's twelve-year-old son.

"Yeah, hit them rims for me, playboy, and we don't give niggas discounts 'round these parts. You know better. What I tell you about that?" he asked.

"My price is my price," the kid answered.

Meek peeled out a band of money and handed the kid a twenty. "Your pops in there?" Meek asked.

"Nah, he out back with my mama," the kid said.

Ahmeek rounded the house. The shadows of the overgrown bushes cooled the temperature, but he was still on fire. His temper was like a raging fire. Only one thing would douse it. Get back.

He pulled up on Beans and Tammy like he was invited.

"Heyyy, Meek!" Tammy greeted, seeing him first.

"What up, sis?" he answered.

Beans's face fell as he sat up straight in the lawn chair and put the Heineken he was sipping onto the glass patio table.

"You smelling good, boy. What's that you wearing?" Tammy asked.

It never failed. Women just loved him. They could be standing right next to their man and would still find ways to let Meek know that he could get it if he wanted it. He didn't want it. Tammy was pretty as hell, but that pussy had been run down back in the day.

Meek gave her a kiss to one cheek and a friendly hug. "Nothing special," he answered. His conversation was normal, but his eyes were lethal, and they may as well have been crosshairs. He had them trained on Beans. Tension filled the air.

"Yo, baby, go season that meat so I can get this grill started," Beans instructed.

"Okay. Meek, you want anything? A beer or something?" Tammy offered.

"I'm good, sis. Thanks," he said. He pulled out a chair and sat silently across from Beans until Tammy dismissed herself.

"Yo, bruh, just to let you know, the burner sitting in my lap. A nigga ain't got no problem pulling the trigger," Beans informed.

"You ain't gon' do that. Or perhaps your stupid ass will, cuz you've definitely lost ya' fucking mind," Ahmeek stated. "Little Bernard out front cleaning my rims. The beam already on him. If I don't walk out of here, he don't either. So tuck your shit and let's talk before I put the play down anyway for the disrespect alone."

Beans gritted his teeth as he put his gun back in his waistline.

"You butt-hurt over that ass whooping, clearly. That's why you sent hitters to the dance studio?" Meek asked. "Help me understand. Help me help you, G, because the way I'm feeling, I'm about to send your whole family on a trip."

"It wasn't my order, man," Beans conceded.

Ahmeek's brow raised. That information surprised him. It meant he had enemies he didn't know about.

"Who called the play?"

"Man, I need your word. You got to let the shit go, man. Nobody got hit at the studio. It was my fuckup. I'll make that up, bruh. On my kids. If I give you the rundown, you got to give me the chance to get back right."

"Niggas show you who they are, you believe 'em. You know my code," Ahmeek answered. "You negotiating the lives of your kids right now, Beans. Yours is already off the table. Never will a nigga send bullets in the direction of Morgan Atkins and live to get clout from the story."

Beans bit back fear and lifted his chin slightly, but Ahmeek sensed the terror. Any man would feel it when facing the grim reaper. He didn't judge Beans for the tremble of his chin. It was natural. At the end of the day, every man feared death.

"It was Messiah, man. After the L I took on the truck that was robbed, he said he would give me a better split if he was back over seventy-five. Said he needed you out the way, though. Told me to get at everybody you love and clear the throne so he could get his seat back. He replaced the money I lost."

"You a lying-ass nigga, Beans. Messiah would do a lot of things, but he wouldn't send you at Mo. He would never fucking touch her."

"He sent me at you, and everybody know how you feel about her. Weaken the king, then kill him. We were supposed to hit everybody you fuck with. He never named her, but she's first when it comes to you."

The news rocked Ahmeek. Touched him right behind his gangster, where he kept the sentiment for his family. Messiah lived there. His entire chest ached. He was unmoved on the outside, but his heart exploded inside. He felt like someone had snatched his stomach out. He bit into his bottom lip, nodding as he finally put together a clear picture of the puzzle in his mind. He gripped the sides of the chair, fighting emotion, but he showed none. Rage and devastation swirled in him. It was a hot-boy summer, and he was about to cool niggas off. It was time to make it rain. Bullets. Murder Meek wanted to change the forecast and make it rain bullets. This feeling, this news was the worst thing he'd ever felt. It was worse than Mo cutting him off. It hurt more than the discovery of Messiah's empty hospital room all those years ago. It ached more than the day his father got locked up. This shit was the worst pain he'd ever dealt with.

"This is what we're gonna do. You gon' go inside and find a real quiet spot. You gon' put your fucking pistol in your mouth and pull the trigger. I'ma sit right here until I hear the shot. You got three minutes. One to say goodbye to your son. One to kiss your bitch. One to build up a little courage, cuz the shit gonna feel impossible to do. It's going to be the scariest shit you've ever done, but you gon' eat that bullet, or baby boy and wifey gon' pay that price for you."

"Meek, man . . ."

"Nah, G. Too late for all 'at." Ahmeek pulled out his phone and set the timer. He turned the screen to Beans. Three minutes and not a second more. "Make the most of it."

Beans stood from the table, and Ahmeek sat there watching the numbers of the timer wind down. It went ten seconds past the deadline. Tension filled him. He didn't want to execute Beans's woman and child, but he would if it came to that. Before it even became a consideration.

Boom!

"Beanssss!"

The sound of Tammy's wails filled the air, and Ahmeek stood. He walked back to his car, catching Beans's son before he rushed into the house.

"Yo, sit here. Sit on this step and don't move, you hear me?" Ahmeek said. "Don't move until your mother comes for you. Shit might get hard for you. Shit might hurt a lot after today. You or your mother ever need something, you come see me. You hear me?"

Beans's son nodded as tears filled his eyes.

The sound of sirens filled the air, and as Ahmeek turned around, he saw a Range Rover pull up behind his car. The window rolled down, and Ethic's face appeared. Their eye contact was brief, but in the stare down, Ahmeek sensed acceptance.

Ahmeek had gotten there first. He had put in work on behalf of Morgan. Ethic's presence wasn't needed. Ethic gave a subtle nod as if he were drawing conclusions in his mind, and then the window rose as the Range Rover disappeared down the block.

Whatever Ethic had come to do had already been done, but Beans was only the middleman to the problem. Ahmeek had to go to the source. Messiah had crossed a line, and he had to come to terms with the fact that a man he considered a brother wanted him dead.

Knock-knock.

Aria turned toward the door of her apartment, and her heart stalled. She knew who was knocking, and she dreaded dealing with him. She walked over and pulled the door open to find Isa standing in front of her.

He was so tall that her neck stretched all the way back just to look at him.

"You know niggas died behind you, right?" he asked.

She nodded. He crossed the threshold, picking her up by the pits of her arms so that she was eye level with him as his lips covered hers.

"Who I got to see about this face?" he asked.

"No one," she answered as he set her on the island in her kitchen. She could barely look at him. "My brother snatched me to prove he could, Isa. He doesn't think you will keep me safe."

"You know better than that," Isa stated.

Aria was silent, and she looked off only for Isa to cup her face and pull her gaze back to him.

"I'm leaving town, Isa." She slid her engagement ring off her finger, and Isa took a step back.

"Man, put that shit back on your hand before I get upset," he stated.

"I can't, Isa." Her brow furrowed, and her pretty eyes glistened as she looked at him. "He's my family. He's all I've got. If I stay here, he'll cut me off. He's always been there for me."

Her words might as well had been bullets the way they went right through him. He staggered a bit. "And you're choosing him over me?" Isa asked.

Her silence cut him even more. The fact that she seemed so sure was alcohol over the wound.

"Fuck it, then," Isa spat. "Pussy was trash anyway."

Aria's neck snaked so far back it felt like it would break. She hopped down off the island and marched toward the door, opening it for him. "Then you shouldn't have a problem letting go. Since you in your feelings, get the fuck out," Aria said.

Isa loomed over her, pausing to stare her down, but Aria wouldn't look at him.

"Little-ass girl, man," he scoffed before walking out.

Aria slammed the door behind him, and damn if her eyes didn't betray her, but she refused to let a tear fall. There was no point in crying. She couldn't stay, and although she knew Isa was being crass because he was hurt, she would rather have an angry goodbye than a regretful one, so she would take his insults. It only made her feel better about choosing her brother over her man.

4

I remember when my heart broke
I remember when I gave up loving you

Morgan sat at her vanity; her earbuds filled her ears with a ballad that told the secrets of her heart. It was so loud it drowned out all sound. She gripped the pen in her hand and wrote the lyrics across the paper in front of her. She didn't know why she wanted to write them down. It just seemed appropriate. It seemed like these lyrics were ripped right out of her diary. Was heartbreak universal? Did men just hurt women to the point where the pain was recognizable by other women? Shared experiences of heartbreak connecting her to a sorority of other broken hearts? She hated that this song was so on point. She hated that she had been inducted into the sisterhood at all.

Morgan was restless. Every time she closed her eyes, she heard gunshots. Her heart had been running rampant ever since the shooting, pounding, overbeating it felt like. It felt like she was having a heart attack, and she just wanted the panic to

ease some. She was fine. Her kids were fine. Still, she felt it. The
anxiety. The pure terror of what could have happened that day.
It could have been her or the twins in a grave right now. Even
losing Aria would have obliterated Morgan. Even the thought
caused her room to shrink. Morgan cinched her eyes and took
in deep breaths, but she was choking. She glanced back at the
bed where Bash slept. She couldn't breathe. She wanted to wake
him, but he no longer felt like peace. He was a part of her storm
too. Her entire life was so fucked up. The chaos felt unending,
and Morgan didn't know the way out. She stood, creeping quietly from the room. She didn't even put on shoes as she slipped
out her front door. She couldn't wait on the elevator. She took
the stairs all the way to the bottom, bursting out the door to her
building and gulping in air. She fisted her hair with one hand
and placed the other to her heart as she sucked in oxygen.

It took a while for her to still her heart.

Beep! Beep!

It was odd that she recognized the sound of the horn. In-
sane that she knew it was Messiah before she even looked up.
He popped open the driver's door of his BMW and climbed out.
She didn't know if she should run inside or stand her ground.
Her feet seemed to be rooted as he approached.

"What are you doing here?" she asked.

Messiah scooped Morgan up, forcing her thighs to butterfly his waist as he pushed her back into the building. He stood
there. Eye to eye. Nose to nose.

"I can't sleep, shorty, cuz you over here in your feelings,"
Messiah said. "When you used to tell me you couldn't sleep, I
used to come through to put you to bed," he said, half smiling
as he buried his face in the groove of her neck.

"Messiah, stop," she whispered. She peered behind her
through the glass door, and Messiah peered right with her.

"It's a problem, shorty?" he asked, voice dripping in aggression because he had been itching to put a nigga on his back.

He turned. She might as well have been Pebbles to his Bamm-Bamm because she was sure he would club her and drag her, kicking and screaming, with him. He didn't even risk putting her on her feet because he was afraid she would run from him.

Morgan blushed and leaned her head against his forehead. She just didn't have it in her to protest at the moment. "I dreamed about you coming back so many times," she said, scoffing. "It was nothing like this, though. I didn't hate you in my dreams."

Morgan was silent, and Messiah was at a loss for words. They made it to the car, and he tucked her inside before going to the driver's seat. He sat there, staring at her, making her uncomfortable as she turned her gaze out the window.

"The gunshots are ringing in my head, Messiah," she murmured. "My babies were in there. I had to—"

"I know, Mo. I know about having to do shit you don't really want to do," Messiah said, his tone low, reminiscent. He was filled with remorse. Time and his selfishness had diluted their bond. He could feel her mistrust of him. It rotted in the passenger seat of his car, and it was so potent it brought emotion to his eyes. He was grateful for the dark of night. It concealed his anguish. "If it's ever you or another nigga, you choose you, Mo. Every time. You're not equal to nobody, shorty. You did what you had to do, and you'll never have to do it again. I swear on my life as long as I'm breathing, you'll never have to protect yourself again. I'ma be there, wherever you are, no matter who you're with, to protect you. I'm taking niggas' heads off over you, shorty."

Morgan sniffed and lifted a trembling hand to her cheek to clear tears.

"How could you leave me?" she whispered.

Messiah gripped the steering wheel and turned his body to face her.

"I just had to handle some shit, Mo. I had to. You couldn't come with me. Every day, I thought about you, though, shorty. That's no lie. Every single fucking minute."

"I died here without you."

"Yeah, well, it don't seem that way to me, shorty. Seem like you were living just fine," he said.

She heard his disdain. His judgment. Silence. Discomfort. This had never been them. They were practically strangers, and it felt horrible because no one knew her better than he did. The intimacies they had shared in the midnight hours all those years ago had made them experts on each other. Well. He was an expert on her. Morgan didn't know much at all about the man who had stolen her heart.

"Your kids. They're two?"

"They are," she said. Her stomach tensed because she already knew where this was going.

"I bet you were pretty as fuck pregnant. I was supposed to know what that looked like. You letting another nigga live my life, Mo," Messiah said in disbelief.

Morgan didn't respond to that. She didn't even give him her eyes.

"And you named your son after me?" he asked. "Are they mine, Mo?"

She was silent. Her heart screamed, but her mouth didn't open.

"Either they're mine, or you were with him the whole time you were fucking with me? Is that why he was so comfortable with you back then? You were fucking the nigga?"

Morgan's throat closed. It was as good of an opportunity

as any to tell him the truth. That he was a father and his kids were upstairs. She couldn't, however. She didn't trust Messiah. She didn't know him. The threat he posed if he had a hidden motive could destroy her entire family. What if he didn't stick around this time? If she told him, and he abandoned her again? What if she told him, and Bash was so slighted that he told what he knew about Ethic? No. Morgan couldn't say anything. It was best for everyone.

"I won't apologize for how I moved when you were moving dirty yourself," she said, remaining vague.

"So that's the word? You were fucking that nigga while we were together?" Messiah asked.

Morgan wanted to defend herself. She wanted to yell that she was stupid in love with him, and that she hadn't dismissed what they had shared the way he had.

Silence.

Nothing.

"Never knew you had so much ho in you, shorty. I would have handled you different," Messiah snapped.

Morgan scoffed. Two years ago, that statement would have gutted her. It would have destroyed her, but today, she was different. He had changed her. He had already taken her through the absolute worst. He had beaten her down so low that she had surpassed bottom. Her feelings had been annihilated. He had mismanaged her heart so badly that she had boarded it up. She had already felt the greatest pain in life. His judgment of her didn't even compare. She didn't even really care.

"I never knew you had so much snake in you, Messiah. I would have kept my grass lower," she shot back. She reached for the door handle and pushed it open. She had one foot to the pavement when he reached for her.

"I'm sorry, shorty. Just close the door," he said, yielding.

It was so hard for him to tuck his anger. Ever since seeing her with Ahmeek, he had wanted to kill someone. He had known he would get his girl back when he had seen her with Bash, but Ahmeek wasn't the type to submit without a fight. He knew Morgan like the back of his hand, and Meek's name on her tongue was said with too much affection. He could hear her adoration, and it sickened him. She had no idea the restraint he was showing.

"Maybe I am a ho, Messiah," she said, void of emotion as she pulled her foot back inside and closed the door. Morgan was checked out. She was a shell. "Maybe after you left, I just broke. You broke me. Bash was there. Meek was . . ." She paused and swallowed down turmoil. Her voice trembled. "Ahmeek put me back together." She barely said it. She was afraid to say it. Messiah was the last person who would ever understand.

"You can't love a nigga from the grave," Messiah answered.

"Exactly, Messiah," she shot back. "You haven't existed for two years. You were in a grave. You ran out on me for two whole years. I would have forgiven you for lying about being Mizan's brother, but the shit you said to me at Bleu's house that day. The way you handled me?" Morgan shook her head and closed her eyes. "Then you left, and when I thought you were dead, that was agony. It was unbearable, but now you're here! You've been out there! Without me! You *chose* to be without me, Messiah. I would have never left you. You don't exist at all to me anymore. I'll never forgive you for the way you deserted me. You're a cheater and a liar." Morgan went to exit the car, and Messiah snatched her hand, pulling her back to him. He hit the locks, trapping her inside.

"I told some lies, Mo, so I'ma have to eat that, but I never cheated on you, shorty. Don't burn my name," Messiah said.

"Yeah, well, bitches who show up with babies in the middle

of the night say otherwise," Morgan shot back. That fateful night played back in her mind. It was the moment her life changed forever. The moment love became hate. The day destiny was erased. Everything they had built came tumbling down that fateful night.

"That girl with the baby wasn't a bitch I was fucking," Messiah said.

"Sure," Morgan said sarcastically. "She flexed on your doorstep in the middle of the night, talking about you were hiding your family. Your lying ass has a baby and a bitch tucked away somewhere, and you act like I'm supposed to just forget that part, like you can separate the two and pretend they don't exist." Morgan scoffed. Rehashing these moments only built her resentment.

"It ain't like that, Mo," Messiah said.

"Then what is it like?" Morgan asked. Her eyes prickled, swelling so much that she couldn't stop the tears from falling. "Just be honest with me, Messiah! How could you let that happen to us? How did we get here?"

Messiah leaned across the center console. A fist to her hair kept Morgan in place as he pressed his forehead to hers.

She knew him well enough to see the struggle tearing through him like a storm. He gritted his teeth. He was holding her so tightly it hurt, but she would rather feel the pain than to disconnect.

"I loved you. It's like you want to say something to me, but you won't. You want me to trust you, but you shut me out of your life for two years. You left me out in the world without you, alone, on purpose. I'd never do that to you. Why won't you just talk to me?"

"I can't, Mo," he said. "But fuck with me anyway, like you used to, Mo. Believe in me, shorty. Over everything, over what you think you know. Trust me when I tell you, you don't."

She wanted to give in to him. She wanted to go back and be who they used to be. M&M. Forever. The fucking scheduled tweet still went out every week.

"I can't," she whispered.

"I love you, Shorty Doo Wop. Like it's an obsession or something. I don't give a fuck about nothing else except getting back to you. I don't even need inside the home, Mo. A nigga will lay his head down on your porch as long as I'm near you. You go be mad. You keep playing with that bitch-ass nigga Bash, and you keep making Meek play your side piece. When you're done acting out, when you're done showing out, I'm fucking coming home. Ain't shit you or nobody else can do to stop that. I'm sorry. Should have never given me that bone if you were going to want it back. I'm a dog-ass nigga, but I'm your dog-ass nigga, Mo."

Morgan closed her eyes. It felt so good to feel his breath on her lips. To hear his voice. Even the tightness from him pulling her hair felt like a gift. He was back. Her man was back, and she didn't even trust him enough to give him the key to her heart.

"I gave you all my love, and you wasted it!" she cried. "It's not our time anymore. It's too late. I couldn't if I wanted to." She thought of Bash, of the web he had her caught in. "Let me go, Messiah."

"I ain't letting shit go," he said. "You know better. I'm coming for mine, shorty." He unlocked the car. "You don't lose sleep over nobody that ever means you harm. You go close your pretty eyes and dream well. Leave the nightmares for the people who deserve 'em."

Morgan got out and rushed inside.

5

Ahmeek sat on Bleu's porch. The lights were off inside, so he didn't knock. He wasn't there for her anyway. He was there for Messiah, and he knew his routine so well that he knew he would be pulling up to her house any moment now. He had put eyes on Messiah. The news that he was behind the shooting at the dance studio told Meek he couldn't afford not to know his every move. Messiah was unpredictable, and Ahmeek couldn't afford to underestimate Messiah's malice again.

He didn't expect headlights to light up the block, because they lived by the same code—pull up without announcement always—but he heard the hum of the BMW. He recognized it from down the block because it matched his own. That's how close they had been. Matching cars. Hood niggas, getting money together, buying foreigns together. One girl had come between all that. A girl who was worth it. Ahmeek would have liked to say he would take it all back, but he wouldn't. What he had experienced with Morgan had been glorious. It didn't matter to him that it had ended. Even the short time he had spent with her was worth all the discord.

Messiah parked on the curb, another Crew rule: never get blocked into a driveway. Messiah climbed out, and he strolled up the sidewalk and stopped halfway up.

"Any nigga ever surprised me got met with a bullet. Better quit playing hide-and-seek, bitch-ass nigga," Messiah said.

Ahmeek stood from Bleu's porch swing. "Only nigga hiding is you," Ahmeek countered. "I ain't ever thrown a rock and hid my hand. I paid Beans a visit."

"Fuck Beans, and fuck you too," Messiah said, hawking up a wad of spit and watering Bleu's lawn.

Ahmeek came off the porch. "You want to kill me? You pull the trigger yourself. You breathe on Mo the wrong way and I'ma put you down. She get caught up in some stupid shit again because you in your feels and I'ma look you in your motherfucking face and blow your head off," he said.

"Fuck is you talking about? Mo always been good with me."

"That nigga Beans sent the shooters to the studio! The hitters that *you* paid to take care of me. Me and everybody I love? That's the order you put down my nigga. I love *her*! Every nigga in this city know the shit! I done spun Mo through every block in the hood! You came for my head, and they came for hers!"

Meek was shouting. Exasperated. He was boiling, and the spit that flew from his mouth as he barked on Messiah told him he was out of control. Messiah's face changed, just slightly. A flash of guilt bent his brow as the revelation hit him. He had almost gotten Morgan Atkins, the love of his life, killed.

The porch light illuminated the yard as the front door

swung open. Bleu stood there in a long T-shirt and knee-high socks. She pushed opened the screen door and stepped out onto the porch.

"Saviour is in here asleep. Y'all gon' wake up my whole block!" she hissed.

"My bad, Bleu. You right. It's late," Ahmeek said, his eyes never leaving Messiah's. "You looking real cozy over here, boy. You sure you even worried about Mo?" Ahmeek asked, voice low as he walked past Messiah, disappearing into the night.

Aria sat in the back seat of Nahvid's Maybach. Her head rested against the leather seats as she looked out the window. I-80 East passed her by out the window. Her chest was so tight that she could barely breathe. She felt every mile that separated her from Isa as Nahvid carried her back to D.C.

"You'll be safer back home, Aria. Where I can see you. Where I can reach out and touch you if I need to," Nahvid said.

Aria didn't respond. She knew Nahvid was right, but she no longer had the desire to be right. She enjoyed the rightness in Isa's wrong. Aria had changed since meeting Isa. She knew he was dangerous and reckless, but instead of running away from him, she gravitated toward him. His energy revitalized her. Getting a man like Isa to propose was like a miracle. He had stepped into the unknown for her, and here she was, leaving him. Her phone was nestled between her thighs, and Aria unlocked it. She clicked on Isa's messages.

> *Ali, u got me stuck, no lie.*
> *What u want me to do, Ali? I been a goon. That's all I know how to be. I can't change that, but I still want u.*
> *I ain't gon' let shit happen to u, Ali. Come home, man.*

*U can't even answer my shit? Fuck it. Wasting my fuck-
ing time.*

*U was never my bitch, Ali. You choosing niggas over
me. Fuck u.*

Aria wasn't even offended. Isa was livid with her, and he
had every right to be. The fact that she hadn't responded once
had only added fuel to his fire. Each message was more aggressive than the one before it. Her lack of communication had Isa
losing his mind.

Aria was torn. Her brother had been her everything for so
long. He had loved her and supported her. He had looked out
for her. He had been her very first love because the man they
shared relation with had been absent. In every way, he was like
her father. She had never defied his wishes.

They rode in silence. Her anger and stubbornness wouldn't
even allow her to ask him to have the driver stop so she could
pee. The farther away they got from Flint, the more regret settled into her bones.

"Excuse me," Aria said to the driver. "Can you pull over?"

"You need a break?" Nahvid asked.

"I'm going back," Aria answered. Her eyes filled with tears.

"You're not going back. Yo, my man, keep driving," he
said.

"No, I'm not going back to D.C. with you," she clarified. "I
love you, Nah. You're my brother, and I respect you and I trust
you, but I have to follow my heart. My heart is pointing in the
other direction," she said.

"Your heart is going to get you fucking hurt. I taught you
to use your head," Nahvid said. "I've seen plenty of good girls
lose their lives over niggas like the one you trying to run back
to. He's no good for you. You've got to listen to me, Aria. You're

my responsibility. Something's going to happen to you on his watch."

"And it'll be worth it," Aria said. She sounded like such a girl in love. "I'd rather die right now than live the rest of my life without him. If I get a day with him and nothing else, it's worth it. So stop the car."

"I'm not stopping the car," Nahvid said without looking at her.

"Fine," Aria said, opening the door while the driver was going eighty miles per hour. The driver swerved.

"Yo! What the fuck are you doing?" Nahvid shouted. "Close the door!"

"Let me out, Nahvid! I'm not a little-ass girl. I'm going home to my man," Aria argued.

"If you do this, that's it. I'm done with it. I'm not doing the sleepless nights, the back and forth coming to bail you out when the nigga go upside your head—"

"He'd never," Aria defended.

"Until he does," Nahvid scoffed. "You make this choice, and that's it."

"Then it's been real, brother, because my heart won't let me not love him," Aria said, her eyes misting. Aria was betting big on Isa and calling Nahvid's bluff, only Nahvid didn't bluff. He said what he meant and meant what he said. If Aria got out of this car, he would be done with her. "You're my brother. I don't want to lose you," Aria said as a tear slipped down her face.

"I'm not into watching people I love self-destruct, and that nigga can't be around me. He don't think before he act. So if you get out this car, don't call me, Aria. I love you, but I know when to love from afar," Nahvid said.

"You can pull over on the next exit," Aria said. Her chin quivered, and a tear fell against her will as the driver veered off the highway. They pulled into a gas station, and Aria opened the door.

"Nah. I'm not going to let my little sister find a way across three states. You take the car, and then we're done," Nahvid said as he opened his door. "I'm disappointed as fuck, Aria. You're better than this." He pushed open the door, and Aria sobbed when it slammed closed.

"Back to Michigan, please," she said.

She turned around in her seat, staring at Nahvid as he placed a call while she rode away. She hoped one day he would change his mind, or that she could prove that Isa wasn't as bad as Nahvid thought.

6

Aria walked through the door of Isa's house carrying two heavy suitcases, one in each hand. His eyes lifted from the blunt, and he kicked back on the leather couch as they stared at each other. He pulled the smoke into his mouth, then lifted one foot to the coffee table and blew the smoke up into the air.

"Fuck you doing here?" he asked. "Walking your lil' ugly ass up in here like this yo' crib. You lucky I ain't blow your head off."

She set down her bags. "Shut up and come here, boy."

Isa wasn't quick to move. Despite the fact that his heart was beating so hard he could hear it in his ears. He had never been happier to see someone in his life. He hated that Aria had the power to ruin or revive his day with just her presence. He turned his gaze to the big screen on his wall.

Fucking stubborn-ass man, she thought.

"Oh, so you're in your feelings? You're just going to ignore me?" she asked. She nodded. "Okay."

She stepped high-heeled feet over his legs.

"Move, man!" Isa fussed as he pushed her out of the way so he could see the basketball game playing.

Aria waltzed right over to the television and picked up the baseball bat he kept hanging on the wall. An autographed A-Rod bat from a World Series game. His pride and joy. One of many because Isa was a sports junkie.

"Fuck you doing, yo?" he asked, irritation playing in his tone. "That shit signed as fuck. Shit ain't no toy."

"Oh, it's signed?" she mocked. "You care about this bat, huh? You were just being a big-ass baby and ignoring me seconds ago. Now you can speak?"

"Man gone with that shit," Isa grumbled, scratching the top of his head as he lifted the blunt to his lips. "Ain't you supposed to be with your people? You can't fuck with me. You said that. I'm over it. Take ya' ass back to ya' folk and get from in front of the TV. A nigga got ten bands on this game."

Aria swung the bat, cracking the TV screen, then tossed the bat at him as he stood from the couch.

"You done lost your fucking mind!" he barked.

"Next time, you better act like you see me when I walk in this bitch!" she shouted.

She started to walk away, but he caught her wrist and pulled her into him roughly. Aria slapped him, and Isa wrapped her. His one hand was large enough to capture both of hers.

"Go home to your people before I knock your head off," Isa said.

"I fucking dare you." Tears built in her eyes, and he frowned. "I chose you, you asshole. Over my brother. I picked you." She broke down, and Isa loosened his hold, placing a hand to the back of her head. "He thinks you're bad for me, but you're so good to me. He cut me off, Isa. I've never fought with my brother ever. He's all I have."

Weakness wasn't Aria. She didn't allow herself to feel it often, but this one hurt. This one hit differently.

"Aye." He pulled her attention, but she could barely see him through her tears. "He ain't all you got."

He bent down and hoisted her up, opening her thighs until she wrapped them around his waist. Aria held on to his neck and rested her face over his shoulder as he took wide steps toward the bedroom. "You got me 'til they drop me, Ali."

She cried on his shoulder, and he consoled her as if she were a baby, and she was. She was his baby. The first woman he had ever cared for.

"You picked a nigga, Ali? Over your blood?" he asked as he sat on the edge of the bed. She was in his lap, still straddling him. She nodded, and his thumb cleared the wetness from her face.

"I picked you," she confirmed while sniffing. She was sad about that, about the rift between her and Nahvid. He was her family, and he meant everything to her. She prayed one day he would accept her choices because she was sure they wouldn't change. Her love for Isa wasn't going anywhere, and she hoped to earn Nahvid's respect again. She didn't know how, but she and Isa would prove him wrong. She would make sure of it.

He kissed her aggressively as he gripped the back of her neck.

"Is this going to last, Isa?" she asked.

"As long as you'll put up with me, Ali."

She placed her hands on the sides of his face and looked into his eyes. "I hate you." She closed her eyes because this wasn't her. This vulnerability. It was uncontrollable.

"Nah. Not tonight. I love you, Ali. Like on some real shit. I'll chop some shit up over you. Die behind you. I need you to know you ain't waste your pick. You gon' be my wife, and I'ma put babies in here." He touched her stomach. "And we gon' live,

Ali. We gon' ball the fuck out, and you ain't gon' never want for nothing. I'ma take care of you cuz you mine. So wipe your eyes, a'ight?"

She nodded.

"Broke my motherfucking TV. I'ma break yo' little ass," he snickered.

Aria reached down and gripped the bottom of her shirt, then lifted it over her head.

"Break me, baby," Aria whispered. She bit her bottom lip as Isa buried his face between her breasts, planting a kiss to her left one as he palmed it before moving to her right. His tattooed hands rubbed upward until his fingers were wrapped around her neck. The valley of her throat tensed, deepened as she held her breath. She expected him to tighten his hold. He liked to choke women, and to her surprise, he went behind her neck and untied the knot of the head scarf that was tied on her head. Her lids fluttered as he removed it and lowered his head to kiss one breast, then her areola, enticing it, until it was taut between his teeth. Then he bit her. She gasped as it throbbed. His teeth pulled just hard enough, and Aria's thighs opened wider in his lap.

"Who am I, Ali?" he asked.

"You the king, baby," she whispered. He wrapped the scarf around her wrists. Bondage. If he was the king, she was his captive, enslaved to this shit, and Aria didn't want to be freed.

"Nah, Ali. A nigga ain't never wanted to be king. I kill the kings. I chop niggas' heads off, baby. Ya' nigga a goon."

"The Kingslayer," Aria whispered. He snickered at her *Game of Thrones* reference.

"Queenslayer too," he said, palming a handful of her behind so roughly that it hurt. "Lay down, Ali, and say a nigga name before I make you scream it."

"The god, baby. Isa the god," she moaned.

Aria stood, and Isa unbuttoned her jeans, rolling them over her ass and then down her legs as she stepped out of them. Her hands hung, uselessly bound in front of her. He leaned into her stomach, biting it, with more pressure, enough to leave teeth marks.

"Isa..."

Isa stood and wrapped a hand around her throat, stopping further protests, further everything, because Aria couldn't breathe. "We ain't talking, Ali. We 'bout to do something else," he said.

He circled her body, slowly, biting her shoulder, the back of her neck, and then running his tongue down the dip of her toned back. Aria's body was incredible. A true dancer, every part was defined. The only part of her that had weight to it was the ass that stopped her from being a ballerina, but she got it from her mama, so unfortunately, it was there to stay. Isa ran his tongue all the way down to the crack of her ass and then lifted one of her thighs.

He slapped her ass. The sting it caused felt like punishment. The chill of his saliva as he licked the injury before blowing on it made goose bumps prickle her skin.

"Lay down," he instructed. Aria climbed on the bed. With her wrists tied, she put her weight on her elbows and knees, but Isa snatched one ankle, leveling her. Aria put her hands above her head and clasped them together. She didn't know what to expect, and she wanted to hold on to something, but with her wrists tied, all she could do was cling to herself.

The anticipation was the worst part. The kink he was into sometimes took her breath away, but Aria was a control freak; the not knowing of it all scared her. He had never done anything to her that hadn't brought her to a screaming orgasm.

It had never hurt beyond her limitations, but Aria feared the day he wanted to take it up a notch. Her body tensed, and she squeezed her eyes shut, and then . . .

"Isa!"

He hated the yelling. The protesting. The smack to her ass told her so.

Aria bit her lip.

Hot. Wet. Burning. She whimpered as the skin on her ass smoldered for a few seconds.

Then his tongue, extinguishing the feeling.

"It's wax, Ali. It's edible," he groaned as his teeth peeled back the hardening chocolate flavor. "Let me eat in peace, baby."

Aria gasped when he poured more, this time down the crack of her ass.

It burned, but oddly, her pussy throbbed.

Aria didn't scream this time, and Isa ate every piece of wax, then blew on the tender spots it left behind.

"Open." There was no saying no, so her shaky legs opened. The air kissed her clit. She was so exposed.

"Isa . . ."

He came up her body, and the weight of him pressed her into the bed. He removed the scarf from her wrists, then bound her mouth with it.

"You know what to say when you want it to stop," he whispered in her ear. Aria thought about saying it, about ending this, but she was too curious to what it would feel like . . . the place he was going to pour the wax next. Aria whimpered as she bit down on the fabric, and he traveled back down her body, planting bites and then kisses along the way.

"I want my name on you, Ali. Down your back," he whispered. He kept one hand wrapped around her long ponytail, pulling her neck back as Ali gripped the edge of the bed.

He didn't even let it go as he poured the wax on her.

Aria's pussy exploded. The feeling of the wax tightening around her clit felt like heaven. She came before he even touched her. She whimpered in ecstasy.

Isa's hands opened her, and then his face conquered her. For a man who hadn't eaten pussy before her, he was a motherfucking pro. He put a hand beneath her waist, lifting her off the bed so he went deeper. Isa was like a lion enjoying his catch, and he didn't stop until her legs shook. The screaming orgasm rippled through her entire body. Isa's dick dragging up her back as he came up felt glorious. He wanted her, and Aria rose, elbows and knees as he entered her.

He fucked every insecurity from her pretty little head.

"Oh fuck!" he growled. Heavy breathing. This nigga beasted her every time, and Aria loved it.

He collapsed onto her back, pressing her into the mattress as his fingers relieved her mouth of the gag.

"Don't leave again, Ali. You fucked me up."

Aria turned and pierced him with shocked eyes. She had hurt him. It was clear as day in his gaze. She touched his face and then rolled over onto him. He wrapped his arms around her body as she stared him down.

"Queenslayer," she said, a smirk playing at the corner of her mouth. "I'm not going anywhere."

7

I'm calling you daddy, daddy
Can you be my daddy, daddy
Come and make it rain down onnnn meeee

Isa sat on the leather couch. He sank into the plush cushions as he held the Styrofoam cup in his hand. His neck was lazy, and he let it rest against the pillows as his low eyes hawked her. Ali. Chocolate ass. Little ass. He would war with any nigga over her. She was a soldier. His most loyal. The shit he felt for her he would never speak, but she knew. She had chosen him over her blood family, and for that, Isa would always be hers to command. Whatever she wanted. He'd wet niggas up to go get it. Every time. Whatever lil' baby wanted, lil' baby would receive. She moved her body to precision. That ass sat high and fucking round as she rode the beat. She laced that bitch like her body was one with the music. He hardly noticed Morgan next to her. Ali was all he saw. She was truth over a lifetime full of bullshit.

"One, two, three, four . . . on every offbeat, you pop, Mo,"

Aria instructed while showing her the move, executing it with nothing less than perfection.

Morgan shook the fog from her mind as she tried to keep up with the choreography.

"What's up, Mo? You distracted like hell," Aria said.

"I know," Morgan admitted. "Run it back."

They practiced in Isa's basement. Isa refused to let Aria back in the studio, so he had turned his entire basement into one. Mirrors had been installed as well as hardwood floors.

"Uncle Isa, let's playyyyy!" Messari yelled as he jumped all over Isa's luxury furniture.

"Ssari, no. Feet belong on the floor," Morgan chastised.

"Get yo' stiletto-wearing ass on somewhere," Isa said. "Come on, Yolly. Let's fuck up some furniture." Isa bent down to scoop Yara from the floor and then stood on top of his own sofa. "Hop all over this bitch, lil' nigga," Isa said. "Fuck what yo' mama mean-ass talking about."

He took one of the pillows and tossed it at Messari. His little body went flying, Isa hit him so hard.

"Hey!" Messari shouted. "Mommy, him hit me!"

"Quit snitching," Isa said, popping Messari again. "Man up, G. A nigga hit you, you hit him back. Ain't that right, Yolly?" he asked. Yara laughed as Isa handed her a pillow. "Hit his ass."

Yara tossed the pillow in delight.

"Hey!"

Isa pushed him down, and Messari scrambled up. He laughed as he grabbed a pillow and tossed it at Isa.

"This nigga is a big kid. Be careful with my boyfriend," Aria said. "I'ma beat ya' ass if he gets hurt, Isa."

The pillow that met the side of her head shut her up instantly.

"See, you want me to fuck you up," Aria said.

Yara giggled away in Isa's arms, and Aria stole her away as Messari attacked Isa.

"That's right. You don't let nobody punk you," Isa said, using an open palm to slap the side of Messari's face. He used just enough force to knock him off balance. "Psk, psk," Isa antagonized.

"My baby is not a dog, Isa!" Morgan shouted.

"Shut up, Mo. You gon' have my lil' nigga soft. His daddy already pussy. I got this," Isa protested as Messari got up and charged at him. "That's right. Buck up, lil' nigga." Morgan shook her head as Messari went toe-to-toe with Isa. Messari got knocked down repeatedly, but he got up every time. There was no doubt about it, there was not a single ounce of bitch in his blood.

Isa snickered as he antagonized Messari.

"Uncle Isa, stop it!" Messari shouted. He ran up on Isa, and Isa pushed him down again.

Isa was getting the best of Messari, and Morgan could see her son's eyes welling in frustration.

"Isa!" Aria shouted.

"That's enough, Isa," Morgan warned. "I swear if you push my baby one more time."

"He got it, Mo. This gangster business right here, and yo' crybaby ass ain't a gangster," Isa teased.

"She got hittas, though, nigga. Don't get fucked up," Meek said as he descended the basement stairs.

Morgan's entire body steeled.

"Meek!" Messari shouted as he scrambled from the couch. His little legs couldn't carry him to Meek quickly enough. "Him hit me!"

Ahmeek bent to scoop Messari. "You hit him back?" Ahmeek asked.

"Mmm-hmm," Messari said.

"Show me how hard," Ahmeek said, holding up one open hand.

Messari threw the hardest punch his little body could, and as soon as his little hand connected with Meek's, Meek took that hand and slapped Isa with it.

"That's how you get with these bitch-ass niggas out here, lil' homie," Ahmeek stated.

Aria hollered in laughter as Messari high-fived Ahmeek and hugged his neck tightly.

"Damn, nigga," Isa complained. "I should shoot the shit out ya' ass," he snickered. "You know I'm light-skinned. Got yo' mu'fuckin' handprint on my shit like I'm a bitch out here."

Ahmeek laughed as he slapped hands with Isa and pulled him in as they tapped shoulders. Isa rustled Messari's head.

"You lucky yo' backup came, nephew."

Messari hugged Ahmeek tighter, hiding from Isa.

Morgan's entire body froze. It was a sin to love someone the way she loved him. Ahmeek didn't even look her way. Her last words to him had been so cruel she couldn't say she blamed him.

"Okkayyy," Aria said, cutting through the awkward vibes in the room. "Let's get focused, Mo. You been fucking up all day. We could have been done. I'm gonna run it back."

Aria handed Yara to Isa, and Ahmeek stepped back. He still held Messari as he made room for Aria and Morgan to finish their routine.

The music started, and Morgan turned on. She had been so distracted before, she'd missed every step the first few rounds of practicing. With Meek's attention on her, she was flawless. He was pretending not to watch her, but she knew he hadn't missed a beat, because if he loved nothing else about her . . . he loved when she danced, and Mo was showing out. Whenever he was in the room, the stakes tripled. She loved to see the look in his eyes. It was more than lust. It was pride.

By the time the song ended, Morgan was sweating she had danced so hard. Her heavy breathing made her chest rise and fall.

"That's all that ass you carrying around that got you tired like that," Aria teased. Morgan blushed. The music changed, and Aria turned up the volume. Music lived in her soul, and her moods fluctuated with the harmonies of her day.

See I don't need n'aan nigga jocking me,
    slowing me down and stopping me
Climbing all on top of me,
    if he ain't gon' fuck me properly

"Don't write no check that ass can't cash, Ali," Isa said as he snatched her by the waist, pulling her to the couch.

"That's a bit much for them, yo," Meek stated, nodding to the twins as he picked up the remote control and pressed the arrow skipping the song. "Trina got to keep that bad-bitch shit to herself."

"Mmkay, Meek. Look out for your babies, boy. You better step!" Aria snickered.

"Slapping niggas behind they asses," Isa snickered as he lifted his red cup to his lips. He tapped Aria on the ass, and she pulled away from him as the next song faded in.

The song changed, and a sensual mood filled the air as Vedo crooned through the speaker system.

Yeah I like when she get nasty,
    but I love when she keep it classy.

It was Morgan's turn to choreograph, and it was so natural for her to slow down the tempo.

"Shit's ridiculous, yo," Ahmeek muttered, shaking his head. She had him. Caught his ass right in her web. He could ignore everything about her except this . . . when she made her body move like this . . . when she made art of her body like this. Like fucking this. Morgan danced her heart out because she knew he liked it. She knew he loved it. His eyes on her made Morgan give her all. She never held back when he was watching. He was all the audience she needed. His support made her feel beautiful. He took her in differently than other men did. His gaze wasn't lust filled but awe filled, like he appreciated the effort it took for her to put the count together.

Do it nasty, do it, do it nasty, she gon' do it nasty.

"These mu'fuckas," Isa snickered as he rose from his seat. "Come on, bruh." The fellas moved to a different part of the basement, allowing the girls to finish their rehearsal. Aria and Morgan put on unbelievable performances. They were a package deal, and a valuable one. They set every stage they ever graced on fire.

They practiced for an hour before wrapping up. When they were done, Morgan walked to the next room. She knocked on the doorframe, and all conversation ceased.

"Come on, guys," she both signed and spoke. "Time to go."

Ahmeek didn't even look at her. There was so much she wanted to say to him. So much to explain, only she couldn't. Bash didn't even know where she was. If he had any clue she was rehearsing for a Stiletto Gang show, he would have a fit. If he knew Ahmeek was present, he would ruin her life. Morgan was walking a tightrope here. She couldn't spare Ahmeek's feelings. Their time had come, and it had passed. There was nothing else to be done. It didn't stop it from hurting, however.

"Tell everyone bye."

It tugged at her heart the way her children hugged both men before they came to her.

"A'ight, Mo. I'll see you, sis," Isa said without looking as he stayed focused on the money on the table.

"You're coming to graduation, right?" The question was for Isa, but she hoped Ahmeek answered. She prayed he would come. She didn't know why she wanted him there. They weren't even on speaking terms, but she wanted to share the moment with him, needed him to witness her accomplishment. She missed him so much. There was an incredible void in her life without him. Above all else, she missed the way he looked at her. His stare was so full of pride and appreciation. He hyped her up like nobody else, and she wanted him to root for her as she walked across the stage. He didn't speak, however. Didn't even glance her way. He focused on the twins. Tying Messari's shoe and then accepting a hug from him before sending him on his way. No acknowledgment for Mo.

"Ssari, grab your sister's hand, and go up the stairs slowly," Morgan said as she grabbed her gym bag and then reached for her purse as well as the twins' bag. "Come on, Ssari, let's go. Help Yolly."

She felt Ahmeek relieving her of the bags before grabbing Yara and heading up the stairs. She felt his disdain.

He hates me.

The thought broke her in half. She wished that things could be different. There were so many things, so many outsiders that kept them apart. Morgan helped Messari make it to the top of the staircase and followed Ahmeek to her car. Once the twins were strapped in and safe, Morgan started the car, then turned to Ahmeek. He stood outside her window, gripping the roof, leaning down like he wanted to say something, and then he stood up straight. He ran one hand down his head, and Morgan climbed from the car. She could see every bit of angst he felt. She was the cause, but she couldn't be the cure. Restraint was the hardest thing she had ever had to show. He turned to leave, and Morgan reached for him, catching the bottom of his shirt. He looked back at her, biting his bottom lip as his brow dipped. He was struggling with this. With her. Morgan pulled him into her space, and he lingered there. She couldn't even look at him. Her head was down, but his finger lifted it and forced the connection they both craved. Neither spoke. They just stood there. Morgan was sure this was what death felt like. To want something so badly but be denied of it. To be denied because you wouldn't let yourself have it. His thumb graced her lip, and Morgan closed her eyes. When she opened them, he was already halfway up the driveway, and he had taken her soul with him. He had stolen her heart, and Morgan would let him keep it because it gave her an excuse to come back to him one day.

Isa pulled the blunt, holding the smoke before blowing it out. Ahmeek sauntered down the steps and fell right into rotation as Isa passed the weed. It dangled from his lips as he sat, then he reached for another stack of bills.

"You on with it with Mo? Thought you was falling back," Isa said.

"Mo for the games. A nigga ain't got time," Ahmeek answered. "She'll drive a nigga crazy, man. If she got to go back and forth with it, it ain't mine."

"Real shit," Isa said.

"Back to this money, nigga," Ahmeek choked out with his weed smoke as he passed the blunt.

"We on track to pay this month's tab to the nigga Hak?" Isa asked.

"We on track. Ya man almost fucked shit up, but I covered it. No lie, bruh, I'm this close to blowing that nigga head off," Ahmeek stated, pinching his fingers together to measure his lack of restraint.

"Shit's out of hand, G. You and him," Isa stated, pausing to toke the blunt. "Fighting over Mo. The shit put a nigga in a real bad spot. You my mans. He my mans. Fuck I'm supposed to do with a war between y'all?"

"Stay out of it," Ahmeek answered.

8

Bleu sat on her sofa, flipping through case files in front of her. The highlighter in her hands slid over the pages. It was late, too late to be up, but she couldn't sleep. A candle flickered, causing shadows to dance against her ceiling as crickets chirped outside. The breeze that snuck through her window caused goose bumps to form on her arms. She heard the sound of his engine before the headlights that turned into her driveway illuminated her living room. She didn't even rise from her seat. She kept working as the sound of the car door slamming filled the air, then heavy thuds against the wood of her porch as he ascended the steps.

"What you doing up?" he asked.

"Working," she said without looking at him. "I have to help a lady get her kid back tomorrow. Be a character witness in court on her behalf. I'm just making sure I have everything together."

He came into view, and Bleu rolled tired eyes up to him. He took the papers from her hands.

"Messiah, I don't feel like hearing anybody's problems but my own right now," she sighed.

He sat on the edge of the ottoman directly in front of her and then tossed the papers to the floor. "Nigga, this shit ain't no one-sided shit where I just dump my shit on you but you can't give me some of yours. Start talking," Messiah barked. "What problems?"

Bleu sighed and let her head fall back against the couch cushions. "Iman wants me and Saviour to move to LA." The room grew so silent you could hear a pin drop.

"Nah," Messiah answered. "Next problem."

The laugh that fell from Bleu's lips made Messiah smirk as he rose slightly to pull the ottoman closer to the couch.

"Just like that, huh?" Bleu asked. "I shouldn't even consider it?"

"You can't consider it. I said no. Now what else keeping you up?" Messiah asked.

Bleu didn't respond right away. She just looked at Messiah. Never the one to back down, the stare down was returned. Bleu looked away first. She wasn't sure if Messiah always won their battles because she let him or because he was simply in charge, but either way, she yielded.

"This woman who's fighting for her daughter is a recovering addict," Bleu said. "It just reminds me of myself. This could have easily been me, Messiah. They're trying to take her kid forever, and I'm rooting for her, but what if she gets her baby back and she goes back to getting high? Any little thing can make an addict backslide, Messiah. What happens to her kid if she messes up? What happens to Saviour if I mess up?" she whispered the last part. This wasn't about the case. It was about her life, about the things that were at stake for her.

"And that's why you want to move?" Messiah asked.

"Because you want him close to Iman in case you start using again?"

Bleu didn't answer, but she lowered her head as tears filled her eyes. She didn't let one fall. "I'm not saying I will. I don't want to, but it's certain shit that terrifies me, Messiah. Like sometimes it's the smallest thing that triggers me. Like when I turn on the stove to cook. There's this sparking sound, this click that reminds me of the sound the lighter would make when . . ." Bleu's voice disconnected, breaking up as her lip trembled. She looked at him with so much angst. "It's just not as easy as it looks, Messiah."

Messiah nodded. "I believe that, B," he said. "That it's hard as fuck. What you need from me to make sure that don't happen?"

She nodded. "Nothing. Nobody can carry this but me," she said.

"And apparently Iman," Messiah said. "He's a good nigga, B. No lie. I fuck with Iman. I know the nigga love you. He's a good father to Saviour. He do his job, B, but Cali? I ain't with that shit, man."

"I don't really need permission, Messiah," she answered.

"The hell you don't," Messiah uttered. He frowned, and he cracked the knuckles on his big hands then stood. He didn't know what to do with this energy she was giving. "You trying to make it work with him, B? Or this just about Saviour?" he asked.

"I don't know, Messiah. We aren't really the same as we used to be. He couldn't even look at me after I told him I was pregnant by you. He's just now speaking to me again. I don't know what me moving there would mean, but damn, I don't want to be by myself forever."

"You ain't by yourself," Messiah muttered.

Bleu half smiled because she knew he believed that to be true.

"I swear sometimes it feel like I should just . . ." Messiah stopped speaking and shook his head.

"You should just what?" she asked.

"You the only one seem to appreciate the fact that a nigga back," Messiah said. "Everything around me changed, B, but you're the same. You tryna move all the way to fucking Cali? Can't see that. Can't see me letting that happen at all, B."

"Why?" Bleu asked. "What am I missing here? You've got your life, Messiah. You have your plans, you know what you came back for. You want Ethic and Mo, and that's an entire family for you. It's just me and Saviour over here. What are we around for? There is nothing keeping me here."

Messiah stood and hitched up his pants, looking off as he rubbed his fingers in irritation. Thumb to middle finger, they circled.

"Leave then, B. If that's how you feel, pack ya' shit and dip," Messiah said.

"Why are you mad?" she asked as she stood too. "Everything isn't about what you need. I need things. Saviour needs things."

Messiah pulled a wad of money from his back pocket and began flicking through the bills. "What you need, B? Huh?" he asked, tossing hundred-dollar bills at her. "That enough?" He kept peeling off money. Bleu slapped the entire roll out of his hands. He didn't even bother to pick it up.

"I will hurt you, Messiah," Bleu sneered. "Throwing money at me like you're crazy."

"I am crazy, mu'fucka, so stop playing with me. Cali ain't the play." He moved through her home and headed to the kitchen. She followed him and stood in the doorway as he

helped himself to the orange juice, tilting the half-gallon car-
ton to his mouth like he had purchased it.

"Saviour needs a father, you asshole," Bleu said. "You gon'
be that? You gon' do that, Messiah?"

"I'll be whatever the fuck he need me to be!" Messiah
barked. He didn't know shit about fathering a human being,
but shit, if that was what her friendship required, he would
try. He had tried to be something to her son, he didn't know
what—neither did she—but somehow he had become a staple
for Saviour.

"And what about me?" Bleu shouted. She didn't even mean
to. It just flew out of her mouth, her emotions overriding intel-
lect because Messiah was driving her crazy.

"Whatever the fuck you need me to be too. What you
want me to be, B?" he yelled. Bleu's temper had her heaving.
Her eyes misted. This had gone too far. She shook her head.

"Nah, don't shake your head. Answer the question. Keep
it a stack with me. What you want from me? I ain't never not
delivered when you asked me for something. What you want
me to be to you, B?"

Bleu hesitated. She froze because she didn't know the
answer to that question. She just knew she couldn't stay. She
couldn't stay in Michigan and keep doing what she had been
doing. With him. For years. The casual nature of friendship,
the unspoken bond they shared, the dependency they had created . . . nah, she couldn't do that at all . . . not anymore.

"Nobody. I want you to go back to being nobody to me,"
she said. "Lock my door on your way out." She bumped past
him, rushing up the stairs and out of sight.

9

Morgan sat at the rectangular table. Squared shoulders, legs crossed at the ankles, not the knee, and perfect posture. Her hair was swept back in a long French braid, and she wore Yves Saint Laurent. She was perfection. Christiana had laid out her graduation look and had left nothing undone. Morgan Atkins looked like an accomplished woman, a royal woman. She looked like the valedictorian of Michigan State's graduating class of 2020.

"Thank you for making the trip to see me walk, David," Morgan said, giving kind eyes to Bash's father. She didn't see him often. He didn't split his time between the States and England the way Christiana did.

"I wouldn't miss it, Morgan. We all watched you work extremely hard for this over the past two years. You earned it," David answered.

Morgan smiled graciously. He seemed to be the only Fredrick who thought she deserved this degree. Christiana and Bash acted like she hadn't done anything at all.

"Well, that's a bit generous, but either way, there is cause for celebration today. Matriculation is always a reason to bring out the good china. Which I would have done if you had chosen to have your dinner here. We have to drive all the way to Detroit for a decent meal when the staff could have prepared it, but I digress," Christiana said.

Morgan opted for silence. She didn't feel like starting her graduation day on a bad note, so instead of arguing, she pushed back from the table.

"I'm going to head out. I've got to be there early, and I need to drop the twins off at Ethic's beforehand," Morgan said.

Bash caught her hand before she walked by his chair. "I can drive you, and the twins can ride to the ceremony with me," Bash insisted.

"Ethic wants them. Do you want to tell him no?" she asked.

Bash released her hand. He stood to help her.

"I've got it. You can finish breakfast with your parents. I'll see you guys later."

Morgan walked out of the massive dining room and hurried to grab the twins from the adjoining room. Messari's little slacks, collared shirt, and suspenders warmed her heart. Yara was pretty in pink, but she had already taken off her tights and kicked off her shoes. Morgan shook her head. She grabbed Yara, tossed her shoes and tights inside their bag, then headed for the door.

"Come on, Mommy's Ssari," she sang, knowing he would follow.

He came running.

Morgan couldn't get away fast enough. Bash had been possessive lately, calling every time she left his parents' estate and picking a fight every time she wanted to go back to her own apartment. Morgan hadn't slept in her own bed in days, and when she left him, she could have sworn he was having her followed. She felt like eyes were on her all the time. She even felt like he was checking her phone at night. She had never been more on edge. She wasn't comfortable anywhere, but she knew she couldn't leave. So, she endured.

Morgan felt the tension leave her chest when she finally made it to Ethic's. Just the sight of the house behind the gate eased her. She typed in the code and eased her car through. After she unloaded the twins, they took off running toward the front door. Morgan used her key and went inside.

"I'm home!" she shouted. She had been on her own for a few years, but this would always be home.

"Mo's here!" Eazy shouted as he grinned while approaching her with excitement. "Hey, Mo!"

"Hey, Eazy," she replied as she received the quick hug he gave before he bent to pick up Yara.

"Come on, man," Eazy said to Messari. The three took off up the stairs as Ethic came waltzing down.

"You look beautiful, baby girl," he greeted. "Fucking college graduate." He said it like he couldn't believe it. He shook his head. "Justine and Benny are smiling today, Mo. Raven too."

"Thanks, Ethic," she said. "I've got to go, but I'll see you guys there."

The crowd was massive. The stadium was filled to capacity, and Morgan could hear the eager chatter that filled the building from where she stood. She didn't know why she was so nervous. She could hardly stand still as she waited in the reception area where the other graduates congregated.

"Can you believe we did it?" Aria asked. "I hate to admit that I'm going to miss this shit."

"Yeah, me too," Morgan said, smiling. "Is Isa here?"

"I invited my brother. He and Isa can't be in the same place at once. He had a run to make anyway," Aria said. "But my brother didn't even show, so he could have come."

"Aria, I'm sorry," Morgan said. "Come celebrate with me afterward. We're going to Ocean Prime for dinner. It's a small thing, but we did this together, so we're going to be acknowledged together."

"I might have plans, but I'll try," Aria answered, forcing a smile as she looked around the arena hopefully. "Is Meek coming?"

"We haven't talked," Morgan admitted. Her voice was sad, and Aria reached for her hand.

"How about we forget all of them today, Mo? It's not about them; it's about us. We did this. We deserve to go into this day with clear heads and proud hearts. Fuck Messiah, fuck Isa, fuck Meek, and fuck Bash ass too. Fuck everybody except Ethic, cuz that's zaddy," Aria teased.

Morgan groaned.

"It's about us today. It's not about them. It's about us. Black girls sprinkling magic across this stage as we get our degrees. I'm chassé-ing my pretty ass across that damn stage when they call my name," Aria said. "You write your big speech?"

"I did," Morgan said. "My stomach is in knots, though. I'll be right back, okay?"

Morgan hurried away from the crowd and found solace in the restroom. She was overwhelmed and underwhelmed all at the same time. It was the most accomplished moment of her life, but the fact that she was commemorating it with Bash cheapened it. He wasn't who she wanted to run to when she received her degree. She didn't want to smile for his cameras or hear his voice singing her praises. She had really bound herself to a man she didn't love, and she was miserable.

She had perfected the art of the fake smile so well that not even Ethic could detect something was wrong. The bathroom door opened, and Morgan spun around as his reflection hit the mirror.

"Shorty Doo Wop." In Messiah's hands, he held a turquoise box. He locked the bathroom door.

"What are you doing here?" Morgan asked.

He walked up behind her and opened the box. He didn't answer her question, and he got so close that Morgan held her breath. Her heart raced as he pressed his body into the back of her.

"Messiah, don't," she whispered.

"Don't what, shorty?" he asked. She closed her eyes and gripped the sink, releasing a shaky breath. Something cold hit her collarbone, and she opened her eyes to find Messiah fastening a necklace around her neck.

"It's from Tiffany's. Your favorite store. I think you said that it was. It's been a while since we had that conversation, but I don't think I forgot," Messiah said.

Her fingers went to her neck, touching the gold butterfly charm that hung from the thin necklace.

"I don't want it," she whispered, but her heart was fluttering. She swallowed the lump in her throat as she stared at Messiah's reflection. "I don't want anything from you," she said stubbornly.

He stared back, moving her braid out the way as he placed his lips to the nape of her neck. It felt like the kiss of death. She spun on him.

"Don't," she warned, pushing him backward. He stepped

toward her anyway, and Morgan pushed him again. "I don't want shit from you. Stop coming around like things are good between us, Messiah," she whispered. "I can't even stand the sight of you." Her voice trembled.

"I know," he answered as he lifted her onto the sink, opening her legs so he could slide between her thighs. "But you gon' end up fucking with the kid anyway, so might as well stop playing tough, shorty."

Morgan was livid at his arrogance. Before she could even stop herself she spit in his face. Messiah pulled back and froze as Morgan stood. She watched him process the disrespect in his mind. She saw the anger flicker in his eyes like a light bulb struggling to illuminate. He used his tongue to lick her spit from around his mouth and then wiped one hand down his face. Anger dissipated, and amusement pulled at the corner of his lips. Nothing about Morgan disgusted him. No part of her turned him off.

"Let me taste something else wet, shorty," he said.

Morgan turned red, inside and out. She hated that he loved every part of her. She bled for this nigga here. Through the good, bad, and ugly, she loved him. Even when she hated him. There was no part of her that disgusted him. Messiah advanced on her, wrapping one hand around her neck and forcing her against the wall as Morgan's eyes lifted to the ceiling.

Please, God, she thought.

She needed God to shake the table, open the floor, and swallow her whole, shit, something! Anything! To stop her from wetting for him, because her body ignited. There was an exhilaration about the danger of Messiah that pulled her to him like metal to magnet. It didn't matter that she hated him. She resented him with her entire soul, but her panties still soaked.

"Ahh," she moaned against her will. Messiah was a beast, and he was about to capture her. She felt how much he wanted her. God, she felt it. He couldn't do this. Not today. She was supposed to be graduating today. She had her entire family sitting in the front row. Her boyfriend was sitting on the stage. Messiah was turning her into a whole whore, but she couldn't say no. The words evaded her. She couldn't even find her voice to protest. He lifted her onto the bathroom sink and lowered his Nike joggers as he pressed his dark fingers into her light skin. He entered her without thinking twice about hitting her unprotected.

"Fuck!" Messiah groaned.

He filled her as his hand tightened around her throat, and he pressed the back of her head against the mirror.

Morgan was filled with an odd feeling. Shame and desire. No way should he be touching her like this . . . fucking her like this, but her mouth fell open as he provided a high she hadn't experienced in years. His sex was like a free fall. Terrifying and exhilarating. It was more than she could handle and made her feel like she were risking it all, but once you jumped out the plane, you just had to pray the parachute opened. Deprivation made Messiah weak, and he came inside her like no time had passed at all. He pulled back, adjusting his clothes as she refused to lend him her gaze. When had they become this awkward? When had sex become such a sin between people who used to partake in it like an addiction?

"This is a mistake," Morgan whispered as she placed both hands over her face in disgrace.

Messiah fingered the scratches she had put on his neck. They were raw, bleeding. Like her heart. He bit his lip and then lifted sad eyes to Morgan. It wrecked him that so much had changed. Years ago, Morgan and Messiah hadn't been able to keep their hands off each other. Anytime. Anyplace. They had allowed themselves to indulge in lovemaking. Today, however, things felt so different it almost felt like he had crossed a line. Somberness filled him. Morgan was so different now.

"I'm real proud of you, Shorty Doo Wop," he mumbled.

She was panting. Spent. Her eyes were misted in an emotion she didn't quite know how to identify as she pulled her dress down and turned toward the sink.

"Everything feels so different!" she cried. "You waited too long to come back for me, Messiah. You're too late."

She gripped the edges of the porcelain as she looked into the black abyss of the drain. Her feelings were so hurt. Messiah made Morgan feel so worthless, not with bathroom sex, because she had always been down to make love whenever and wherever, but by abandonment. He had discarded her without even thinking twice. She couldn't even look at him in the reflection of the mirror. Then she felt him, on his knees, between her legs. His tongue parted her sex, cleaning up the mess he'd made of her, sucking her soul out of her body and swallowing it . . . trapping it. Checkmate, bitch. Soul mates, bitch. An apology for being so cruel. Morgan's eyes snapped closed; her grip tightened on the sink as Messiah maneuvered underneath her as if he were a plumber coming to tighten her leaky pipes. She bit her lips as he pulled on her pierced clit. He played with the piece of jewelry. The tiny M she kept there. Messiah's pussy. She hadn't forgotten. She'd made sure she'd tagged it so she would never forget. Even in his absence, it had been his for so long. She had waited, and then one day, the hood came to London. Ahmeek stepped off a plane, and his reintroduction into her life made Morgan not want to wait anymore. The thought of him caused Morgan's body to tense, and she was grateful for the knock at the door that interrupted them.

"Morgan, are you in there? The ceremony is about to begin," Aria called out. "Mo!"

Morgan scrambled. "Stop," she pleaded weakly, but Messiah kept licking, kept sucking. "Messiah, you have to . . ."

Morgan's mouth fell open as she came.

"Just like that, Mo. Some things don't change, shorty," he moaned, still eating, still face-deep in her.

Morgan pushed his head away, and Messiah smirked as he stood to his feet, wiping his face with one hand. "Head of the class like a mu'fucka," he snickered. "Enjoy graduation, shorty."

He unlocked the door and walked out, bumping into Aria along the way.

Aria stepped inside. "We've got to go, Mo," she said, knowing better than to ask questions.

Morgan pulled paper towels from the holder and wet them.

"I'll be right out. Just give me a few minutes," she stammered, flustered.

Aria looked at Morgan in concern but said nothing as she let the door close.

"What the hell am I doing?" she asked herself.

Morgan cleaned up as best as she could before rushing out. Leave it to Messiah to bombard her greatest achievement with mixed emotions, but she knew she had to tuck them away so that she could make it through the day.

10

Morgan was so deep in her feelings she was drowning. The ceremony was torture. She couldn't sit still as she waited for her name to be called. She kept turning to look in the crowd, her eyes scanning hundreds of faces, looking for just one. Her heart ached and eyes clouded as she tapped her foot against the concrete floor in angst. Her eyes found Aria, who was seated two rows behind. Her brows knitted in concern as she swiped a tear from her cheek.

"You okay?" Aria mouthed the words as she held up her hands and frowned at Morgan's distressed face.

Morgan couldn't breathe. She stood abruptly, interrupting the speaker onstage, and bolted for the door. She caused a slight disruption as people whispered as she ran past them. She burst out of the auditorium doors and raced for her car. She hopped in and peeled off just as Ethic rushed out of the building. Morgan's tears flowed as she pressed her gas pedal to the floor. She reached to the passenger seat, grabbing her phone, her eyes barely on the road as she tried to unlock it. She went to her favorite contacts. He was still the only number on the list, even after all this time. She had never erased it. She hadn't used it in years. She hoped the number was the same. She touched his name SSIAH and held the phone to her ear. Voice mail. Morgan drove faster. When she pulled up to his trap house, she saw him. He stood at the back of an SUV, removing boxes that she knew from experience were filled with a load they had just robbed. Same Messiah. Still thugging. Still risking it all . . . risking even more since she was no longer a factor. She pulled up recklessly behind the truck, blocking it in and throwing her car in park. The men standing beside him turned to her in surprise as she hopped out in her cap and gown.

Messiah stepped up and Morgan ran to him, practically knocking him over as she threw her arms around his neck. She kissed him so deeply, giving him years' worth of passion. He knocked that square hat off her head as he grabbed her braid and returned the kiss.

"Hmm," he groaned as she attacked those lips with aggression, aggression she had hidden, aggression he had taught her and that she had locked inside for years. She pulled back, placing her hands on his cheeks as he gripped the side of her face desperately. Their foreheads connected as she cried.

"What are you doing, shorty?" he asked in disbelief.

"I don't know," she answered while stroking his face gently.

He turned to the man behind him. "Yo, park the truck in the garage and lock shit down. Move her car around the block. I'll meet you back here tonight. I'ma text the details. Be ready," he said in a low tone. "Come on," he said, focusing back on her.

He grabbed her hand as they rushed to his bike. He handed her his only helmet, and she strapped it on in haste before climbing on the back without hesitation. He kicked off the stand as Morgan wrapped her arms around his body. She leaned into him, and he took off.

He took her hand and laced his fingers through hers, then balled his fist. Morgan closed her eyes because he took her breath away, and she held him tightly as the thrill of the high speeds caused nervous jitters to fill her. An hour outside of the city, they retreated to a hotel, and Morgan climbed down, removing the helmet. She sniffed away her emotions, wiping her eyes, and then ran her hands through her hair as Messiah held her under his scrutiny. Morgan looked away, unable to withstand the eye contact. It was like she didn't know him . . . like she was afraid to be alone with him. He reached for her hand, and her feet didn't move.

"I need to keep your gun. In my bag," she finished.

Her words were like a jab to Messiah's chin. He recoiled, stunned. Morgan Atkins, the one person on earth that he would never lay a finger on, feared he would hurt her. She saw the flicker of emotion in his eyes. No one else would have, but she did.

"I've been around you since I've been back," he said, looking for an explanation as to why she felt unsafe all of a sudden.

"Never alone," she answered.

It was a blow to his soul . . . the fact that she thought he would hurt her, but he reached into his waistline and held it out for her. He wouldn't protest. This was as calm as she had been around him in a long time. This was reminiscent of times past.

"It's your world, shorty. You hold the power," he said.

Morgan took it from his hand, clicked the safety on because Messiah never used his safety, and then put it in her purse. "The other one too."

It was an order. Her tone let him know it wasn't optional. Messiah's lips lifted on one side, a smirk . . . a disbelieving smirk.

Nobody had ever relieved him of his pistol. Not even the police. Morgan fucking Atkins had disarmed him merely with words. He removed it and handed it to her. She removed the clip and checked the chamber, putting the ammunition in her bag, then handed it back to him, empty. He had taught her that. Apparently, he had taught her well. He remembered the days she had been terrified to handle a gun.

Messiah scoffed, then led the way into the hotel. They were silent until they entered the room. He went to the bed and sat on it as she stayed near the door.

"I ain't gon' bite you, Mo," he said.

"Are you sure, Messiah?" she asked. "I barely know you."

"Nah, everybody outside these four walls barely knows me. You know, Mo," he said. "What you doing here? You pulled up on a nigga. What you want, shorty?"

"I don't know," she said, breathless, eyes prickling, as she rustled her hair and turned toward the door. She reached for the handle.

"Let go of the door and bring yo' ass over here," Messiah said.

Morgan's hand froze, and she closed her eyes. She turned and leaned her back against the door. "Don't tell me what to do. It's been a long time since you've seen me, so I know you don't know, but nobody tells me what to do."

"You let that fucking door go, didn't you?" he baited. "Now bring that shit over here so I can finish eating."

Morgan's feet had a mind of their own, and she crossed the room. She stood between his legs, and shaky hands reached for the top of his head as he unzipped the graduation gown. The dress beneath hugged her curves as if it were molded to her frame. She was so damn nervous. Everything was heightened, her senses on alert because this was new for them, reconnection over anger, over resentment . . . none of that had existed before between them, but it crowded the space between them now. Still, this moment was inevitable. He had been home too long without this happening. Flashes of what they used to be to each other caused her eyes to prickle. They would spend hours stuck between four walls with each other as the itinerary for entertainment. Trapped in a bubble. Their love had grown without sunlight, without water . . . like the plants that grew between the cracks of urban concrete. They had been resilient until a terrible storm had destroyed them.

"Damn, shorty," he groaned in appreciation. Morgan had filled all the way out. It had been years since he had left her in that hotel room, and she had transformed. He hated that somebody else was hitting it. He knew Meek was in it, and it burned him. He suspected Bash may be hitting it too. Not well. He was almost positive the lame nigga was trying, and the thought set a small fire inside his chest. Little Morgan had some ho in her with the juggling of two men, and oddly, it turned him on. He lifted the dress above her hips as Morgan stifled her breaths in anticipation. She held his ears, her thumbs caressing the side of his face, a familiar stroke she hadn't done in a long time. His eyes closed. Morgan was such comfort. She knew exactly where to touch, and he felt his nose burn as his emotions tried to push to the surface. He pushed them back down. Buried. Always unexposed beneath years of bullshit. Morgan knew this was wrong. She was already stretched too thin. Pieces of her were everywhere. Stuck to Bash like lint to a black shirt, attached to Ahmeek emotionally because even now he was in the back of her mind, but she couldn't stop herself because Messiah owned pieces too. He possessed the most broken parts. At one point, he had held them all because the pieces used to be whole . . . the pieces used to make up a heart. A heart that beat for him.

She straddled him. She pulled back, lifting his face, forcing him to look at her as she sat in his lap while his hands rubbed her behind. She saw a new tattoo on his neck. Two M's. One inked on top of the other like a logo. Branded on his body like she was the last woman he would ever be accountable to. Like he didn't have the rest of his life to find another one who would dislike the imprint of Morgan on his skin.

"Why did you pull up on me, Mo?"

"I don't know," she answered again, looking off at the ugly painting on the wall. It was hideous, and Morgan took in every detail of its ugliness to avoid looking at him. She couldn't face him.

"You know, shorty. Don't do that. You're supposed to be walking across a stage right now, but you're here. Why?" he asked.

"Because . . . ," she started, then stopped. There was a lump in her throat. So much resentment existed between them.

"You know how my patience is set up, Mo. Because what?" he pushed. She marked him with angry eyes.

"Because, Messiah," she said weakly. Her lip quivered because she couldn't even admit that she needed him. She hated that she loved the feel of his hands on her body. She hated that his eyes on hers felt incredible. Having him back was a miracle. She had never thought she would see him again, feel him again. Her anger had been masking how grateful she was that he was even alive. "You came back!" she cried. Her lashes were so heavy from the tears that clung to them. "What took you so long?"

Messiah stole her mouth, not giving one fuck about her resistance because he still owned every part of her. He would own her forever. Morgan withered under his touch. She bit him. Hard. He pulled back and caressed his lip as she pushed him down onto the bed, eyes glossing, angry tears spilling from her . . . challenging him. He reached up, gripping her neck, and flipped her onto the bed, dominating, hovering over her, one hand squeezing slightly on her throat. Morgan tried to lift, but Messiah grabbed her wrists and pushed her back down against the bed.

"It's been two years," she said, shaking her head. "And you just show up." Tears rolled from her eyes and pooled in her ears as Messiah hovered over her. Morgan's sobs escaped her, and she turned her head to the side as her chest quaked. "You should have left me alone."

"I can't, shorty," he groaned as he lowered to her ear. Messiah licked the side of her neck, while still holding her wrists hostage. "I'm sorry. I'm a reckless-ass nigga, but I'm your reckless-ass nigga, and you're a spoiled-ass brat . . ."

"But I'm your spoiled-ass brat." She barely managed the words. They were a ghost on her lips. Morgan pinched her eyes closed as he released one of her hands. She used her newfound freedom to grip his head and push him south. Messiah obliged, rolling down her panties and taking her swollen clit between his lips. She was like a pink Starburst . . . the motherfucking best out of the bunch. "I miss this shit, shorty. Damn," he groaned as he pulled on it with his full lips, hoisting up her hips to press her into him, adding pressure. Morgan's back arched clean off the bed as she grunted. This was wrong. She was in love with someone else, but damn it, how could she deny that behind all that anger for Messiah was indeed the love he had abandoned? She loved his bitch ass too. She didn't know if she was cheating on her fiancé, cheating on Meek, or cheating on Messiah, but she was definitely cheating. Perhaps herself. She was cheating on her soul, but she couldn't stop. Messiah smeared his face in her wet. Nasty. Nasty as ever for her, especially after all this time. She reached for his shirt, pulling it over his head, and the reflection of his back in the mirror made her eyes mist in disbelief. A mural of her face was staring back at her in the reflection. His body was a canvas dedicated to her. It hadn't been there two years ago. That tattoo was proof that he had thought of her while he was away. Her heart ached. It was bawling. She could feel her soul bleeding. How had they lost touch with each other for so long? How had he let it occur? How could he not need her? Not once had he reached out. Morgan had so many questions.

"Your back, Messiah," she gasped.

He paused and came up for air, his eyes meeting hers. "Every inch of me belongs to you, Mo," he said.

A streak of guilt flashed in her eyes because they both knew she had given her body away. He rubbed a gentle finger on the cover-up tattoo where his name used to be. She didn't know what to say.

"Lay down, shorty," he said as he went back down. Any grudge he held he took out on her clit. He made light work of her body, sucking that first orgasm out of her so fast Morgan had no time to do anything but bask in it. Colors exploded behind her lids as his soft tongue lapped at the small piece of flesh between her swollen labia.

"Ugh!" she groaned. "Agh!"

Messiah came up her body, peeling that dress up along the way. The feeling of his erection dragging against her skin made Morgan weak. Her head spun like an addict's, pining for her first hit. Hoisting her legs over his shoulders, Messiah entered her.

"Oh my God," she moaned as her head rolled left, then right. He filled her, every part of her, and Morgan felt him tap on the window to her soul as the familiar aching pleasure made her bite her lip. It was a feeling she hadn't had the privilege of indulging in since him. The pain that came with the pleasure of his lovemaking was uniquely his. Only he could make something this rough feel so good. Ahmeek gave her orgasms, back to back, sometimes all night, but Messiah punished her pussy without remorse. He made her take dick even when she couldn't handle it, even when it was a little past her limit, he made her bite down and endure the ride because, like a roller coaster, once it started, it didn't stop. He kissed the insides of her knees as he dug into her middle, hitting her with deep strokes. He brought her left foot to his mouth, and Morgan wanted to stop him . . . because she knew what he would do next. Her feet had been cramped in heels all day, but when he wrapped his mouth around her big toe, you would have thought she was fresh out of the shower. Her face collapsed in pleasure. Messiah's tongue worked its way between every single one of her pretty phalanges, a word she had learned doing something exactly like this with him during a sex-study session. His rhythm never changed. His stroke never altered. He sucked those toes and worked her middle at the same time, and Morgan could feel her temperature rising. Morgan fisted her hair, going crazy from delirium, her head whipping back and forth, her bottom lip lowering slowly as he led her toward a glorious orgasm. Her forehead pinched, and she held her breath as he released her legs and lowered to her ear.

"Give me that nut, shorty." His voice. Demanding. Aggressive. Messiah's mean ass held the key to her pleasure. Who was she to defy him? Her body jerked as she rained all over him. "A fucking super soaker, shorty," he groaned as he put one arm beneath her body and hit it deeper. *Harder.* "Oh, fuck," he groaned. *Deeper.*

"Messiah, I'm cumming." Morgan let the words escape her glossy lips. They were pulled tight in a grimace across her pretty face. Her desperate plea. Was there such a thing as too much pleasure? He was making up for lost time. He owed her a couple, and he planned to deliver. Morgan's nails dug into his back as she shuddered beneath him. His fingers entangled in her hair. The braid was nonexistent now from the pulling as he gripped her tightly, burying himself in the pocket of her neck as he came too.

Morgan was destroyed as she looked off to the side, tremors never leaving her because now she was crying, and crying hard, crying and riding a wave of euphoria at the same damn time. Bawling . . . the one thing he hated to see her do.

"Mo," he whispered as he rose slightly, hovering over her. She was trapped in the prison of his biceps as they stretched out on the sides of her head. She noticed another tattoo. The words *Doo Wop* on the inside of his arm. She covered her face with both hands, her chest quaking as she cried from her soul, emotion rattling her and hindering him. The sight of her distress was bringing out things in him that he had been able to tamp down in her absence. He had been unfeeling for two years because if he allowed himself to feel anything about her, he would murder everyone in his path that kept him from her.

"I've got to go. This is fucked up. I've got to get the fuck up and go." She pushed him off of her and scrambled into her clothes. Messiah wasn't quick to go after her. He sat on the edge of the bed, elbows to knees, head lowered.

"I didn't come back for this," he said. The emotions she brought out in him weakened him. He wasn't comfortable with the control she had over him. This fucking tender spot in the middle of his chest that ached so terribly when she was around, even worse when she wasn't. He couldn't get rid of the shit. It made him feel as if he were having a fucking heart attack.

Morgan fumbled with the tight dress, pulling it down and

then flipping pillows and covers in frustration. "Where the fuck are my panties?"

Messiah held them up on one finger, and she stalked over to him. She reached for them, but he snatched them out of her grasp, bringing them to his nose, then balling them in his fist, trapping them between those chocolate fingers. "Nah, shorty, these on me."

Morgan shook her head, enraged. "Nigga, give me my underwear."

He stood, dwarfing her with his height, but Morgan didn't back down. He was so close that her breath caught in her throat. Her stomach tightened. Nervous. He made her nervous.

"You got my mind all messed up," she said, lip quivering.

He lifted her chin with one finger, and she moved her face.

"You should have stayed gone, Messiah!" she cried. "I was moving on. I was putting things back together."

"I just want to be a part of your important days, shorty. A part of your life. A part of you. Like I used to be," Messiah said.

Morgan's lashes fluttered as she sucked in air.

"Today was too much. My bad. I know we ain't there yet, but shorty, it's been two years. A nigga dick get hard every time he see you, Mo. That pussy so sweet, shorty. I just wanted to taste you. Every time I see you, Mo, I want it," he whispered. The angst in his voice told her it was true. He hadn't been able to help himself. He took her hand and placed it on his dick. Morgan gasped. "Feel that," he groaned. "I don't want to fight with you, Mo. I just want to fuck, shorty. Love you and fuck you. That's it." Morgan's hand massaged him. He was so damn strong. Hard. Big-dick-ass nigga. Lust made her breaths heavy as she felt her skin flush. His mouth. It was disgusting. The things he did with it . . . just filthy. She felt her pulse in her clit, then she felt his coarse hands as they slid up her thigh, then two fingers, middle and ring, as he wet them inside her. Morgan went up on her tiptoes to run from those two fingers, but he chased her, catching her. Her teeth pinched into her bottom lip as she grimaced from the tune-up he was giving her. His thumb circled her bud.

She was goddamned ruined by this man, even after all this time. The mind control he had over her was uncanny. She guarded the part of her heart that he had touched. No one else could access those depths; she would never allow it because the last time someone had trespassed there she had been hurt, but he had the key. He could come and go as he pleased.

"Now stop talking all that shit and nut for me, shorty. Make a mess so I can clean it up." He growled the words to her as her legs weakened, and he wrapped his other hand around her waist to hold her up. She had always been a good student—a follow-every-rule, raise-your-hand-to-answer-every-question, obedient type of girl—so she did as he asked. The faces she made as she rained all over his fingers were hideous, but she didn't care. He took those fingers and just like every other time he had ever touched her there, he put them inside his mouth.

"You're disgusting. You don't know who you're eating after," she said. She knew what the notion would do to him before the words ever left her tongue. Her eyes blazed with challenge. Like a hood nigga who fought pit bulls to make them tough by inciting them, slapping them around a little bit, to get them to snap. She was tagging Messiah's ass with those words. Yanking his chain. Provoking his rage.

Her words were like the first strike of a match, the practice strike, the one that made the sound but didn't find its blaze. She was testing him, playing with fire. He could see the challenge in her; she was different, harder, and he smirked.

"Be careful, shorty," he warned. "That's a big trigger you trying to pull."

He grabbed her roughly, a thumb caressing her cheek and four fingers around the back of her neck. She pulled away, and he jerked her toward him.

"I swear you love when I send niggas up outta here over you," he said as he looked down the bridge of his nose at her through low lids. She pulled away again, and he pulled her right back.

"Messiah," she gasped. Those ss's for zz's. His heart fluttered, and he scooped her, hands under her ass, and pushed her back against the wall. Their lips met, and she was weakened again, by his presence, by his kisses. Morgan slapped him. She had a fit as she jumped out of his arms and pushed him, then socked him upside his big-ass head, as he lifted his hands to block her attack. She was bawling, distraught, as he captured her wrists and pinned them above her head.

"Stop!" he shouted.

"You left me for two years!" she cried. "Where were you when I needed you? There were so many days that I needed you, and now I don't anymore!"

"You didn't need me, Mo. Look at you. You're a big girl now. You're graduating. You're living. You're—"

"Getting married, Messiah, and fucking your friend on the side," she finished in a weak admission of guilt. He released her. Her words were like a cannonball, jolting him back. Like a bullet . . . no, he had been shot before. This was worse than that. The hurt and confusion that took over his face hollowed her stomach. "I thought you were dead, and now I'm getting married." She shrugged and held out her arms in defeat.

He snickered. "Yeah, you want me to kill a mu'fucka today, shorty," he said with a nod. Then his eyes went to her ring finger. The brilliance of the diamond sparkled. It was like it had magically appeared there; he hadn't noticed it until now. He had known she was engaged. This wasn't new information, but he'd never thought she would actually go through with it. He always thought she was playing games, seeking attention, because, well, that's what Mo did, but hearing her speak the words so frankly . . . like it was inevitable for her to be another man's wife . . . it hit him differently. It hurt with significance. It hurt worse than the molestation he had survived as a young boy. It ached more than the day he'd found his mother murdered. It tortured him more than the look of betrayal he had seen in Ethic's eyes when he had snaked him all those years ago. It affected him more than killing his own sister. Morgan hurt him most with just words.

Match two. He felt that fire trying to start, and he smothered it as the words he was trying to form got stuck in his throat. He gritted his teeth, jaw locked, fist closed unintentionally as if he were preparing to knock a nigga out.

"You left me," she said, defeated.

"I ain't worried. You can't marry a nigga that's no longer breathing," he said.

"Messiah!" His name on her lips like she were chastising a child she had birthed, but hadn't she? He was a by-product of her love. That counted. She was his family, his Shorty Doo Wop, and she was engaged. He'd thought he had more time. "You're going to murder every man I ever meet?"

She didn't even know why she was defending Bash. His death would mean her freedom. She wanted to tell Messiah to go ahead, to pull triggers for her because Bash was hurting her, but she knew it wouldn't truly mean freedom. It would just be a transfer of power. From Bash to Messiah she would go. Messiah would kill him for her without a second thought, but then he would expect to take Bash's place, and Morgan wasn't ready for that. Letting Messiah in again, indulging in their obsession for each other, would kill her. She had fought hard to breathe without him, and he would suffocate her all over again.

"Pretty much," he said. He was so nonchalant that Morgan knew he meant it.

Messiah snatched up his jeans and sat on the edge of the bed as he dressed.

"How long did you expect me to wait?" she asked. "You never even called."

"I had shit to get in order, Mo. Shit to handle," he said.

"Shit that took two years?" she asked in disbelief as she spun toward the door. She opened it, and he came behind her and closed it. Apparently, she wasn't going anywhere.

"Yeah, Mo. The shit took two years. Two long-ass, hard-ass years. I wasn't out fucking with no hoes. I didn't move on. Every day I was on my shit, so I could come back for you . . . so I could get right for you!" he shouted. He was frustrated. She could see it rising in him, and the guilt she felt eroded her as she stood in front of him, half of the woman she had walked in as.

"You're too late. It's too late," she whispered.

"How you let this happen, shorty?" he asked.

Match three, only it was Morgan's fire that came alive.

"How did *I* let it happen? No, nigga, how did *you* let it happen?" she shouted as she pushed him. She opened one palm and slapped her other hand inside it as she spoke. "Bash was there for me, Messiah. He ain't the best man. He has his ways, but he was consistent!"

"Bash." Messiah scoffed and shook his head. "Fucking corny-ass college boy?"

"Yes, Messiah, the corny college boy! You disappeared, and he didn't. He was solid. On days when I felt like taking a razor to my wrists, he would show up out of nowhere. We talked. We went to the movies. He cooked for me. We read books together. He was my friend. He saw me through depression. He welcomed me into his family, helped me keep up with homework while raising two babies. He put in the time, Messiah . . . with the space and opportunity you gave him!" She shook her head and stopped speaking as she turned away from him so he wouldn't see her tears. She couldn't believe she was advocating for Bash after what he'd done to her. After the threats and him being physical with her, she was defending him vehemently. It hadn't always been bad between them, and if she was honest, she'd played a role in the way things had changed for the worst. She was wrecked, decimated by the cloud Messiah had cast over her life. She hadn't been happy without him, but she hadn't been sad either. She had just been coasting, on autopilot, through each day. His strong hand on the back of her neck, massaging, coercing her to face him made her feel like she couldn't breathe. She knew he liked to hijack shit. Semis, her heart, now her air. Damn him for being so good at it. "I think about what would have happened if that girl never showed up at your house that day. I think about it every day. When would you have killed Ethic? Would you have killed me? Eazy? B? How would it have all gone down? Would I have seen it coming?"

She closed her eyes as her lip trembled. The thought alone destroyed her. Messiah blew out his exasperation and stumbled backward until he felt the bed behind him. He sat and leaned forward, dragging his hands down his face. It was time to address what he had avoided for years.

"No. You wouldn't have seen it coming," Messiah said. "Cuz I'm good at the shit. You wouldn't have known shit until everybody was in the dirt. You only know because I told you the shit . . . because I loved you too much to keep hiding it, Mo. Hitting you was never an option, shorty. My issue was with Ethic. Day one I saw you, I wanted you, shorty. You were young, though, and I knew what I was there for, so it wasn't even an option, but your ass kept chasing it. You kept begging me to pop that, and when I did, it was over. You got in my head that night at the falls, and then I fucked with you and everything changed. I couldn't figure out how to touch Ethic without it tearing you apart. Then I started questioning if it was even worth it in the first place. Ethic was more of a brother than Mizan ever was, but there was pressure on me to make that right. Either I made it right or somebody else was gon' come through and make it right, but somebody else might not play fair. Somebody else might touch you or B or Eazy. I was never touching you, though. Touching you is like touching myself."

He sat there so pitiful, so dejected, and Morgan was conflicted. Eighteen-year-old Mo would have wrapped her arms around him. She would have broken every rule to have him a part of her world, but he had proved to be a disappointment. He had burned her, and she hadn't been the same since. At twenty-one, she was a bit older, a bit wiser, a bit tarnished, and she held some resentments. She couldn't deny that she loved him still. Even after 912 days, he made her entire body react just by being in her vicinity. He activated her spirit whenever he was around. She didn't know what to say to him, what to do with him.

The buzzing of her phone caught her attention, and she picked it up to find she had missed calls. Bash. Ethic. Alani. Even Bella had been trying to reach her. "I've got to go," she said.

"Don't marry him, Mo." Messiah's words stopped her feet from working.

She was in the threshold of the door—all she had to do

was keep walking—but her fucking feet wouldn't move. His hands around her waist, pulling her back into the room, back into his arms, as he kissed the back of her head. He breathed deeply, inhaling her scent because he didn't know if she would ever let him get this close again.

She turned around and marked him with sad eyes. She reached into her purse and removed his guns, placing them on the stand by the door. "There is a part of me that's going to always wonder what we could have been, Messiah, but there is also a part of me that will always wonder who I could have been if Mizan had never come into my sister's life. If my daddy and my mama and Raven were alive, and I had them. When I look at you now, I see him. I don't know how I didn't see him in you before. The anger issues, the quick temper. I've always been afraid of him, Messiah. I used to be extra good when he was home. Try to be extra nice to him so he wouldn't get mad and blow up on my sister. He thought I liked him, because I used to pretend to try to keep him in a good mood so he wouldn't hurt her. I was terrified of him, though, and with you being here, it's like I'm a little-ass girl again, staring at him, pretending that my heart isn't in my throat. I'm afraid of you now, Messiah."

Messiah nodded as his temple throbbed, and he sniffed away his emotion. He was trying his hardest to keep it together. She could see his struggle, but damn if antipathy didn't stop her from soothing him.

"You know I wouldn't hurt you, Morgan," he said, pained as he caressed her face. She rested her cheek in the palm of his hand, relishing the moment, holding on to it because it was going to pass soon. He never called her *Morgan*. He barely called her *Mo*. It was *Shorty Doo Wop*. Just *shorty* when he was being lazy. He was serious, dead serious, because this was serious. She was giving herself away to another man.

"That's the problem, Messiah. I don't know that at all," she replied.

"I'm trying to fix shit," he said, his voice catching. He cleared his throat. "I swear to God, shorty, I'ma make it right. I'ma make up for all my wrongs."

She shook her head.

"Messiah." She sighed. He kissed her forehead, and her eyes lowered until the black behind her lids greeted her. He lived there too. He haunted her. There was nowhere to run, because he existed everywhere. He kissed her nose, and she gasped. Her stomach lurched as he moved to the valley above her lips, the oddest place, but he deemed it worthy to kiss as well. Her stomach went crazy with anxiety. There was no aggression in his touch. This time, she felt weakness. He took her lips, and she let him. It was a soul-stirring kiss. The kind that made electricity shoot through her nerves and made the slightest touch feel erotic. This was the gentlest he had ever been, and it felt so good. It felt earned. Morgan melted.

Morgan's head was cloudy, spinning, as confusion made a mess of her. She placed both hands on his chest and pushed softly, not really wanting space, but wanting their lips to disconnect so she could breathe . . . so she could think . . . so she could find her *no* . . . but as he looked at her, brows dipped low in pain, cheeks heavy in devastation, all Morgan felt was *yes*. She lunged for him, unleashing the aggression he had taught her, the aggression she had locked away since the last time she had seen him.

The buzzing of her cell phone snapped her back into reality. *What am I doing?*

She pulled away, breaking the trance he had her under. "I can't do this," she said.

"I can't not do this, shorty, so what we gon' do?" Messiah

asked. "I'm ready, Mo. I'm ready for you, ready to do whatever I got to do to make it right . . . to be your man, shorty."

"I have a man, Messiah," she said as she shook her head. He thought she was talking about Bash, but her heart had given the title to Ahmeek. Ahmeek was her man. Yes, she was trapped by Bash, but she was trying to figure out how to escape. One day, when she was able to break free, she would be Ahmeek Harris's woman. "And I ain't shit because I'm here with you. He doesn't deserve this. I've got to go," she said.

Every step she took away from Messiah burned him. He had walked away from her many times before, and if she had felt like this, like she was suffocating, he was sorry as hell because the ache was unbearable.

"Yo, shorty," he called out as he stepped into the hall, shirtless, tattoos covering him, marking him up, proving he was a glutton for pain.

She pressed the elevator button repeatedly as he strolled up to her.

"Just let me go, please."

"I'ma let you go. You got a wedding to plan and all," Messiah said with a scoff as he caressed his lips, his lips that still tasted like her. "But yo, while you at it, plan a funeral too, shorty. You gon' need a black dress that day, because the day I watch you walk down the aisle to that lame-ass nigga is the day he takes his last breath." Messiah kissed the side of her head and then walked back to his room, leaving her standing in the hallway, heart racing, feeling more alive than she had in two years.

11

Morgan glanced down at her phone. She was so late. Taking the Uber to retrieve her car had taken some time. Everyone was waiting for her at the restaurant, and she was over an hour late. Bash had been calling repeatedly. She reluctantly answered.

"I'm pulling up to the restaurant now." Seconds later, she saw him emerge from the building as she parked. The look on his face told her he was pissed. She couldn't say she blamed him.

"Where have you been, Mo?" Bash asked. "What the hell was that? You just run out in the middle of your graduation?"

"I felt like I would be sick," Morgan said. It was only half a lie. Messiah had thrown her world off-kilter and left her stomach in knots. That much was true. "I couldn't breathe up there. I just needed to get out of there. I just needed some time to myself."

"Where did you go?" he asked.

"To the cemetery," she answered. It was a low thing to use her dead family as a cover, but it was one of the few excuses that people would understand. No one would ask anything further after she said that, and she needed Bash to back off. She was drowning in lies.

"Get your shit together, Mo. You're embarrassing yourself and my family," Bash said. He turned to the restaurant, and Morgan trailed him. She felt see-through, like everything she had just done, or rather that had been done to her, was written all over her body. She still had Messiah's scent all over her, and she was filled with shame as she followed Bash into the restaurant.

Alani had reserved the private room in the five-star establishment, and Morgan followed Bash to the section as she pulled on her clothes insecurely. As soon as she walked into the room, everyone in attendance cheered for her. Morgan turned red, and she gave up a fake smile. Her eyes immediately found Ethic's. He sat at the head of the table, and the stare he pierced her with made her heart tremble. He spoke without even moving his lips. He nodded.

You good?

Morgan sighed because she realized that with him in the room, she was always safe, always secure. She nodded back and smiled. A real smile.

"Congrats, Mo Money!" Bella said, standing to hug Morgan. "My sister did it, everybody!"

The pride in Bella's eyes made Morgan emotional. She hadn't always done the right things. She hadn't always been the girl that Bella could look up to, but this accomplishment was one Bella could aspire to. She moved around the table, speaking to everyone, delivering kisses to cheeks and shaking hands of Christiana's associates. Morgan hugged Eazy and Nannie, then moved on to Ethic and Alani.

"Thank you so much, Alani, for throwing me this," she said.

"You deserve it, Mo," Alani answered.

"He almost done cooking in there?" Morgan asked.

Alani blew out a sharp breath and placed both hands on her round belly. "Almost. A few more weeks. Thank God, because I'm so ready."

Morgan laughed and moved to Ethic, who stood to receive her.

"I'm proud of you. You know that?" he asked as he held her close. Morgan nodded and pulled back.

"Morgan, we saved you a seat next to Sebastian," David said.

Morgan rounded the table, and Bash pulled out her chair as she sat down.

"So, Morgan. What's next for you?"

The question came from the white woman sitting at the other end of the table beside Christiana. A senator for the state and the keynote speaker at graduation.

"I honestly have no idea," Morgan said, smiling as she moved the tassel to her graduation cap out of her face. She beamed as servers came around serving a five-star meal. She didn't even know most of the thirty guests seated at the table, but she was happy to have them there. To her surprise, the vibe was easy. She laughed and conversed with her family, and even Christiana seemed to be in good spirits. Morgan tried to imagine her life with Bash. The rest of her days at his side. His baritone in her ear, laughing, praising her. Her family mixing with his. Her twins bouncing around the table, being doted over. This was legacy at this table. It was royalty. There was power of vast proportions present, and Morgan had a seat among the elite. It was one she didn't even know if she wanted. In fact, she was sure it didn't suit her at all, and somehow here she sat.

Aria walked in, still wearing her graduation cap, but the

gown was gone. She wore a green pantsuit that complemented her skin so well she radiated.

"Hey, everybody!" she greeted. She instantly gravitated to Morgan's family, hugging Bella and waving to the rest before taking a seat as well.

"I thought you had plans!" Morgan exclaimed.

"You think I'm missing the opportunity to say ya' fine-ass daddy bought me dinner?" she answered, beaming. She quickly turned to Alani. "Sorry, Alani. I love you, I do, but you know your husband is fine, and he's clearly married and got a billion kids, but he still fine. Speaking of fine"—Aria turned to Morgan—"where is ya' fine-ass uncle? Will the good pastor be coming to bless the food? He can bless this plate all day." Aria lifted a hand like she were praising Jesus, and Alani snickered as Christiana cleared her throat in discomfort. Aria was always the life of the party. The smallest at the table with the biggest personality, she shone in every room.

"Where is Ny?" Morgan asked.

"Can't show up to Morgan Atkins's graduation dinner empty-handed."

Everyone turned their attention to the door, and Morgan rose from her seat. Nyair stood holding a silver Saks bag.

"Ny!" She ran into his arms.

"My bad, Mo. I know I'm late. I had to stop off and make sure I came through right for you," he said. He held up an envelope that was so thick it wouldn't close. It was stuffed with hundred-dollar bills. "A bag to stuff the bag," he said as he handed over the Saks bag. Morgan beamed as she peeked inside to see a new YSL purse.

"I miss you," she said. "I'm so happy you came. Thank you for the gift, Ny."

"Wouldn't miss it, Mo. We real proud of you, baby girl," he

said. "I want to see you more often now that you're home. Like we used to. Once a week, Mo." She nodded, and he kissed her cheek and then graciously infected the room. The scent of his cologne made the ladies at the table swoon as he shook hands. A kiss to Alani's cheek and a gangster's salute to Ethic before kissing Bella and Eazy. Nyair was energy. He always commanded all eyes when he entered a room. Good looks, charm, and regality followed him everywhere he went.

Morgan watched him work the room. Nyair was still the same. Gracious and welcoming and comforting. She loved him, and as he took a seat on the other side of her empty chair, her heart swelled. Ethic had built a small village for her, for all of them. They had made it to the other side. She remembered her other graduations. At her sixth-grade graduation, only Ethic had been present. At her high school graduation, it had only been Ethic, Bella, and Eazy. Today, however, this table was full of support, and even if only half of it was wanted, she had to give them all credit for showing up. There had been so many days when no one had shown up at all. No one but Ethic.

Morgan took her seat, but before she could get comfortable, she felt Bash's hand tighten against her thigh. He was squeezing so tightly under the tablecloth that she knew he would leave bruises on her skin. She turned to him, frowning, but she got stuck when her eyes landed on the door.

Ahmeek Harris.

Black pants, tailored fit, black shirt, no tie, and a leather jacket with leather boots. Morgan knew he'd ridden his bike, and she wanted nothing more than to run out of the restaurant and ride off with him.

Morgan's eyes misted as they met his, but Bash's hand kept her seated. She felt like absolute shit. She had felt nothing when facing Bash after sleeping with Messiah, but looking at Ahmeek, seeing him, hearing him, he brought the aura of love into the room, and it infected her just by looking in his eyes. She had been disloyal to him. Letting Messiah touch her the way he had, if Ahmeek knew, he would never forgive her. Morgan loved this man. She loved them both, and it was killing her. She couldn't even breathe as he stood there staring at her. She was transfixed, under a spell. Meek shit, as he called it. He was too good for her. He had come to see her despite how angry he was at her, and Morgan had just finished having sex with another man. She felt horrible. She regretted it now, in this moment; she wanted to take the past two hours of her life back. Rewind the clock and make a different decision. How had she forgotten how much she loved him? How could she do such a terrible thing to him? Even when he wasn't around . . . even when he was mad at her, he still loved her; she could feel it in the air. It was so potent it choked her. Everyone at the table felt it too, so they didn't dare disrespect the moment with words. It was silent, and Bash's hand was so tight around her thigh, and it hurt so badly that Morgan wanted to scream.

"I don't mean to interrupt," Ahmeek stated. "I'ma be quick cuz this ain't really my scene, but I just wanted to say congratulations, Mo."

Morgan couldn't look away, and words evaded her.

The energy between them was loud despite the silence that stilled the room. It was like someone had cast a spell over the room, because no one spoke. The heartbeat of their connection pulsed through the air. It was felt. Morgan could hear it beating in her ears.

I'm fucking up so bad. I'm going to lose him.

She felt so much guilt. She had just given her body to Messiah moments ago, and now Meek stood in front of her, and it felt like he could see her lies. Her eyes glossed as emotion built in her, rising and rising and rising as she bobbed for air in her mind.

"Umm, Meek, why don't you join us?" Alani said, filling the awkward silence. Meek ran one hand down his head. Morgan waited. Would he stay?

"This is a private dinner; I doubt that's appropriate," Christiana added.

"And since I'm the hostess and you're a guest, I don't really think your approval is required," Alani said.

Morgan couldn't even believe he was there. He had heard her. At Aria's. He hadn't forgotten that she was graduating today. Her emotions were already heightened. Messiah had already sent her mind spinning today, but Ahmeek standing in front of her, staring at her like she were the only person in the room, left her breathless. The tension thickened the air as everyone awaited an answer.

"Thanks, but I'ma break out," he answered without looking to Alani. No one existed but Morgan. She felt it. The intention he looked at her with. The focus. There was so much she wished she could say.

"You came all this way. Might as well have a seat," Bash said. "We know your neighborhood is nowhere near here. Grab a chair, man."

Morgan finally broke eye contact as she looked at Bash in shock. The smug look he wore on his face sent Morgan's temper through the roof. He thought he had the upper hand. He was seated in a five-star restaurant, and his family had a tableful of power sitting among them. Morgan could see the contempt burning in Bash as he sat back in his chair and threw an arm around her shoulder.

"A friend of Mo's is a friend of mine, right, love?"

Morgan's eyes widened in alarm. He had never called her

that before; in fact, she knew he knew that Ahmeek called her that all the time. It was such a passive-aggressive blow that Morgan interrupted him. "Bash, please stop," she said in a hushed, pleading tone.

Bash stood, grabbing a champagne flute and holding it in the air. "I'd like to propose a toast. Mo, you have accomplished something great today, and I'm looking forward to building a beautiful life with you. While we have our friends and family here, we might as well make the announcement."

Morgan squinted in confusion. "Bash, what are you—"

"Come on, Mo, we might as well share," Bash continued. "The reason why Mo won't be entering medical school immediately is because we've decided to expand our family. After the wedding, we're going to try for a baby."

"Ohhh, shit," Aria whispered, astonished.

Morgan died on the inside.

Mixed reactions erupted from the table, but Morgan only cared about one. The revelation landed like a blow to Ahmeek. She saw the fire coming from him. She detected every bit of restraint he used to stop himself from reacting. He hid it well. The devastation. No one else knew. He was too smooth to show his discontent, but Morgan knew. She felt it.

"Bash, stop," she pleaded, whispering as she leaned into his ear. "I'm here with you. He gets it. Please just stop."

"Stop what, *love*?" Bash asked.

"Stop while you're ahead," Ethic added, scratching his head and grimacing like the scene in front of him was hard to watch. He stood from his chair and leaned down to Alani. "I'ma grab a drink at the bar. I'll be right back, baby." A peck to her lips before he walked around the table and put a hand on Meek's shoulder. "Not the time nor place," Ethic said in a low tone that only Ahmeek could hear.

Ahmeek walked out, and Morgan wanted to go after him, but Bash's hand was like a vise on her thigh. Morgan looked down into her lap, then up at him. Her vision blurred as he brought a gentle hand to her cheek, then wrapped four fingers behind her neck, pulling her face to his. A kiss. It felt like the kiss of death. He had just killed everything she and Ahmeek were. Or had she done that? Had she done it when she had turned him away? Morgan struggled to put the fake smile back on her face, but she did it. She sat there at Bash's side, smiling because he wasn't leaving her any choice. She watched Ethic walk Ahmeek to the bar and then darted eyes over to Alani. Alani sat with an elbow to the table. Her chin rested on top of a closed fist.

"Morgan," Alani called.

Morgan's forehead dipped. She was having such a hard time controlling her runaway emotions. She had lost him. She knew it, and it hurt. It hurt more than anything she had ever felt before because it was a hurt she'd chosen. She looked at Alani again. Alani used her finger to lift her own head. A sign.

Morgan nodded and lifted her head, pulling in a deep breath. She had to find her way out of this mess because she couldn't live without Ahmeek. She needed to tell the truth and ask Ethic for help, but fear stopped her. Fear that he would hate her for exposing his secrets in the first place, fear that he would think she'd done it to be vindictive against his marriage. Fear of being shunned by him altogether. She had pillow talked to Bash in a moment of insecurity, and she was terrified it would be considered betrayal. Morgan watched as Ethic spoke to Ahmeek. She had no idea what was said, and the anxiety from that made her chest tight. She hoped Ethic spoke love and not hate. She prayed Ahmeek could feel her heart and see through her actions because everything she did was screaming fuck him. She watched him walk out and then felt Bash's lips on her cheek. Everyone resumed the dinner. They just went about their meal as if her heart weren't breaking, as if her life weren't ruined. She was in a roomful of people, and no one heard her screams. It was as if she were deaf all over again. Nobody heard her. She was saying no, but no one understood her language.

Morgan was grateful when Ethic switched seats with Nyair for the rest of the dinner. Just having him next to her made her feel a little bit better. Ethic made everything better, which was why she couldn't lose him. He went into his jacket pocket and pulled out a box and set it on the table.

"For you to open later," he said. She looked at him in surprise. "When you're alone," he concluded.

She nodded and then placed the small gold box in her handbag. She was able to survive the five courses despite the tension coming from Bash. She kept checking her phone to see if Meek would at least text her, but he didn't, and she knew he wouldn't. His showing up at all surprised her after what she had done to him. The same way Messiah had sold her a dream only to repossess it, Morgan had done the same to Ahmeek. Messiah's words had shredded her apart, and she had used the same weapon to disconnect from Meek. She had never felt so low. Never had she loved someone so cruelly. He was an unknowing victim. Her hurt had blindsided him, and it was killing her that he thought it was true. The dinner concluded, and Morgan hugged her family goodbye before rising from the table. When she got outside, she stopped walking. Her car was surrounded with floral bouquets.

The way Bash's hand tightened around hers crushed her fingers.

"That's some gift. Well played, Sebastian," one of Christiana's friends said.

Bash smiled in acknowledgment, but Morgan could feel the anger coming from him. He hadn't sent them.

"She deserves every petal," he said.

Morgan smiled nervously as he pulled her close for a kiss. Morgan turned red as everyone oohed and aahed, but she knew these flowers weren't from him.

"B, can you help me get them into the car?" Morgan asked.

"Sure," she said. "I'm keeping a bouquet for my room, though," she added.

Morgan half smiled and stepped to her car. She saw the card under her windshield.

Two simple words moved her to tears.

Congratulations, shorty.

They packed up the car, and Morgan said her goodbyes.

"My parents will drive your car back. You can ride with me," Bash instructed.

"I can drive my—"

"Now, Morgan," Bash said. She stilled but didn't budge. It would be a long ride home.

Bash and Morgan sat in the parking lot silently as everyone pulled away. The twins had exhausted themselves, and both slept uncomfortably in their car seats. The silence and tension that filled the car was maddening.

"We used to be really good friends," she said sadly. "This doesn't feel the same anymore, Bash. Why can't we go back to that? We used to laugh all the time. There were days when I couldn't breathe, and you made me laugh. This pressure to be your wife. It's too heavy. I don't want—"

Bash reached out and gripped her chin roughly like she were a child he had to chastise.

"Stop talking," he sneered. "I can't believe he showed up here. You're so ungrateful it's not even funny." He pushed her head away as Morgan's eyes misted. "Did you call him?"

"No," Morgan answered.

"Did you call him?" Bash demanded.

"No!" she shouted again. She didn't know what Bash wanted her to say. She hadn't spoken to Ahmeek, but she wasn't mad that he had shown up. Just seeing him was enough to give her hope that he still cared.

Messari stirred, and Bash turned rage-filled eyes to the road as he threw the car in drive and pulled off recklessly.

"I'm beginning to feel like you're not worth the trouble, Mo," he said. "Not worth it at all."

Morgan turned her head out the window so he couldn't see her tears as he drove her back to his family's estate.

12

"Aria, that dress!" Morgan gasped as Aria pulled back the curtain to the dressing room and stepped out into the boutique.

"Mommy, Auntie Ari is pretty," Yara signed.

"Yes, she is, Yolly," Morgan signed back.

"Tee-Tee, you look like a pwincess!" Messari yelled while jumping up and down in front of Aria, arms reaching up high for her to pick him up. She obliged him and gathered him up in her arms.

"Eww, boyfriend, nobody wants to look like that." Aria frowned, turning to the mirror in the big Cinderella gown.

"You don't like it?" Mo asked. "It's amazing."

"It's one of the most expensive in the store," the bridal associate added. "One of a kind."

"It's so big," Aria said, fluffing the side of it with one hand. "And heavy. I feel like I'm drowning in fabric. I'm not the girl that wants to look like a princess. I want Isa to see me and want to fuck."

"Aria!" Morgan shouted as she stood and took Messari from her best friend's arms.

"My bad," Aria snickered.

"So sexy. So perhaps maybe mermaid style?" the woman asked.

"I don't know, just not this," Aria said, frowning.

"I'll pull some options," the woman answered before heading to the front of the store.

Aria sat down on the floor, causing the dress to pool around her, and Yara rushed over to play in the folds. Aria laughed as she grabbed Yara's small body up, tickling her and then hugging her tightly. Yara got comfortable in Aria's lap.

"So he made you bring them so he could make sure you wasn't going to fuck with a nigga?" Aria asked.

"Basically," Morgan answered.

"He does know that both Messiah and Meek will fuck you with these kids present, don't he?" Aria asked.

Morgan couldn't help but laugh.

"Why haven't you told that man yet, Mo? They're his. He deserves to know that," Aria said. "It's safe to say he's not going to hurt you or them, so what are you waiting for?"

"I'm just not ready yet, Aria. Sharing them with him is letting him back in. I can't handle him barging into my life. I'm already in over my head with Bash. I don't need more problems right now," Morgan reasoned.

"You don't get to decide that, Mo. You're being selfish as fuck," Aria said. "These are his kids." She lowered her voice on the last part so Messari wouldn't overhear. He was the king of repeating what he heard, and Aria didn't want to get Morgan caught up. She stood. "When Messiah busts your ass, don't cry victim, because he's going to fuck you up when he finds out."

Morgan sighed as Aria disappeared behind the curtain to change.

"We're going to head out. I told Bash I wouldn't be gone long," Morgan called out.

"Yeah, whatever, girl. You just don't want to hear what I'm saying because you know I'm right," Aria said. She pulled back the curtain, only wearing panties and a bra. She hugged Morgan. "I'll call you later."

Morgan gathered her twins and headed out into the mall.

"Mommy, Mommy, me want ice cream!" Messari squealed from the double stroller he was seated in.

Morgan pushed them to the food court and purchased one cone for the three of them to share before finding a quiet spot. She let her twins have free rein as they bounced and played around the table while running up to her for free licks of the chocolate treat.

"Mommy, more! I want my own!" Messari shouted as he pushed Yara out of the way. She fell, hitting the tiled floor hard.

"Messari!" Morgan shouted as she bent down to pick Yara up off the floor. Her daughter wasn't as delicate as she seemed. Her pretty face was bunched in a scowl as she reached across Morgan to hit Messari back. Her big baby cried instantly. Messari's little lips trembled as he cocked his head back and cried bloody murder.

"Mommmmyyyyy, Yolly hit me!" he screamed as he climbed up her body and rubbed his chocolate-covered face into Morgan's Gucci T-shirt.

Yolly scrambled up her other leg and tried to reach for Messari, but he was the type to hold grudges, so he turned away from his sister, crying on Morgan's shoulder.

"Him hit me too, Mommy," Yara signed.

Morgan snickered because Messari had indeed passed licks first.

"I know," Morgan said, winking at Yara before pulling Messari off her shoulder and gripping his chin. She kissed his chubby cheeks. "Stop crying, Mommy's Ssari. You can't hit people and get mad if they hit you back."

"But her hits hurt more, Mommy!" Messari wailed.

It took everything in Morgan not to laugh. "Aww, my baby," she cooed as she pulled him close and bounced her leg. She gave Yara a high five behind Messari's back. There was something so special about her baby girl. Yolly was going to give the world hell. Morgan just knew it, and she loved it about her. Yara was a fighter.

"That's right, baby. Beat up the boys," she signed. Yara giggled and then climbed down before getting back in the stroller.

"You want to say sorry to your sister, baby boy?" Morgan asked.

"No," Messari said stubbornly.

"Boys don't hit girls, Ssari. Not ever. Even if she hits you first. So go tell her you're sorry, okay?" Morgan coached.

Messari turned toward Yara. "Sorry!" he mumbled stubbornly before burying his face back into Morgan's shoulder. Morgan shook her head. He was Messiah's son through and through. Do damage, then label everybody else the bad guy while withholding sympathy.

Morgan put Messari down. "Climb up next to Yolly. It's time to go."

Messari did as he was told, and Morgan looked down at her mess of a shirt. Her hair was disheveled, thrown up in a messy bun, and her shirt was now ruined. The boyfriend jeans she wore had melted stains of ice cream from the twins' messy hands. It was definitely time to head out. Morgan was ex-

hausted, and they hadn't even been out that long. Having two
babies was a blessing, but they wore Morgan out on a regular
basis.

Morgan pushed the stroller through the mall and was
halfway to her car when she saw him. In fact, she smelled him
first. Ahmeek Harris wore Bond No. 9, and the way it mixed
with the scent of his sweat flashed through Morgan's mind as
images of him on top of her body caused her to stop walking
abruptly. Her entire body reacted to him. He was across the
corridor, but just his presence made Morgan come alive.

An invisible lump in her throat choked her. What was he
doing here? With her? Morgan was sick. She stood there frozen
in her dirty shirt and raggedy ponytail. She prayed that Meek
didn't see her. The universe wouldn't be cruel to her that way,
but she knew he would turn her way. She knew the magnetic
energy that made it impossible to stop looking at him would
guide his eyes her way. He stilled on her for three seconds before Morgan turned. She had to get out of there. Away from
him. Out of this infected space with this tainted air that made
it hard to breathe, but before she could, Yara shot across the
hallway that separated them.

Ahmeek turned away from his date and met Yara halfway,
scooping her as she wrapped her arms around his neck.

"That's my girl," he said.

Morgan almost hated that her daughter loved this man
so much. She was jealous. She wanted to be the one with her
arms wrapped around his neck. She knew he smelled like
Bond No. 9, and she couldn't wait to snatch her daughter back
because she would undoubtedly smell like him too.

"Who do we have here?"

Morgan's heart ached when Livi stepped up beside Meek.
She was flawless. Redbone, with a blunt-cut bob that was cut

to perfection. Livi switched looks like panties, going from long to short hair by the day because she was pretty enough to pull off any style. A midriff off-white T-shirt and denim laced her. Morgan judged every inch of her perfection, from her toes to the top of her head. She rolled her eyes. She didn't remember this girl being this bad. Their only other encounter, Morgan had such the advantage. Oh, how the tables had turned.

"This the queen of the world," Ahmeek said. "You can finish looking for the bag you want. Let me handle this. I'll catch up."

Livi looked at Morgan. A smirk played on her lips like she was amused, and Morgan knew why. She had gotten the last laugh.

Bitch.

"You never really cancel a good subscription. Like Netflix. You might pause it, but you just keep coming back," Livi said.

"Yo, the flex is unbecoming," Ahmeek said. "Go pick out your shit before I change my mind about buying it."

Livi's face dropped at the warning as she adjusted her purse strap on her shoulder and turned. "Don't be long, babe," she said. She shot Morgan a look of triumph. "Nice shirt." It was a final jab before walking away.

Morgan scoffed and diverted her eyes to Messari, who was sleeping in the double stroller she held on to.

Livi turned on her expensive heels and sashayed back into the Louis Vuitton boutique like she had no worries about leaving her man with Morgan. Like Morgan wasn't even a threat at all.

Morgan reached for Yara, and Ahmeek turned, shrugging her off.

"She's where she wanna be. Why ain't you?" he challenged.

"Why do you care? I see Livi's back, or maybe she never

left," Morgan stated. Her eyes betrayed her, filling with emotion as she shook her head. "It ain't even been that long, and you're already—" Morgan stopped talking and pulled in a deep breath. "Just give me my daughter," she said.

Morgan reached for Yara, who pulled away and wrapped herself around Ahmeek tighter. Morgan huffed in frustration as she cleared hair from her face. Her eyes were burning so badly. He was already moving on, and it hurt.

"Tears and goodbyes don't match, Mo. You stopped fucking with me, not the other way around. Now you're here upset because I'm stepping out with someone else? You out here planning babies with niggas. Ain't that right, Mo? You and your fiancé taking it to the next step. You letting that nigga put babies in you. That's what I heard, right?" Ahmeek asked. His temper rose at just the thought. He had denied every single phone call from Morgan since.

"You know I wouldn't do that," she said defensively.

"I fuck with actions, Mo. Your mouthpiece real good, but you walk different," Meek said.

"You know that's not true," Morgan answered. "You know how I feel about you."

"I know the nigga had you sitting at his side talking about leaving babies in you and calling you *love*. I know that. You lucky I left air in that nigga lungs."

"And you're lucky I didn't snatch that lace front off that bitch head," Morgan shot back. "Just go back in there with your girlfriend and give me my child," she snapped, a tear slipping down her face. She hated that she was so damn emotional all the time. When she was afraid, she cried. Angry . . . she cried . . . sad . . . more tears. Even when Mo was happy, she shed emotion. She just wanted to be strong. "What are you doing with her?" She knew she had no right to demand answers.

"Whatever I want to do, Mo. I'm single. You not my girl. You ended the shit," Ahmeek answered as he rubbed the back of his neck. This was too much drama, too much back and forth for Ahmeek. He had never let a woman play with his emotions the way he allowed Morgan to play. She was in one day and out the next. Morgan could see the stress building in him.

Stunned, Morgan's eyes widened. Most men would have lied. He served her an unfortunate truth. "Right," she whispered, nodding. "I forgot. Ahmeek with all the hoes. Move 'em in, move 'em out, right? You're predictable, and you're disgusting. Bitch probably been in the picture since I started fucking with you."

Ahmeek stepped to Morgan, dwarfing her as he gripped her T-shirt, snatching her close. Her space became his, like he'd paid rent and had a right to occupy it. Yara's head rested peacefully against his shoulder, and he pushed Mo back toward the wall. Jail. She was locked up in Ahmeek, and freedom wasn't an option as he glared at her.

"You're in your feelings, so I'ma let you get that off. Don't feel good, do it? Watching somebody you fuck with heavy give love to somebody that ain't you? It drive you a little crazy, right? Got your blood boiling thinking about me putting my lips on the same places I put them on you? Got you putting together shit in your head that make your chest ache."

"It makes me regret ever fucking with you," she said plainly. "Every single moment."

"Yeah, I'm feeling the same lately, Mo. Real shit. None of this should have even happened because you stay on your bullshit," Meek stated. "Fucking wasting my energy, yo."

"Fuck you, Meek!" Morgan snapped. Morgan's voice echoed through the three-story building, and passersby slowed their stroll to take in the heated argument. She was making a scene. She was so deep in her feelings that she couldn't help it, and he shook his head. This young-ass girl would drive him crazy if he let her.

"We're done," Ahmeek said. "I'm off it, Mo. Coming at me over a bitch when you got niggas in rotation. Ya' ass and your games. Fuck out of here with that shit, man."

Morgan swiped another tear. He was right. She knew it. She didn't care. She was still hurt.

"You're a ho, and I knew you were a ho before I let you in. Ain't nothing special about a whack-ass nigga that's giving out one-size-fits-all dick."

His hand pinched the sides of her face before she could utter another insult. A lesser man would have hurt her. Meek was well aware of her limits. He issued the warning with no pain, but the look in his eyes told her she was pushing him. Mo was lethal when provoked, and her mouth was her weapon of choice.

"I don't even see the point in pretending like this shit even matters anymore. None of it matters." Her sister took over her mind. Would Meek slap her? Would he hit her? Would he destroy her? Bash did it. Even Messiah had hurt her—not physically, but damn if the emotional blows didn't hurt worse than the physical ones. She was so damn tired of building men up in her head for them to not meet her expectations. They always fell short. Defeat was written all over her.

Ahmeek's eyes changed. Her words altered him. Anger melted into concern because he knew that Morgan could be pushed to the edge. He also knew she wasn't afraid to free-fall to the bottom. She had done it before. "You have to tell me what we talking about here, Mo. Keep it a buck with me, cuz it sounds to me like you giving niggas too much power. It sounds like you're going to a place that you almost didn't make it back from last time, and that's never going to happen with me around. Good or bad terms, I'm never going to pretend like I don't see the shit and let you fucking drown, so tell me. Is this for attention, or is this for real? I'm with it either way. You got problems, I got answers, love, either fucking way. You want attention, I got that for you. I got that all day for you. I'll pay real close attention, Morgan Atkins."

Mo tried to roll her eyes and look away, but Ahmeek was in control. He turned her chin back to him. There would be no averting this conversation.

"If it's something else, if this is serious, if you're in trouble, I need to know. You said you would come to me if you felt like that again. Niggas don't deserve you. Not even me, love." He brought his face so close to hers that Morgan sobbed. "What the fuck, Mo? Stop letting niggas ruin you. You're so much better, man. You're so fucking good, yo. I'd love the shit out of you if you let me."

She could see his conflict. Out of everyone, he knew exactly how fragile Mo could be. She bawled right there, hands covering her face, forehead leaned against his chest. The weak spot he had for this girl made no sense. She had him completely caught in her web. Morgan had to be karma for the many hearts he had broken because she stayed fucking his shit up.

"Shit's that bad? It can't be that bad, Mo. Talk to me. If you can't talk to me, I can find you someone, but whatever the fuck is going on that got you shutting me out, we got to settle that."

Morgan trembled. This man holding her daughter in his arms was offering solutions to problems she hadn't even admitted to herself. There was no hiding place when matters of the heart were concerned. Her eyes told all, and they screamed to

Ahmeek for help. Morgan wished she could let him. The truth she was speaking was a lie, and he knew it. It was like no one else in the entire mall existed. Just them and this corner. Just him staring in her eyes. Morgan knew she was see-through.

"There's nothing to settle, Meekie. It was cool. You were something to do, and now I'm done. I'm bored, so just let it go. I can't fuck with you, Ahmeek. I don't want you."

Why the hell couldn't she control her emotions? She wished she could stop crying. Her inner bitch would be so much more believable if she could at least stop her voice from quivering, but damn, without him, she was mourning. She was grieving a loss of love. A loss of trust. Ahmeek had not only wooed her body but the finesse of her soul had been extraordinary. He had mind-fucked her, exposing a level of intimacy that felt like a secret only best friends would share. They had spent so much time together that he had unknowingly become the person whose gaze she sought when she found something funny in a roomful of people. He was the one who reached for her hand when she felt anxiety creeping up her spine. He was the person who finished her sentences before the words could leave her thoughts. The friendship beneath the sex and passion was so solid that the void he left behind was debilitating. Ahmeek was her inside joke, and now she had to let him go. To keep Ethic safe and to stop herself from losing it all, she had to give this up. Return it to the forbidden place it had come from.

He blew out a sharp breath. The tears gutted him. He wanted to hold her at her word. It was *fuck him*, so it should be *fuck her*, but he hated the discomfort that accompanied fighting with Morgan Atkins. Her tears had always done something to him, even before she was his concern.

"Once I let go, ain't no double back," he said. "I ain't with this shit, Mo. The back and forth. I know what I'm about and what I want. That's you, but I don't particularly like the shit you on. I ain't ever let a mu'fucka play with me, love." She tried to turn her head, and his hand steered her chin right back to him. "In my eyes." Morgan melted. Her lip trembled. Even with the mess her feelings had made of her face, she was still the prettiest girl he had ever seen. Ahmeek had been with his fair share of women. He had been with the baddest, but there was something about Morgan Atkins. A daintiness to her that pulled his heart through his chest, that made his dick react when she was around. He lived to hear the melody of her voice. He loved it. It had been far too long since he had indulged in her. "Damn, I want you. You acting the fuck up out here. Come home with me, Mo."

"I can't, Ahmeek." Her voice was so pained that it made his forehead pinch in concern.

"I wanna devour you, love," he admitted.

Her pulse raced. Her body hummed.

"Meekie, no." Why did this man speak to her this way? He was so close. He wanted it, she wanted it more. A life with him seemed impossible, but a day, a day and a long night they could have anytime. Only she couldn't. Too much was at stake. She had to let him go. Her easy love, her steady love, and she couldn't fucking have him. She had never wanted to throw a temper tantrum more.

"Yeah, love," he countered. He was close enough to breathe her air, and Morgan's lashes fluttered.

"Why are you with her?" she cried.

"Why ain't I with *you* is the better question?" he shot back.

"Because I can't be, Meekie. Just leave it alone. Forget we even happened." Morgan sobbed.

Morgan felt his lips touch hers, and her knees went weak. She reached for his beard and curled her fingers through it, hurting him, gripping tightly for dear life as she indulged in him.

I love him so much.

Ahmeek pulled back. "You're fucking me up," he admitted.

"Meek!"

His temple throbbed as he pressed his forehead to hers as Livi's voice echoed behind him.

"Tell me what you want me to do," he said. Morgan knew he would end things with Livi if she asked him to. She couldn't ask him to, however. Not this time. Bash had set a trap she couldn't escape from.

"I don't want you to do anything," Mo said. She pulled Yara from his arms and wiped her eyes before squeezing out of his trap. She grabbed the handles of the stroller and walked around it, placing Yara inside. He stood there, watching her. Frowning. Rubbing both hands down his waves and then caressing his lips where the taste of her lingered.

"Mo . . ." His voice held so much dread that Morgan couldn't stop herself from crying.

"No," she answered as she rushed away.

"Yo, love!" he shouted after her. Her feet stopped moving, and she looked back. "I dig the shirt. You should go back to wherever you got it from and cop another one," he said.

It was his shirt. A shirt she'd gotten from his loft because she didn't have clothes there.

"Or not," Livi said as she looped her arm through Ahmeek's.

Morgan turned and retreated with her feelings as Ahmeek walked the other way. They were putting distance between themselves. With every step they grew farther apart, but it felt as if she were still trapped against that wall, still staring in his eyes. Her heart beat for him, and she couldn't have him. He was walking away with another girl because Morgan was pushing him out.

13

Ahmeek's mood had soured. Seeing Morgan and the twins unnerved him. His gut pulled at him.

"You're quiet," Livi said as she sat in his passenger seat.

He leaned against his door, whipping the BMW with one hand as he kept his eyes on the road. "I'm good."

"Are you, Meek? Cuz you been acting real shitty since we left the mall," she snapped. "And FYI, I don't appreciate you and your ex having hushed conversations. The shit was mad rude and disrespectful."

"Yo, you doing a lot," Ahmeek stated. "Let me drop yo' ass off."

Livi folded her arms across her chest and huffed her displeasure. "I thought we were making progress, Meek. One glance at this bitch, and you back on your bullshit."

"Ain't no progress with me. I told you about asking me for tomorrow. All I got is today to give," he said.

"But she gets tomorrow?" Livi asked.

"She ain't ya' concern," he snapped.

"Fuck you, nigga. Take me home. You got me fucked up. I have feelings. I'm not some bird out here. I enjoy you, but I don't want to date casually anymore. I want to settle down. I want to get married . . ."

The frown that crossed his face couldn't be stopped. "I ain't with none of that. You know that. Where the fuck is this shit coming from? Cuz we ain't never kept that type of time, Livi."

"We could, though. We could be good together if you'd let us," she whispered. "I saw how you looked at her. I've known ever since that night in the club. When she's around, it's like nothing else even matters. I've been down for years. Why don't you feel that for me?"

Ahmeek blew out a sharp breath. He pulled the car over and threw it in park, then turned to her. Livi was stubborn, so she didn't let her tears fall. She was pretty as hell. A little bad, redbone, with wide eyes and flawless everything. His type. His type before Morgan.

"Look. If I was disrespectful, I apologize. You're a good woman, Liv. You are. You got your shit together. Your salon and shit. You on your hustle. You're smart and low-key. I fuck with it. I enjoy your vibe, but we were cruising. We were after the club with it, real casual with it. Good sex, a little shopping and breakfast. You've never even been to my crib. Now you telling me you want to marry me, and that ain't supposed to scare a nigga?"

"Not now, Meek! I'm not saying I want a ring tomorrow. I'm just saying I'm not the type of girl to just do this shit for fun. I want to build toward something with a man, not just have sex. I'd like to do that with you. I know what it's been between us, but I'm telling you my feelings are involved, and I'd like for it to be more. Anything that isn't growing is dead, Meek. You growing with Morgan Atkins?"

Her question dug a hole straight through him. He had no response. He pulled in a deep breath. All this back and forth gave him a headache. He swiped a hand down his face as he rubbed his beard.

"This is getting heavy, Liv," he said. "The timing is bad. What you want and what I can give right now . . . it don't match."

"Then take me home," she said. "Cuz now that I see what you'll give the next bitch that ain't even half of me, I want more."

Ahmeek nodded and merged back into traffic. The ride was silent. Tense. Awkward. Something they had never been. He hated that women did this. Compared. Measured. He couldn't give Livi what he gave Morgan. He hadn't even known he could give it to Mo until he'd experienced her for himself. He wanted to settle down, he did. He wanted to exit the game, but damn if he hadn't built the frame in his mind and inserted Morgan's picture inside. She was already a part of the picture in his mind of how good life should be. Every time he made a run, touched a brick, hit a semi, or spoke to Hak, he had her in the back of his mind. She had become his motivation. Morgan had become the goal. To do it a while longer so he could eventually come out on the other side with her on his arm. Could he replace her? If Morgan never came back around, could he open up to the possibility of Livi or perhaps a woman he had yet to meet being "the one"? He wasn't in the business of making women feel like they were being shortchanged. He enjoyed spending time with Livi, but her ticket had just gone up. She had upped the price on him when she discovered he was valuing another more than her, and because of that, the casualness of a fling was no longer enough. He pulled up to her home, the downtown one-bedroom condo she had purchased for herself.

Ahmeek scratched his head as his brow hiked in confusion. Shit had just been good, and now it wasn't. They had been smooth, and now because of a run-in at the local mall, their night was full of emotional turbulence.

"Yo, Liv. I didn't know it was like that for you. Serious. I didn't know you were getting serious," he stammered.

"Sticking around watching you give love and commitment to someone else, meanwhile all I get is a handbag or two and a trip to Benihana. I'm not a back-burner type of girl. I'll pass, but thanks, babe; it's been fun."

A bad bitch, indeed. Livi slid out of his passenger seat and closed the door before strutting into the lobby of her building.

Meek wondered if he was a fool. To give up the potential that could exist between him and Livi. He was hung up on Morgan. He wished he had stuck to his guns and kept his distance from her. Two years had gone by before he had been in the same space as she had, and at first sight, she had affected him. Those sad eyes had pulled him in, and he had been stuck ever since. Meek idled on the curb of Livi's building as the seconds ticked away and he stroked his chin. A million thoughts ran through his head. To stay or pull away. Livi was as good as any. She was beautiful. Another man would have staked a claim a long time ago.

She ain't her, though.

Meek put his car in drive and pulled off.

Morgan heard the key slide into the lock of the front door, and she stood. Eager eyes watched him cross over the threshold, and when he looked at her, she closed her eyes to savor the seconds that passed as he took her in. She fluttered them open, and he was still across the room. The blank expression on his face made Morgan wring her fingers in anxiety.

"You said to come to where I got the shirt from. I got it from you," she said. Her voice barely worked. She had prayed he would come home. She had hoped he wouldn't stay out with Livi. That he wouldn't fuck Livi.

God, don't let him love Livi.

"Where are the twins?" he asked.

"Ethic's," she answered.

Ahmeek's jaw clenched, and he ran both hands down his wavy head. "You say one thing and do another, Morgan Atkins. The circles I don't love, Mo."

He stayed on his side of the room. He was thinking real hard. She could see him. Weighing the options of what her presence meant in his head.

"I ain't fucking with it," he said.

Morgan deflated. The air left her. It wasn't what she had expected to hear.

Ahmeek tossed his keys on the table near the door and crossed the room, passing her. Morgan couldn't even speak as he ignored her. He pulled open his Sub-Zero refrigerator and pulled out a Heineken and then bypassed Morgan again as he headed to the couch.

"So you're going to ignore me?" she asked, voice small.

"Fuck you here for, Mo, huh?" he asked.

His tone stunned her.

"I just wanted to see you . . . to . . . I don't know . . . seeing you with . . . you said to come . . ." Morgan was searching for an explanation.

"I fucked over a good girl for you today," he said.

"Fuck her," Morgan said. "I don't care about her."

"What about me? Huh? How you feel about me?" he asked.

"You know how I feel about you," she defended.

"I know you stay bullshitting. I know Livi don't bullshit. I dismissed a bitch today that'll lace up her boots and ride with a nigga over anybody. When I asked myself why I'd give that up, the shit didn't even make sense. I don't do shit that don't make sense."

"So, you want her?" Morgan asked. She held her breath because she knew Ahmeek wouldn't lie to her. If he desired Livi, he would let it be known. He wouldn't deny it to protect her feelings. Deceit just wasn't his game. He put his cards on the table faceup every time. If he said yes, Morgan would be destroyed.

"Nah, but she want me, and I ain't got to second-guess the shit. I ain't got to think about her with other niggas. I ain't got to stop myself from killing a mu'fucka behind her, cuz she solid," Ahmeek stated.

Morgan didn't know what to say. His praise of Livi made her sick to her stomach. She had no defense. She couldn't even pretend he wasn't right. She couldn't convince herself that he deserved her half-commitment. She may not be with him all the time physically, but he owned every part of her. If only he could measure the loyalty of her heart. He had no idea how much of it he occupied. She was just in a jam, a trap, a maze that she couldn't find her way out of, and she couldn't ask for help. It was something she had to figure out alone. She understood his impatience. It didn't stop it from hurting, however.

"I want you," Morgan said. "It's more than a want, Ahmeek. I dream about you every night. Having you in my life in this way—" She paused. "It was never supposed to happen. It's fucked up, and it crosses so many lines, but it's like a dream. The way you make me feel is . . ." She closed her eyes. "I want you, Ahmeek."

Ahmeek tilted the green beer bottle to his lips. "You like

to play with a nigga head, Morgan. With your back and forth. You in and out with it. You make a man feel like he on top of the world. Love on a nigga real good. Say all the right shit. Stroke his ego, put pussy on him, scream his name, smile at him like you can't see shit else," Ahmeek stated. He sat with legs wide, beer tilted to his lips and not even looking her. His eyes were on the floor as he inventoried the things she had done to him. "Then you go back home to another man. Then you compare me to Messiah like I ain't loving you with everything I got, like what I been doing ain't shit—"

"It's everything," Morgan interrupted. She crossed the room and straddled him, removing the beer bottle from his hands. He was uncooperative as he leaned back against the couch. "Nobody compares to you. I don't love anyone the way that I love you. I've felt a lot of things for a lot of people before, but never this. I love Messiah, I do; I can't help that or stop that. It's a history I can't rewrite. Even if I could, I don't know if I would because I wouldn't know you, Ahmeek. If I didn't hurt with him, I wouldn't know what it feels like to heal with you. I have a situation with Bash. It feels like I can't help that or stop that either. I'm sorry about all of that, but none of that stops me from thinking about you. I know I don't deserve you. I don't, because I'm wasting you, but every day, I think about you. Every day, I dream about you. Every other man that you think I put over you has created storms in my life. You're the calm. You're my peace. I just can't get to you."

Ahmeek's head was leaned against the back of the couch, and Morgan leaned into him, resting her head over his shoulder. Ahmeek pulled her closer, one hand to the back of her neck, the other to the small of her back. He was so lenient with her. Hard to the world, fucking soft with this one girl. He hated it. His body went rigid as he slid Morgan out of his lap.

"Ahmeek..."

"You should go home to your fiancé, Morgan. Or Messiah. Or whoever you belong to, cuz it ain't me."

"I don't know how to respond to you when you're like this."

"Ain't shit to say. Show me. You staying or you going back to your nigga, Mo? Cuz unless you about that action, all these words are just words. You selling niggas dreams. I told you how I was going to be behind you. I will murder that nigga, Morgan. I don't want to because it's reckless, and it's out of emotion, not necessity, but I will—but then what? Then there's Messiah. A nigga you telling me you still love and one I can't just put down. I can't erase him, Morgan, cuz I love that nigga. He is me. A blood pact at ten fucking years old. The nigga DNA is somewhere in me. You got me out here at war with my man over you, and I'm like, fuck it, cuz you worth fighting for, but you ain't even fucking here. You ain't even mine. You ain't nobody's, Mo. You for everybody."

Morgan recoiled. He didn't even mean for the insult to land so viciously. He hadn't even meant to say it. It wasn't how he felt. Wasn't how he looked at her, but somewhere in her soul, Morgan connected those words with her self-worth. He saw the injury his words caused, and he immediately wanted to take them back. It wasn't like him to speak without thinking. Especially with her. His anger had gotten the best of him. Only Morgan could make him lose control this way.

"Wow," she uttered in disbelief.

A knock at the door made Morgan turn, and her gut hollowed when Livi peeked in.

"Hey, Meek, I got your text. I—"

Morgan turned tear-filled eyes back to him. Livi. He had invited Livi to his loft. Her loft. Their motherfucking loft. He had never brought a girl home before. That's what Ms. Marilyn had said, yet here Livi stood. Morgan knew it was a double standard, but she couldn't help feeling betrayed. Her feelings were on the shiny hardwood floors they were so hurt.

"Am I interrupting something?" Livi asked.

"Nah, you not interrupting anything, sis. He's all yours. Thanks for letting me know how you feel. I'm done." Morgan's voice quivered as she looked at Ahmeek.

"I been done." He hated that his pride offered up the response. There was a hint of regret in his eyes, and he bit his bottom lip before looking away from her. He knew if she walked out that door, it was over, and the throbbing in his chest was begging him to stop her. The pit in his stomach was screaming for her. The girl he loved had hurt him, and he was purposefully trying to hurt her back. His ego was bigger than every emotion in the room. So much so that even the prickling of Morgan's eyes didn't force him to back down. He was on some bullshit, and he knew it and he didn't stop it. He was destroying her simply to break the connection they shared. Her eyes pleaded with him, but Ahmeek couldn't take more nights of lying in bed without her by his side. He could barely get through his days without killing anyone because she had him trapped in an emotional well so deep that he was drowning. When he was here and she was there, life felt like a prison sentence, and he needed to break free. He knew it hurt her because it made a grown man feel like crying, but if she wasn't going to stay for good, then he had to end it.

The devastation he saw in her eyes made him feel like shit. Seconds felt like an eternity as he memorized her in this moment. Such a beautiful fucking girl. The outside was obvious. The inside of her, the most magnificent part, was so opulent it beamed through, reaching the darkest places. Touching the pits, the shadows, the heartless . . . men like Messiah. Men like him. They gravitated to Morgan because after being in the dark for their whole lives, the light felt miraculous. He fucking loved this girl. He would have taken good care of her. Ahmeek would have given it his all to try to be what she needed. Her only crime was allowing others to lead her instead of following her heart. He sniffed and flicked his nose as Morgan turned, walking right past Livi, who stood smirking at the door. Morgan may not have been able to end it, but Ahmeek certainly was capable, and he had. It destroyed them both.

"You always wanted to wrap a ball and chain around a nigga leg?" Isa asked. Aria paused mid-stroke, turning to him with the paintbrush in her hand.

"Is that what I'm doing?" Aria asked, chuckling.

"I mean, yeah. Dealing with one woman for the rest of my life sound a little bit like prison. Same four walls for the rest of my life. That's a life sentence for my dick," Isa stated.

Aria laughed from her soul. "You make it sound horrible!" she exclaimed. "Why would you ask me to marry you if this is how you feel about it?"

Isa kicked one foot up on the coffee table in front of him as one hand went behind his head and the other hand brought a lit blunt to his lips. He took his time answering her. Brows bent. Deep in thought.

"That was the price of admission, and I wanted in," Isa answered.

Aria bent down and dipped her paintbrush into the red paint. She turned to the wall. She didn't know how she felt about him marrying her for such shallow reasons. "So love had nothing to do with it. Wow. Doesn't seem like a good reason to choose someone forever."

Isa heard her feelings crack as if they had shattered all over the floor. He knew he wasn't a Prince Charming type. He came off callous and cold. His love language hadn't been discovered yet. It definitely wasn't one out of the book he saw Aria reading at night. His love language was protection. He guarded everything that meant something to him. Aria was an asset in his life; therefore, she had a shooter on her team. Before she even knew he would wage wars over her, it was already established. He knew she would be something special when he first saw her onstage, and when she gave him attitude while walking by him all those years ago, Isa knew she had potential. The chase had been a plus because it proved she wasn't easy. She was a challenge, and when he finally caught her, he realized she was a diamond among stones. You protect a jewel. Especially the rare ones, so Isa went into beast mode with her. Any other nigga that got close got snuffed, because she was his whether she knew it or not. His way might not have been conventional, but it was his expression of love. He didn't have a mushy bone in his body. If she wanted romance, he wasn't the one for her, but that protection she had for life. He rose from the couch and walked up behind her. He wrapped tattooed arms around her small frame, bending some because she was so short.

"Stop, Isa," she said softly. Yeah, she was upset. Aria didn't do anything soft. She hid behind a tough-girl façade.

"You know what it is with us, Ali," Isa said, moving her hair out the way so he could kiss the back of her neck. He bit her, teeth sinking into her shoulder just enough to cause a slight pinch. "Don't you?"

She turned to him and took the paintbrush and painted a wide smile on his face.

He grimaced and nodded before bringing the blunt to his lips, then puffed it between red paint, staining the tip. She laughed.

"You stay on bullshit," he said, tilting his head back and blowing smoke into the air.

"You on some clown shit; thought I'd put your face on for you," Aria stated. "Don't be evasive with me. I always knew I'd either marry for love or marry for money. I'm not against either—just let me know what it is. If all I am is sex to you, then you can be my bank."

Fire danced in his eyes. The equivalent to reducing her to a loveless wife was reducing him to a lick.

"Don't like that, huh?" Aria asked.

"I ain't tricked on a bitch ever," Isa stated.

"I ain't been a bitch ever, baby. You tricking on a queen, paying me for my time, or you loving me? You tell me what we're doing," Aria stated.

Isa reached around her body and palmed her ass. "I'm loving you, Ali. Now quit talking reckless before you make me mad." He leaned into her, paint everywhere. Red. The color she hated. All over her neck as he planted a kiss there.

"Go wash your face." Aria laughed.

"Come wash it for me." He picked her up, hands under her ass as Aria dropped the paintbrush. His lips on hers. She didn't even care that he was getting paint everywhere. That she tasted it a bit as he carried her to the bathroom.

He placed her on her feet, then took a step back before pulling his fitted white tee over his head. Isa's light skin was covered. Crew shit, affiliation pieces, tributes to Aria, guns, Jesus, you name it—Isa had it tattooed on him. It looked like someone had come to tag him. He was skinny—frail, even—but as he stepped out of his Gucci jeans, he revealed all his weight. Dick like that made Aria coy. She would never get used to the size of him.

"I hate you so much," she moaned as he closed the lid and

took a seat. He was completely nude except for Nike socks, and Aria smiled, shaking her head. She had no idea how she had ended up with his ghetto ass, but she was enjoying the ride. Every single minute with Isa was a roller coaster. Their love for each other was a thrill. If they ever ended, Aria would struggle to find this much stimulation in a different man. The challenge was incredible.

"Come show me how much," Isa said. Red paint still smeared his face and now decorated hers too.

Aria toed her way to him and straddled him. She wore his boxers. A habit. A bad one, according to him. "I don't want to see all that ass in no drawers, Ali," he would fuss. Tonight, he didn't seem to mind.

"Yo, take these off," he ordered. Aria stood, turned her back to him, then slid them down. Before she knew it, his large hands were around her waist. She yelped in surprise as he lifted her onto him. "Spell something on it."

F-U-C-K-U-B-O-Y

Aria wound her hips around the curve of every letter.

Isa smacked her ass so hard Aria clenched her teeth. "Fuck you too," he answered. "You ain't slick."

"I didn't know you knew how to read." She laughed.

D-A-G-O-D

"That's right, Ali," he moaned as she made light work of him. "Shit so good, baby. Swimming in chocolate. It's wet and sweet."

Aria moved her body as if she were putting together eight counts, and the friction of his fingers in the right places made her called out his name. "Isa, baby!"

"All on that dick like a good girl, Ali," he groaned.

She came first. It was one fight Isa didn't mind losing. He took his time, picking her up again and then bending her over the sink, snickering as he looked in the mirror at his red face. He slapped her ass again. Payback for the clown shit. He was putting dick in Aria so good his name was bouncing off the walls. Her cries took him all the way, and he didn't even care to pull out. She was his. She said no babies. He said fuck it.

"Isaaa!" she protested, standing and spinning to punch him.

"Got to know you up real good. Put a baby in you and that's mine forever," he stated, laughing because he knew she was pissed.

He pecked her lips and then made his way to the shower as Aria sat down on the toilet to pee. She shook her head in distress, reminding herself to get on birth control as soon as possible because otherwise, messing around with Isa, she'd be somebody's baby mama in the near future.

"Boy, if you don't get your ass up and clean this mess up, you better. I don't care if you bought this loft; you know better than this," Marilyn fussed as she made her way from the front door to the kitchen. Ahmeek groaned as he rubbed a hand down his face. He had just gone to bed two hours ago. A night of fucking his feelings away with a girl he hardly cared for, he had forgotten all about Sunday breakfast. Marilyn frowned as she turned to the refrigerator and found the pair of thong panties clipped to the magnet. "Now I know damn well these ain't Morgan's."

Her voice was so loud. Like nails on a chalkboard. He hadn't drunk like this in years. A hangover plagued him as he stood from the couch where he had given in to sleep.

"Morgan isn't a thing no more, Ma," Ahmeek said.

"Morgan is the thing that led to these empty bottles, these tacky panties, and that sad look on your face, boy," Marilyn said. "Come get rid of these trifling thangs and clean this mess up so I can cook."

Ahmeek didn't protest. He scratched the top of his head in irritation, but he knew better than to vocalize it. Ms. Marilyn was the real gangster between them. "Let me hit a shower and get myself together first. I'll be right back," he said.

He dressed quickly, showering and brushing his teeth before emerging.

"I told you that young girl was going to run circles around you," Marilyn snickered. "Little Morgan Atkins." She shook her head. "Who do the panties belong to?"

"Just some girl I see from time to time, Ma. Don't make it a big deal," Ahmeek answered.

"Oh, I know it isn't a big deal. I know you better than you know yourself. You're moping around here because Morgan done hurt your feelings, and you trying to be tough, act like you the man and you can just replace her. You can deal with ten women after her, and it won't make you want her less, Ahmeek. I've seen you with her. She brings out my little boy. Not the man you became too fast. You laugh with her. You smile with her. You're better for her. Don't run around tangling yourself up in temporary flings thinking it's going to replace somebody that made you think about forever."

"Mo ain't forever, Ma. She won't let it be that. What I'm supposed to do? Sit back and wait?" Ahmeek asked.

"She's a baby, Ahmeek. She's not where you are mentally," Marilyn said.

"She's engaged," Ahmeek answered.

"And she's not ready for whoever she's engaged to or to be what you're ready for her to be," Marilyn said. "She hasn't lived. If you love her, you have to let her learn to use her wings. You might have to watch her love another. Might have to watch her lose another. Maybe she'll contact you every now and then, maybe she won't. You got to give that baby time to grow. If what

I felt between the two of you is as potent as it seemed, she'll come back to you one day. You can't rush her transformation, son. Every man who has ever tried to do that to any woman has been left disappointed."

Ahmeek was silent as he processed his mother's words. Maybe it wasn't their time. Perhaps time had to pass for them to catch each other at the exact moment when serendipity would cut them a break. That was hard on a man like Ahmeek, who was used to having what he wanted, when he wanted. He couldn't guarantee he would wait. In fact, he was sure he wouldn't. His pride wouldn't let him, but his heart wouldn't soon forget little Morgan. Loving her would be a nostalgia he craved for a while. Some women were simply irreplaceable.

14

Morgan was back in her cocoon. No Meek. No Messiah. Just herself and the family she had fabricated. She had never felt so unsafe, not even when she had been under Mizan's roof. A touch that had once felt loving froze Morgan instantly. Bash's ability to run hot and then cold terrified her. She was just on edge around him, but Ethic was safe. That was all that mattered. She would play her position to keep him that way. No one knew she was unhappy. Sometimes she even questioned if she was just being ungrateful. Bash had never been horrible to her. He was handsome and rich and esteemed. She should have been grateful. Things could have been worse. Sure, he was controlling and his temper sparked sometimes, but he wasn't unbearable. Only, after Ahmeek Harris, it was impossible to settle for less. She tried not to think of the men she had loved before. The Messiahs and Meeks of the world who gave love in intense waves, leaving a girl drunk at just the thought of them. She missed them both. She loved them dearly. It was the part of her that didn't want to have to choose between them that made settling seem like the only option. She was hurting herself but neither of them, or so she thought. She had no idea the ways their days were extended by her absence, prolonged by thoughts of what she was doing and who she was doing it with. Twenty-four hours without Morgan was like a life sentence for Ahmeek. For Messiah Williams, it was like death. The no-contact orders that they were forced to abide by because she had been whisked off to the Fredrick family home had put moods on the hearts of gangsters. The solitude gave Morgan time to think. She had never really considered how she had contributed to the chaos in her life. She had always been the type to follow her heart, wherever it may lead, but this time, it had gotten her lost.

"I'm glad things are settled," Bash said as he stood in front of the floor-length mirror and adjusted his necktie.

Morgan hated his arrogance. She had never noticed it before coming back to Michigan. The entitlement he walked around with. The fake authority. Bash's respect had been inherited, not earned. She knew real kings who had either stolen or hustled for every jewel in their crown. Men like Ethic, Messiah, Isa, and Ahmeek. Her father. All the men she respected had come up in the trenches. They had waged wars and earned their honor in battle. Bash's was given, and the way he carried it— as if he were worth more because of what he was born into— turned Morgan's stomach.

"Are they?" she asked.

He turned to her, pausing, but before he could form words, Yara came flying into the room. Morgan was grateful for the interruption.

Bash picked her up, and Morgan stood from the bed, hurrying over to take her daughter from his arms.

"I can't just sit here and do nothing, Bash. The applications," she said. "To medical school. I should be starting a program by now. You don't have to stop that anymore. I get what's at stake. I've been here with you. For weeks, I haven't left this house. Can you at least stop your mom from freezing my apps? Bash, I worked hard for this."

Morgan had put her all into those two years at Cambridge. Flying back and forth between Michigan and London, keeping her GPA high enough to remain eligible to participate in the exchange program. It had done her well to focus on her studies instead of on the pain Messiah had left behind. Morgan was sure it was the reason she hadn't noticed that things were awry with Bash. She had been too focused to focus on him. Now that her options were being taken away, all she could think about was how she didn't belong here.

"Medical school will be a distraction," Bash said.

"A distraction from what?" Morgan replied. "I'm not doing anything here but sipping tea and smiling for your mama and her old-ass friends."

"You have a wedding to plan," Bash stated. "Focus on that. After the wedding and the baby, we'll talk about school."

"You can't be serious," Morgan protested.

"It's your role, Mo. I'm a man that's expected to marry and build a legacy. I love the twins, but they're not my bloodline. I need a son. We'll try until you give me one."

Morgan scoffed. The notion was ridiculous. The expectation, outrageous. Morgan was only sexually free with men she trusted not to enslave her. She had trusted Messiah's touch. He had been her first willing sexual encounter, and although Ahmeek was never supposed to be one she experienced at all, he touched her with such love that Morgan had no regrets. Bash could never. Bash would never. Sex was mental for Morgan. Her emotions were expensive, and Bash, although royal, was cheap. She would never have his children.

"I have two kids, Bash. I'm twenty-one years old. I want to do more than lay on my back and have babies. If not school, what about dancing? I could be auditioning—"

"You're better than that, Mo. It was sexy when I met you. It was a hobby. It's not a career. Your ear for music is a little off anyway, don't you think? I mean, the gimmick is cool. The whole deaf dancer thing, but next to professional dancers at an audition? You really think you'd make the cut? It's time to be realistic."

Morgan shrank before his eyes. Doubt crept into her mind. Dancing made Morgan feel as if she were yelling, like she were using a voice she hadn't always been brave enough to share. The way he crushed her feelings made her tremble in rage. Morgan had been misunderstood her entire life. Only three people made her feel otherwise. Ethic interpreted her soul, reading through her thoughts like they were printed in ink on the outside. Messiah had learned to speak her language, and the effort of communication had been a gift that made Mo feel like no matter what, at least one person could understand her. Ahmeek was fluent in her body language because he appreciated the way she moved, both on and offstage. He was fluent in the way she spoke without speaking at all. A sixteen count to music was an entire conversation if he was watching, and now Bash was telling her that was a lie. He was telling her the praise was sympathy, and Morgan hated for anyone to feel sorry for her. She could tell he wasn't even trying to offend her. He was giving his perception of truth. He didn't believe in her. She wondered if he ever had. Had he been good at faking, or was he simply fed up? Morgan never claimed to be innocent. She had done him wrong. This much she knew. She just wanted to let this go so they could both move on.

"Wow," she answered. "Good to know I have your support." Her sarcasm wasn't missed. She gathered her bag and fumbled with Yara on her hip as she headed toward the door. "I'm going to spend a few days at my apartment."

"You sure you want to do that?" he asked.

Morgan recognized the threat. "Don't worry. You've pushed every man who's ever loved me away, Bash. After the things I've done"—she shook her head—"all I've got is you left. Mission accomplished. You have a key, warden. You know where to find me. I just need some air."

She hated that she was a crier. Didn't matter that this was anger and not sadness, those tears were coming. Morgan pushed out of the bedroom and stormed through the house to find her son.

"Ssari, let's go. We're going home for a little while," Morgan said as she entered the living room where Messari sat on the floor in front of Christiana. He played quietly with his toys as she sat with readers on while enjoying a crossword puzzle. It could all be so simple. Only her heart wouldn't let it. These people didn't love her. They wanted to control her. Morgan couldn't figure out why. She shouldn't be important enough for them to force this the way they were. The longer she stayed, the more creeped out by them she became.

"Why you must rile this boy up every time he's calm, I'll never understand," Christiana commented without looking up.

"Because he's mine, Christiana. He's my son. I can do whatever I want to do with my child," Morgan stated.

Christiana lifted her eyes slowly until she was staring Morgan directly in the eyes. "The amount of authority you think you have over these children is cute, Morgan Atkins. You're soon to be a Fredrick. Mrs. Sebastian Fredrick. The power in that is leased. I own it. I own you. I own them. The sooner you realize that, the more you'll begin to fit your new life. Use the name he's giving you. Stop running back to that mediocre lifestyle you used to lead. When you're ready, I'll open the world to you. Until then, no medical school, no nothing. You'll be a wife and mother and nothing else."

The chill she spoke with made Morgan's eyes prickle. When she had first met Christiana, she had admired her. Morgan had respected her. To be a black royal had seemed so honorable—like a privilege—but Morgan hadn't recognized the price. It wasn't until Christiana began stripping Morgan of the things that made her *her* that Morgan began to see the cost of prestige. It started with her clothes. Then her hair. Then her posture. Then the places she could and couldn't go. Now the people she could and couldn't see. Another girl might be willing to erase her past, but Morgan's past meant everything to her, despite how painful it had been. Her past was where her family lived. All she had were the memories of them to get her by. She couldn't erase that part of her if she wanted to.

"Yeah, let me get out of here real fast," Morgan scoffed. "Messari, baby, follow Mommy."

Morgan ran away as if she were never coming back. She drove so fast that dirt kicked up behind her car. Escape. She was looking for a way out, even if it was just temporary. Morgan headed west, hitting the highway that would take her back to Flint. The red rose she had saved sat dried up on her dashboard. The lone survivor of the bouquets Bash had put in the trash.

She wished she could run to him. Once upon a time, she would have. It seemed like so long ago. She picked up her phone and dialed one number. It was like a lifeline. A direct connection to the best listener she knew.

"Hey, baby girl." The voice was instant relief, and Morgan

let out a sigh. She had love. She possessed so much of it outside the walls of Bash's castle.

"Can you meet me somewhere?"

"I could really use you right now, Rae," Morgan whispered. She sat Indian-style on the grass facing her sister's headstone. "It feels like I'm in trouble, and I don't know how to get out of it this time. I can't ask Ethic for help. I can't ask anyone."

"Mommy, who are you talking to?" Yara signed.

Morgan reached out to touch the stone. "Your auntie Raven. She's sleeping here, baby," Morgan signed back.

"When will she wake up?" Messari signed.

"She can't, baby boy," Morgan whispered. The tear that slid down her cheek nestled in the corner of her mouth. Messari turned in her lap and wiped it away as Yara snuggled closer.

"Like Sleeping Beauty, Mommy?" Yara asked.

"Exactly like that," Morgan signed.

The peace she found at the cemetery was odd. Most would be rushing to leave, but Morgan felt at home. The people who shared her last name were there. An entire tribe awaited her.

"Mo?"

Morgan turned her neck to find Alani navigating across the lawn.

"La La!" Messari yelled in excitement as he scrambled to his feet and ran in her direction. Yara wasn't far behind. Morgan laughed as Alani bent down, going to her knees to accept their hugs.

"Be careful," Morgan called after her kids as they swarmed Alani.

"Is he still cooking?" Messari asked impatiently, turning his head to the side as he pressed his ear to Alani's belly.

She laughed, and Morgan smiled.

"Yup. He's still in there holding tight. He'll be here soon, and then he's all yours to love on," Alani said, tapping his little button nose.

"Mine too?" Yara signed.

"Yours too, Yolly Pop," Alani confirmed.

Morgan wondered if Raven would have been this good with her kids. Would they have loved her as much as they loved Alani? Alani was a beautiful addition to their lives. She often wondered if Raven would fill the shoes well or would she fail the way Morgan was failing at life. Atkins girls seemed to be cursed.

Alani climbed to her feet and then made her way to Morgan. "Want some company, or maybe we should go grab a bite to eat somewhere?"

"Is it awkward for you if I say I want to stay here?" Morgan asked, staring up over a crinkled brow as she shielded her eyes from the sun.

"Not at all. Me and Raven have discussions about Ethic's ass once a week," Alani responded. She took a seat, setting her purse next to her and claiming Yara as Morgan pulled her son into her lap.

"Wow, really?"

"Really, Mo," Alani confirmed. "It's important to me to honor her for Eazy, for you." She paused. "And for him. She's a part of him. I love every part."

Morgan was amazed. She didn't have that type of understanding yet. Wasn't old enough to possess such maturity. "Wow," she whispered. "I've always looked at you and Ethic and wanted what you have. Even when I hated the thought of you two together, I always felt the energy between y'all whenever you guys were in the same room. It takes my breath away."

Alani peered at Morgan, focusing on her eyes. "What's

going on, Mo? You say you want those things, but I've seen two men love you with their soul, and you're not with either of them. You're wearing a ring and planning a wedding with Bash. Why?"

Morgan's lip trembled, and she bit down on it, clenching her teeth. "I don't know," she admitted.

"It's time to be honest with yourself," Alani said. "What do you want, Mo?"

"I don't want anyone I love to be hurt," Morgan whispered.

Alani frowned. "Morgan, you're clearly not happy. You're hurting. What about you? What's best for you? Who do you love?"

Morgan closed her eyes and shook her head.

"You love them both," Alani said aloud.

"With everything in me," Morgan admitted. "I miss Messiah. I miss everything about him. How safe I felt with him. How it was just us against the entire world. I haven't even been able to be happy that he's alive because there is all this anger in the way. All this resentment. I'm so mad that he left because if he had stayed, there would be no Bash, there would be no Meek. It would just be us with them," Morgan said, nodding to her children. "And I know it would have been beautiful. He would have been good to us. Right?" Morgan was looking for confirmation.

"There is something valuable about a man who doesn't know how to love anyone but you, Mo. It can still be beautiful, Morgan," Alani said. "If you let it, it could still be beautiful for you both."

"It can't," Morgan said, shaking her head. "Because now I love Ahmeek too. Now Messiah's not the first person I think of when I open my eyes. He left me, and I was so lonely. There were so many days he could have come back, and we could have picked up right where we left off. He waited. He let all those days pass, and now I'm in love with his best friend, Alani. They're brothers. No matter what I do, I'm going to destroy that."

Alani scooted closer to Morgan, and Morgan broke down. She turned her head away from Alani and her twins and stubbornly looked at the rows of graves as her tears flowed. She hated this. Absolutely detested it. The wanting but not having. The craving but being denied. Morgan had never not been given what she desired. Ethic had laid down framework that catered to her every need since she was a child. Not having free will was killing her.

"Mo, why don't you just come home for a little while? I could use your help around the house. I'm getting closer to my due date, and Bella and Eazy have so much on their schedules that I can't keep up with. We love it when you're home. We love having you and the twins close. It killed Ethic when you stayed away in London. Just move back for a while. Help me out with some things before the baby comes. It'll give you space to think. I know you say you're fine, but I don't like that bitch Christiana. It's something about her that I don't trust, and it feels like there's something you aren't saying."

Morgan turned to her in shock, and the concern she saw on Alani's face made her want to confess it all. The intuition of a woman was remarkable, but the intuition of a mother was God given.

"Talk to me, Morgan."

"I can't," Morgan whispered. "I just can't."

Alani reached for Morgan's hand and squeezed it tightly. "I don't really know what you're afraid of, Mo, but let me tell you something about me. I ain't really afraid of shit, and I've been two seconds off Christiana's ass since you introduced us.

You don't have to talk about it, that's fine, but I'm not sending you back there until I know what's wrong." Alani managed to climb to her feet. "Come on, babies. La La has some fresh cookies at home for y'all," she signed as she began walking to her car. "Babies as in all three of you, Mo," Alani called out without looking back at Morgan.

Morgan glanced down at her phone and considered running it by Bash, but if she did that, she would be giving in to a lifetime of that. Of asking permission, of dictatorship. He was already forcing her into something she no longer wanted; she would be damned if he got to decide the frequency with which she visited her family. A little time back home would do her some good. She stood and gathered her belongings before following behind Alani.

15

Messiah rode through the city streets brow bent with his gun lying in his lap, ready for easy access. A nigga had never and would never catch him slipping. So much had changed since he had been gone. He almost questioned if it was worth the effort to make things go back. He was merely a man. He didn't have the power to rewind time. It was lost to him, but he prayed Morgan wasn't. As he pulled into the short driveway and noticed the rented Benz sitting curbside, he prayed another wasn't lost to him as well. Messiah exited the car and approached Bleu's house.

"Fuck this nigga doing here, man?" Messiah mumbled. He had never had an issue with Iman before. They hadn't been friends but friendly on behalf of a shared respect for the girl that stood between them, but today, Messiah felt a fire in his soul. Today, the conversation-turned-argument with Bleu over her moving to California was playing in his head on a loop. He had given her some time. He hadn't wanted to crowd her after their argument, but pulling up seeing Iman was in town ignited him. The heavy hum of a semi engine pulled his attention down the block.

"I know this mu'fucka bet not pull up to this house," Messiah mumbled. Sure enough, the white-and-orange U-Haul truck pulled behind Iman's car.

Messiah turned to the house. On go. His entire mood had changed. The sight of movers flipped his switch. He didn't even knock before snatching open the door.

"Yo, B!" His bark echoed through the house as he stalked through the home like he owned it.

"Uncle Messiah!" Saviour shouted as he came running down the stairs.

Messiah settled a bit at the sight of him. "What up, boi? The locs getting long," Messiah said, wrapping Saviour in a headlock, then dragging him around the first floor in search of Bleu. "Where ya' mama?"

Saviour laughed as he tagged along. "She's upstairs with my dad. Are you going to come visit us in LA?"

Messiah released Saviour and faced him. "Let me ask you something. Do you want to move to Cali?"

"I'm kinda gonna miss my friends and you, but my mom says I'll make new friends," Saviour said.

Messiah bent down, noticing the laces of Saviour's shoes were undone. "What's these, man? We got to get you out of these mu'fuckin' boat shoes and put something proper on your feet. Where the Js I got you?" Messiah asked as he tied Saviour's shoes.

"They're in boxes, and my mom said I can't wear them ever since somebody beat up this boy at school and took his," Saviour explained.

Messiah stood. "Ain't nobody beating you up, nephew."

"How do you know? What if they try to take my shoes?" Saviour asked.

"You a man or you a mouse? Huh?" Messiah grilled. It was a question he had asked Saviour many times before.

"I'm a man," Saviour said, tilting his chin slightly, proudly, because Messiah had taught him that too, over the years. "But what if someone still tries to take them?"

"Niggas run up on people they think won't fight back. You let niggas know you got a little bite behind your bark, and you'll be a'ight. They won't mess with you, and they for damn sure won't try to take no shoes."

"But what if that doesn't work? What if they are ten times bigger than me?" Saviour asked.

"You come get your daddy. They ain't bigger than Daddy," Iman's voice came from behind them.

Messiah stood as Saviour asked, "But what if they are?"

"Then you holler at Unc, cuz I'm coming with something hot for 'em," Messiah said, staring at Iman in the eyes.

"You'd shoot them, Uncle Messiah?!" Saviour asked.

"Blow a nigga head off his shoulders, nephew," Messiah said. He was no longer focused on Saviour, however. "Over you and your mama. I'ma go to ten every time. Niggas ain't never really took nothing from me without it being a problem, so those shoes better stay put. Ain't that right?"

"Definitely!" Saviour agreed, dapping Messiah up.

"That room still need to be packed up," Iman said. "Go take care of that."

Saviour raced up the steps, and Messiah finally addressed Iman. "What up? B here?"

"I been cooling it with you for a minute, laying in the cut cuz I know Bleu rocks with you heavy," Iman said. "But this is my family, nigga."

Messiah halted. People didn't speak to him like that. Ever. It took everything in him to not put Iman's jaw on Bleu's pretty tiled floor.

"They my family too. Them weeks when you gone back to Cali, and it get lonely for her. When he got the doughnut day at school, and you can't fly them three thousand miles . . . or you forgot about them days? She mine too."

Iman scoffed and stepped closer to Messiah. "I only ever want what's best for her. Noah was best, so I fell back. You, you're the worst type of nigga for her. You string her along and come and go as you please. You take advantage of feelings you know she hiding and do what you want with her body cuz you know she ain't gon' say no, then you make her watch while you love the next bitch. So nah, she ain't yours. You put a baby in her and then disappeared for two years. Who the fuck you think was here making sure she made it through that clean? She buried a kid, man. A kid she should have never had cuz y'all just friends, remember? You had Ethic's little daughter to focus on, so you shouldn't have been focused over here. I had a feeling you were the reason she kept me at a distance. The whole friends bullshit. I bought it for a while, because I want to trust her, and she's never lied to me, but it ain't me she's lying to. She's lying to herself about you, but you ain't gon' hold it down with her. You ain't gon' rock with her the way she deserves. So what you here for? You playing. That's what you doing. Playing games like a little-ass boy with my family. That girl is my family. She has my son. I'ma give her a life, a ring one day, my name, nigga, but I'ma need you to step out the way, and I'm tired of asking you nicely. You don't want me to put it to you that other way."

Messiah's eyes flickered, a small fire erupting inside him at the notion of a threat. He saw no need for conflict, because Iman had it all wrong. Iman wasn't describing them right. It wasn't a love thing. It wasn't anything. It was nothing, but somehow just the thought of her moving away was enough to unearth grief in him. If B left town, Messiah would lose a piece of himself. He wondered if she had felt this when he had gone away. Had she felt this sinking in her stomach for two years? It hadn't even been five minutes of discovering her potential move and he was dying a little on the inside. Bleu was the most dependable and consistent friend he had ever had. She never failed him, never judged, never gave up on him. She was such an unconditional presence in his life. She was everything he needed, and he didn't know it.

"We can do it however you want to do it, G. My burner show Cali love too. You ain't exempt," Messiah said. He was unmoved and unafraid, despite Iman's extensive street pedigree.

"Messiah?"

He didn't turn to her immediately. Iman had let it be known it wasn't love, and Messiah would never turn his back to a foe.

Eye to eye. Man to man. They didn't need words to speak the rules of engagement.

"I was going to call you," she said. "I decided to go." She held a cardboard box in her hands, and Messiah removed it, setting it on the floor beside him.

"Let me talk to you," he said. All aggression, he didn't hide his disdain.

Bleu looked at Iman. He was her rock. Messiah was her hard place. Here she was, caught between them.

"We out of here in an hour. I'll let the movers know what's what," Iman stated, unaffected by Messiah's discontent. He slid his cell phone out of his pocket and stepped out of the house, forehead full of wrinkles as he pushed the screen door open.

They were silent as Bleu looked up at him. "I hope you get everything you want, Messiah," she said, eyes glistening.

He flicked his nose and sniffed as he gritted his teeth, temple throbbing. He cleared his throat. He was doing everything to stop the volcano of emotions inside of him from erupting.

"You gon' make me say it?" he asked.

"Say what, Messiah?" she sighed.

"You're all I got, Bleu," Messiah said. He searched for answers in her eyes, but all he saw was confusion.

"And somehow I'm not enough," she said in disbelief, shaking her head. He saw the limit. For the first time, he saw her putting up a boundary; she was fed the fuck up, and it bewildered him because over the years, Bleu had given and given and given. She had never said no, and all of a sudden, she was screaming it loud and clear. He had overlooked her one too many times. She had no more to give without reciprocation.

Bleu bent down to pick up the box and walked by Messiah. He pulled at her elbow. His eyes pleaded with her. They did the begging his lips never would. He was too full of pride to tell her she was destroying him with this move. He had lost every single person he had ever valued. Bleu had been solid. She had been an everyday factor in his life. The only time she hadn't been present was when he had forced her out by disappearing. This cut him deep.

"I swear you on some bullshit, B," he said. "This about Mo?"

Bleu sighed. "Messiah, not everything is about Morgan Atkins," she said, eyes lowering in complete confusion as she shook her head. "It's about me. For once, this is about me."

Two men entered through the front door. They wore gloves

and wheeled in dollies, interrupting Bleu and Messiah with playful banter as they began to gather Bleu's possessions.

"Yo, my nigga, you take one box up out of here and I'ma split ya' shit," Messiah said as he scratched the tip of his nose with his thumb.

"Messiah!" Bleu whined.

"Come here, man," he barked, snatching her hand and pulling her into the garage. He turned toward her once they were alone. "I want to be happy for you, B. I do. You're my family, man. I lost everybody, B. Meek ass, man, he on some snake shit, Isa caught in the fucking middle, Ethic half trust a nigga, and Mo can't even look at me, B. You're the only one I got that's ten toes down. Now you leaving?"

"Iman loves me, Messiah," Bleu whispered, recapturing control of her eyes and lowering her gaze to the concrete floor. Her feet shuffled back and forth as she crossed her arms.

"Look," Messiah said, exhaling as he took a seat on a box Bleu had pushed in a corner. "I know he do. I know that part, and I know it's fucked up for me to ask you to stay, but, B, you ain't fucking with Iman like that. Come on, man, let's keep it a hunnid. You don't love that nigga. You used to, but not no more. I know you, B. I know you better than you know yourself," Messiah said. "That's Saviour's old man. That's your family and I get it, but that shit don't run deep. I saw it run deep with Noah, but that part of you ain't even fucking with Iman like that no more. I know you."

"What do you know, Messiah?" Bleu asked. "Huh?" she raised her voice. "If you knew so much, we wouldn't be here. We wouldn't be saying goodbye. You don't know shit with your stupid ass."

Messiah snickered and glanced up at Bleu. She couldn't

help the stubborn smile that broke out on her face. "You're so stupid," she said, eyes watering as she began to laugh.

He chuckled and nodded. "Stupid as fuck, but I need you, B," Messiah said, a smirk pulling at the side of his mouth. Bleu swiped at the tear that slid down her face. He stood and wiped the second one that chased the first. "Stop crying, man."

"I'm not crying," she answered stubbornly, but she very much was. He pulled her into his space and wrapped strong arms around her as he held her. Bleu sniffed. "One day, you're going to have to let me go."

"One day, but not today," Messiah said. He squeezed her tighter, and Bleu wrapped her arms around him and held on to his T-shirt for dear life.

"When you let go, I'm going to end up hurt, Messiah. How is this fair?" she asked. One strong hand massaged the nape of her neck, and Bleu closed her eyes tighter.

"I don't ever plan on letting go, B. It don't matter who come in and out the door; I'ma be here. You know better," he said. He kissed the side of her head, and Bleu pulled back. Her chin quivered, and she used the back of her hand to clear the snot from her nose as her eyes focused on those white Converse sneakers on her feet. Ironically, Messiah wore the same pair. Saviour had picked them out for both of them one year for Christmas. Two peas, two pods . . . they could never quite become one. Bleu turned her face sideways. Her ear to his chest.

"Your heart is racing," she said. "Your heart is beating." He felt her shudder. "I still can't even believe you're alive. I'm so grateful."

Messiah breathed a sigh of relief, but the churning in his gut told him he was getting in over his head. He had a girl he loved. A girl he couldn't wait to earn back, but here he was with another girl, one who he couldn't quite see a life without. He didn't know what to do with that, but he couldn't let Bleu leave. He placed a hand to the back of her head, locking her in place as they embraced.

"What am I going to tell Iman? And Saviour?" Bleu asked.

"Shit, I'll cut it to homie. You want me to do it, or you want to do it?" Messiah asked.

Bleu laughed, but she didn't let go. Couldn't quite let go because as much as Messiah needed her, she hated to admit that his friendship over the years had been a need too. A necessity that kept her focused, a light in the distance when she felt like she was lost, a listening ear when she felt like her cries fell upon the deaf. What they shared was reciprocal. Give-and-take in a world so cold that two damaged souls found shelter in each other's hollowed hearts. "No. I'll do it. You can't be here for that."

Messiah pulled back. "I'll break out, no problems, B, as long as when I pull up, you're here," he answered.

"Aren't I always?" she sighed. She walked over to the button near the door and pressed it. The garage opened. Iman stood in the yard giving orders as Saviour rode his bike on the sidewalk out front.

Messiah walked out, no nods or salutations given to Iman this time. The cordiality had been thrown out the window. Iman wanted smoke, and Messiah didn't blame him, because Bleu was worth the battle.

"Uncle Messiah, wait! I want to say goodbye!" Saviour shouted as he hopped off his bike, tossing it into the grass handlebars first.

Messiah shook his head. "You ain't going nowhere, nephew. Cuz I'm a man, not a what?" Messiah asked.

"Mouse!" Saviour shouted. "We're really staying?"

"You're really staying," Messiah answered as he glanced at Iman.

"Yes!"

Saviour jumped for joy and ran up to Bleu. "Thanks, Mom!" he shouted as he gave her a quick hug before rushing back into the house.

Messiah didn't stay. He knew Bleu had business to tend to. He pulled out his keys and got back into his car before pulling off.

16

"We need Messiah on this, man. We owe this nigga Hak too much money. We got to do this shit the old way. Two sets of hands ain't enough," Isa said as he wrapped a rubber band around a thick wad of money and tossed it into the pile that was building in the center of the table. "You niggas need to get out your fucking feelings so we can hop in this bag. Mo with her gangster boo ass got you niggas acting real fucking sensitive. That shit is getting in the way of the money."

Ahmeek was silent. The quiet was answer enough. He didn't even acknowledge that Isa was talking as he flipped through the bills in front of him. He was more precise than any teller, quicker than any money machine. He had been counting up thousand-dollar stacks since he was a young boy. "You fuck up my count and that's ya ass," Ahmeek stated.

"Fuck yo' count, nigga," Isa said, jumbling up the bills in front of Ahmeek. Ahmeek blew out a sharp breath and turned stern eyes to Isa. Isa stuck up a middle finger while pulling on the blunt he smoked. He blew smoke into the air and passed it to Ahmeek.

Meek exhaled sharply. "Fuck it."

"Ain't our shit; make that nigga Hak count it," Isa said. "It's all there. I ain't with this shit, though, bruh. Hustling day and night to deliver the shit back to him. Right now, I'm ready to scream, 'Fuck that debt and fuck Hak too.' We can do the shit the hard way and get at him real proper. Send him to get fitted for them wings, real shit."

"We aren't there yet," Ahmeek stated.

"You not there yet. I'm right there, my G," Isa replied.

"Don't misunderstand me, Isa. It's not an option. That's not the move. I've done the digging on Hak. He's connected. We could put him down. My murder game is always proper, so yeah, we could, but we do that and that's war, and I ain't talking no corner-boy-turf shit. We play the game smart, we move fair, in the end, we'll walk away with our respect, a couple Ms, and our life."

"I ain't seeing no Ms paying back this debt," Isa griped.

"That's temporary. We'll climb out. Grind up. We ain't making rash decisions that'll cost us in the long run, bruh. I ain't looking to die in this shit. Just get rich and get out. I got people to protect, man; it ain't just about me now."

"Like Mo?" Isa shot back.

Ahmeek hit the weed and held the smoke as Morgan and the twins ran through his mind. He pushed out a cloud of smoke as he choked out, "Mo don't need me. She got it all figured out." Pride forced those words from his lips, because all he really wanted to do was be the one she called on. She hadn't, however. Not even a text from her had graced his phone, so in return, he hadn't reached out either. Days had been long. Nights had been longer without hearing her voice. He missed the fuck out of Morgan Atkins but would never say it. "But you got a fiancé at home. We hit Hak, that's her head in a bag on your doorstep. We want to move clean with this one. Just be patient. Once we back on track with Hak, the money gon' triple. You got to trust me in this one."

"You keeping that man breathing. He should be paying you for insurance," Isa stated.

Ahmeek leaned back against the couch and kicked one boot up on the table as he lifted glazed eyes to the ceiling. The weed had taken him to another place, and he heard his heart slow as it beat in his ears. He swiped a hand over his mouth and groaned in conflict. A part of him wanted to move recklessly. The part that had some shit to get off his chest wanted to end niggas for no reason than just to make himself feel a little better, but he had outgrown that temperament. He had thought he had leveled up for a purpose . . . for a woman . . . but with her nowhere in sight, he questioned if caution was even necessary. She was his plan. His end goal. He never needed one before her, but once he got a taste of her, he realized it was a craving that had gone unfulfilled his entire life. Love. Ahmeek wanted the love of a woman to force him to get out, but he was learning there were no guarantees when it came to affairs of the heart. If he wanted to go legit, he would have to do it for himself.

Morgan's phone rang, and she felt her heart skip a beat as Bash's name popped up on her phone screen. His persistence was intimidating. Back to back, he had called her for hours. She hated it, and her stubbornness wouldn't allow her to answer. She shouldn't have to. *I just need some space,* she thought.

Voice mail.

Morgan silenced the phone and exhaled as she looked up at the only safe space in her life. Ethic's home. Her eyes prickled a bit because she was home. In his care. He was right inside. Her entire family was within these four walls, and her heart pulled inside her chest. She watched Alani climb out of her Tesla and then walk over to Morgan's door and open it for her.

"Come on. We're prepping for Sunday dinner. You can help," Alani said.

Morgan half smiled. She never thought she would see the day when she would be happy to be in the kitchen with Alani.

Morgan climbed out, grabbing one twin while Alani managed with the other. Morgan almost cried when she saw Ethic coming down the steps. Everything about him was regal and strong. He was so loyal. So loving. Her family. The thought of him being in jeopardy because of her made Morgan feel like crying. *I really messed up this time,* she thought.

"What up, Mo?" he said, kissing her cheek and then bending down to lift Yara off her feet.

"Pop-Pop!" Messari screamed as soon as he and Alani walked through the door.

Ethic was the deadliest man Morgan knew, but with her twins, he turned to putty. His tall frame lowered onto the staircase, taking a seat right where he stood as he pulled them both into his strong arms.

"This is the best surprise I've ever gotten. I didn't know you guys were coming over," Ethic signed. "Who are my favorite little people in the world? Huh?" He roughhoused them as if he were training baby pit pulls, and they loved it.

"Me," Yara signed.

She hated to share him with Messari, and Ethic chuckled as he blew a raspberry on her cheek. She giggled and wrapped her arms around his neck as Messari sat propped on Ethic's log of a thigh.

"Not just you," Ethic signed. "Both of you. You two are my favorites. You know that right? I love you."

"Luh you too!" Messari said, scrambling by him. "Eazyyy! I'm here! Eazy!" Messari took the staircase with his hands and knees until he scrambled all the way to the top. "Where is him? Pop-Pop? Where him is?"

Ethic smiled while standing with Yara. "He's in his room. He has headphones on. Go get him."

Messari took off. He knew the home well enough to find his own way, and he knew the rules even better so he wouldn't make mischief along the way.

"Come on, Pop-Pop. You can watch a movie with your girls," Alani teased. He kissed her lips, a quick peck, but a peck from Ethic Okafor held a lifetime worth of love. Alani led the way into the great room as Ethic wrapped an arm around Morgan's shoulders and pulled her in close. Yeah. Little Morgan was home, and it felt amazing.

"You want to talk about it?" Ethic asked. Morgan didn't know how he knew something was wrong. He had always been a master at all things Morgan Atkins, and he read her effortlessly. He knew at first glance that something was heavy on her heart.

Morgan shook her head. "I want to watch the movie," Morgan said simply. "Just be here with y'all and watch movies."

"Well, when you're ready, you know I'm here. Don't wait too long, or I'ma force the issue. If you're bothered, I'm bothered, Mo, and when I'm bothered, I'ma see about you. You got me?"

Morgan nodded. "I promise. It's nothing. Let's just watch a movie. All of us. Like we used to when I was little. That's exactly what I need right now."

"What about you, Yolly Pop? You want to watch a movie, princess?" Ethic signed.

Yolly's eyes twinkled in interest, and she nodded.

"I'm making popcorn—and don't worry, Mo, I got your ranch seasoning for it. Y'all set it up," Alani said.

Ethic walked toward Alani and placed his free hand to her hip. "I'll grab the popcorn. Get off your feet. Keep my boy in there for a little longer," he said.

Morgan swooned. God, how she wanted what they had. Something beautiful and lasting and true. Something so organic the rain from a storm couldn't destroy it. E&A's love was like a seed—the deeper it was pushed down into the dirt, the more it strove to bloom. She watched Ethic as he whispered something in Alani's ear. The way Alani's brown cheeks deepened to a burgundy and the way her lips pulled in a smile was beautiful. He went from her lips to her belly, and Yara followed suit, planting a kiss on Alani's swollen belly. Morgan wondered if she truly knew what love was, because she wasn't sure she looked as exquisite when love reflected off her. Ethic's love made Alani glow differently, like he shined a light down on her. She was the spotlight of his life. Morgan didn't have a choice but to respect something so potent. She made her way to the great room.

"Where's B?" Morgan asked.

"She's shopping with Nannie. They went to the outlet sale in Birch Run," Alani said.

"Since when is Bella so thrifty?" Morgan asked, chuckling.

"Since Nannie got her hands on her," Ethic answered as he walked in. He set Yara on her feet as Eazy walked in with Messari.

"Y'all watching movies without me?" he asked. "That's cold, Dad."

"Boy, get your ass in here and be quiet," Ethic said, smirking as he gripped the back of Eazy's neck.

"Come on, baby boy," Alani said. "You can sit next to me, cuz Daddy stay hogging the covers. Come on, Ssari. You too," she said, lifting the blanket she was using. Her boys flocked to her, and Ethic opted for a seat beside Morgan. Yara scurried into his lap while Morgan used his shoulder as a cushion.

Ethic was the captain as he flicked through the movie options.

"What are we watching?" Eazy asked.

"*Home Alone*?" Alani asked.

"It ain't Christmas," Ethic said.

"When does it ever have to be Christmas to watch *Home Alone*?" Alani shot back.

"What's *Home Alone*?" Eazy asked.

"I swear before me you are raising these kids ass backward," Alani said in disgust.

Morgan laughed.

"I meannnn," she said, grimacing as she giggled joyously.

"Don't agree with bullshit, Mo," Ethic said.

They laughed, and the room was filled with the sound of love as Eazy wisecracked with Ethic. Morgan felt frozen. Like she was watching outside a glass dome. Like this scene was supposed to go inside a snow globe because it was beautiful. It was family. Something the Okafors had worked hard for. Morgan's phone rang and snatched her focus away. Her heart clenched at the sight of Bash's name.

"I'm going to take this. I'll be right back. Don't start without me!" she shouted as she rushed to her feet and out the door. The makings of fall greeted her as she pulled the door shut behind her. A shiver crept up her spine as she pressed the green button. She had been gone for a few hours and had been ignoring him all day. She knew he was imagining the worst in his head. Morgan wasn't trying to fan the flames; she just wanted a little me time. She put the phone to her ear, but before she could utter one word, a clear threat was made.

"It takes fifty-five minutes to drive from where you are to this doorstep," Bash said.

"How do you know where I am?" she asked. Bash ignored that question, and Morgan felt sick, like she would throw up.

"I'm trying hard with you, Mo. Harder than I've ever tried with anyone before you. I've been patient. I've been understanding. I've been taken for granted and made a fool of. It's not even close to being acceptable anymore. Get home before I get upset."

The line went dead, and Morgan pushed out a timid breath. Her eyes prickled, and she fisted the crown of her head in dismay. He sounded so mad. No doubt she was headed home to a fight. Morgan didn't know what she was feeling, but the walls seemed to be closing in on her.

Beep! Beep!

Morgan rolled her pretty brown eyes toward the long driveway, and her heart ached when she saw Messiah sitting in there in the passenger side of Isa's BMW. She hadn't even heard him pull up. Or had he been there the entire time? She had no clue, but she had an unbelievable urge to run to him. It felt like Bash's eyes were on her. Like he was spying on her. Like if she went to Messiah, he would witness it, and it would only make the situation between them worse.

"Fuck you looking back for like you need permission, shorty?" Messiah asked. "Get over here."

Morgan's feet moved before her mind had time to tell her to stop. "What are you doing here?" she asked as she wrapped herself tighter in her jean jacket to protect against the wind. He popped open the door, and weed smoke drifted out of the car as he placed one wheat Timberland to the pavement. He made no move to stand.

"Come here," he said.

"I can't fit, Messiah," she protested.

He pulled her fingertips, forcing her into the car, right into his lap. He hit the blunt that he pinched between his tattooed fingers and gripped her chin, pulling her near as he blew the smoke out of his mouth slowly into her face. Morgan inhaled it, held it, then tilted her chin to blow it out. She licked her lips, then focused on him.

"Let me get that," Messiah signed, licking his lips, a conceited smirk lifting the corner of his mouth.

"Don't do that," Morgan signed back.

"Is that a yes? Three squares, two snacks, shorty," he reminded.

Morgan's face flushed red as she remembered the things he had done to her body.

"I know it's wet," he signed. "Tell me it ain't."

He pulled his lip into his mouth and licked it so slowly that Morgan felt a jolt travel through her entire vagina.

"Messiah, stop," she whispered, swiping her hair out of her face, tucking it behind both ears. She was frustrated, exasperated, fucking bothered. She didn't want to do too much in front of Isa, because she didn't want things to be misconstrued. She and Messiah were not a thing, and she didn't need Isa or anyone else thinking otherwise. Messiah hit the blunt and chuckled at her discomfort.

"What are you doing here?" Morgan asked, irritated.

"My girl is here. Where else would I be?" he asked.

"Messiah. I haven't been your girl for a long time." The sadness in her tone surprised them both.

He placed his hand to her cheek, staring at her through lidded eyes. He was high. She could see his mind spinning as he took a trip to the past through her stare. "You always gon' be my girl, Mo." He was inches from her face, and Morgan closed her eyes.

"You can't be here," she whispered.

"I can be wherever the fuck I want to be, Mo. That's the difference between me and you. I go where I want. You go where you're told. How that happen, shorty? Where the girl I made a woman out of?"

Messiah kissed her bare skin, where the jacket slid down.

"Yo, that shoulder gon' get you in trouble," he said.

Morgan hollered in laughter. Only Messiah would find her shoulder seductive.

"Keep playing with me," he said. "I know that nigga ain't hitting that shit right."

"Messiah!" she shouted.

"Yep, that too, calling my name and shit. You want a nigga to fuck you real good," he snickered.

Morgan turned so red that she felt her face warm.

"Y'all wild as fuck, man," Isa said, snickering. He popped open the door. "I'm about to go get a plate. I know Alani in there cooking the fuck out of some shit."

"Nigga, ain't you vegan?" Messiah said, laughing. Morgan raised a suspicious brow in Isa's direction.

"Not when Alani's on the stove, my nigga. You brought a nigga one plate one time, and I been jonesing for her shit ever since," Isa said. "I'm vegan-ish, G."

Messiah and Morgan fell out in laughter as Isa climbed from the car.

"Ethic gon' shoot yo' skinny ass!" Messiah yelled after him.

"I'll risk it!" Isa shouted back.

"Just go on in," Morgan said. "They're in the family room." Isa disappeared inside the house, and Morgan focused back on Messiah.

"Ahmeek in there?" Messiah asked.

"He isn't really speaking to me these days," Morgan whispered.

Messiah nodded, biting his bottom lip. "College boy in there?"

She shook her head.

"Good. I ain't got to kill nobody today," he stated as he hit the blunt. He passed it to Morgan, and she reluctantly took it, lifting it to her lips. One hit and she passed it back.

"Not today," she choked out. "Have you talked to Ahmeek?"

Messiah tapped her ass, causing her to rise. "Don't ask me about that nigga, Mo." Messiah's brow bent as he continued to smoke. "Get in on the other side. I want you to drive me somewhere."

"I can't just leave, Messiah," she said.

"We ain't going far, shorty. I just want to rap with you," he said.

Mo bit her bottom lip and looked down at her phone.

"Yo, you look down at your phone one more time and I'm gon' call that nigga and tell him what's good. I don't need permission to do shit with you, Morgan Atkins, you hear me?"

Morgan pushed out a sharp breath and hurried to the driver's side. She started the car, and the sound of a guitar oozed through the speaker.

Love you like the Westside
Fingers out the sunroof, won't you let your wings loose
Look at how your stress fly

Morgan lifted eyes to Messiah, and her heart flipped upside down. He just wrung out her insides. Every time she was in his presence, he made her sick.

"Drive, shorty."

Morgan reversed the car and then switched the gear to drive before pulling off.

"What about Isa? Ethic's really going to kill him." Morgan laughed.

"He'll be a'ight. He's a big boy." Messiah snickered. "Big Homie definitely gonna kill him, though."

Morgan let the windows down and opened the sunroof as Messiah leaned back in his chair. She didn't care that Michigan was skipping fall and heading straight to winter. It was freezing outside, but the heat between these kindred souls kept them warm as Morgan sped down the block. The frigid winds didn't bother Messiah. He liked what she liked and didn't say one word about the air coming inside. His head bobbed to the beat as he licked his lips and hit the blunt. He blew the smoke into the air, and the wind carried it away instantly. Morgan's hair whipped wildly, and Messiah lifted one foot, resting it in the corner of the window. His hand found its way to her thigh, and Morgan sucked in a breath, holding it, because even something as simple as fingertips to her skin ignited her. She stole glances of him, and her eyes thanked her, misting in appreciation because even in anger it was a pleasure to see him. There were days she didn't think she would ever see him again. Just his scent pleased her. It was all in her psyche, and she was so grateful, because she had cried for days when it had disappeared from her memory years ago. He sat beside her, kite high, eyes closed as he rocked to the music. He wore his low cut with a line so sharp that it looked like it had been painted on. He was handsome. Distinctively so, in fact, but Morgan couldn't help but miss his signature locs.

"Stop staring, shorty," he signed without opening his eyes, and then he tossed up double Ms. Morgan fought hard against her smile and drove. She had no idea where she was going until she pulled into the entrance of the old tourist attraction.

"Crossroads Village?" Messiah asked, frowning as he sat up, looking out the windshield. Flint didn't have much, but this was an iconic piece of happiness. Every little girl and boy had memories of this place. It was booming during Christmas season, but on a random fall day, it was a ghost town. There wasn't a soul in sight besides the workers manning the place. Mo and Messiah had the entire place to themselves on this day. The life-size gingerbread-style houses and old-fashioned shops were empty.

"My daddy used to bring me here every year for Christmas. Just me and him. Raven and my mom never came. They hated the snow, but I loved it. It was our time. He would carry me on his back, and we would go from shop to shop eating cotton candy, getting souvenirs, looking at the Christmas lights, riding the carousel and the train. It was my favorite place when I was a kid. I haven't been here since he died. Ethic tried to bring me, but I always said no."

Messiah opened his door, and Morgan didn't move. She just sat there gripping the steering wheel until he opened her door too. Still she sat there frozen. It was as if she were glued to her seat. Messiah reached for her hand, and only then did she slide from the car.

"It's cold outside, Messiah. I'll freeze. I didn't grab my coat," she said.

Messiah took off his Moncler jacket, and helped her into it, then flipped up the hood to the jean jacket he wore beneath.

"Now you'll freeze," she scoffed, smiling.

"I been in Michigan my whole life. I can take a little cold, shorty. Come on," he said, grabbing her hand.

Messiah took one last hit of the weed before extinguishing the tip on a tree, then flicking the roach. He tilted his head back and blew smoke from his mouth as he dragged Mo along to the entrance. He pulled out a knot of money, all hundreds, and paid admission for two.

"It hasn't changed. It seemed bigger when I was six," she said, scoffing again as she folded her arms in front of her chest. Messiah pulled her under one arm.

"It's plenty big, shorty," he said. They walked over the uneven gravel as they made their way through the little town. Her phone rang, and she pulled it out of her purse to see it was Bash.

She silenced it and put it back into her purse.

She saw Messiah's jaw clench, and it surprised her when he didn't say anything. He kissed the side of her head, then pulled her into the trinkets shop.

"I used to have one of these," she whispered as she fingered the antique jewelry box. A hand-carved ballerina stood in the middle of it, and she smiled. "Mizan broke it. He threw it at Raven's head one day when she was late coming home from the hair salon. I cried all night, and she begged me to be quiet so I wouldn't make him mad."

Messiah steeled as their eyes met. He could see the damage hanging from her soul like wet laundry on a clothesline. "I don't want to talk about them, Mo. Why don't we just keep it right here . . . me and you? I don't want to think about nobody else . . . just for a few hours. I ain't never really asked nobody for shit, but if you can give me that, just today, I'll be a happy nigga, Mo. You can go back to hating me as soon as I drop you off."

It would have been easy to just tell her Mizan wasn't his brother, but he knew the timing wasn't right. They had so many things to talk about. There were too many hard conversations to have between them. Morgan barely gave him the time of day. He didn't want to ruin this rare moment of peace between them with mentions of her childhood. He didn't want her to do too much thinking at all because it would cause her to pull back.

She folded her lips inside her mouth and looked off, snatching her stare from his because she got lost in his eyes. They steered her down memory lane. "Okay," she whispered.

Messiah picked up the jewelry box. "Yo, my man," he said to the white man behind the counter. "We'll take one of these."

He paid, and Morgan smiled as he peeled off another hundred-dollar bill. Her eyes sparkled as he turned to her.

"Thank you, Messiah," she said.

He nodded. "You're welcome, shorty," he replied.

He led her back out into the cold, but she turned back for the store. "I'll be right back."

When she emerged, she carried a blanket and two cups of hot chocolate. She handed him the Styrofoam cups and opened the blanket wide. "Come on, we can both fit," she said. "You're going to get sick out here with no coat."

"I'm good, Mo, as long as you're warm," he said.

"You either get under this with me or take your coat. As a matter of fact, it's too cold for this anyway. Let's just go back."

"A'ight, shorty. I'll get under the fucking blanket," he yielded. He took one end and she took the other, hanging it over their shoulders and then tying a knot in the middle in front of them. It forced them to touch, the heat from their bodies warming the space inside. An M&M burrito. She rested her head on his shoulder as she took one of the cups from him.

"I love these lights," she said. "I forgot how much I loved this."

The "this" she was talking about wasn't just the lights. It was him. It was being connected to him while being removed from everything and everyone else. They had loved each other in a bubble, not caring about the risks they had taken or the people who hadn't liked it. M&M forever, like her 1:00 a.m. tweet that went out every Friday. It had been a beautiful thing while it lasted, and then it had ended tragically. Morgan was still struggling with that, their demise, all these years later.

"Yeah, it's dope. Seems like something you'd like," he said. He sipped the hot chocolate. "Yo, this shit needs some liquor in it."

Morgan burst out laughing. "Just like you. Got to corrupt something innocent," she teased.

Messiah bit his lip. "If I remember right, you liked that shit," he snickered.

The cold didn't exist anymore because Morgan's entire body warmed, and her face flushed crimson. "That was a long time ago," she said sadly.

"Yeah, I guess it was," he stated. They strolled through Crossroads Village for hours, picking up trinkets, laughing, talking, joking. It felt like old times. He was taking her on a trip down memory lane, and when she came across the carousel, her heart stopped.

"Wow, Messiah. It hasn't changed. This is the exact same one my daddy used to take me on." He followed her stare to the amusement ride ahead. She closed her eyes to stop the burning she felt. Her nostrils flared, and her chest lurched in emotion.

"Come on," he said.

He walked over to the ticket booth and bought two passes. Mo stalled a bit at the entrance of the ride, and he grabbed her hand, intertwining their fingers, their souls, tied . . . in that moment, she wondered if they had ever really come undone. She had always felt him. Even when she had been told he had died. It was like he was alive inside her, like she felt two hearts beating inside her chest. They tossed the drinks before stepping onto the carousel.

They stood on the platform, and Mo's smile broke through her somberness.

"What you want? A horse, shorty? You want the bench? You want the throne? Where you want to sit?" he asked.

"I want to stand," she said. "I want to stand with you while it spins and close my eyes. I want to feel dizzy like I used to." She bent her head back and looked up at him, surrendering to the moment as the carousel began to turn.

He knew the dizzy feeling she was speaking of. The sick feeling. He had felt it too. He felt it now. Always felt it. Ever since the day he had decided to love her, he had been dizzy over her. This one young-ass girl affected him deeply.

He placed his hands on her hips and pulled her close, bodies touching, sharing a breath, and her eyes sealed. She laughed as the cold wind kissed her skin, and Messiah was glad that she wasn't looking. Had she been paying attention, she would have seen his eyes gloss over as he took her in. He pressed his forehead to hers and closed his eyes too, and the spinning made it seem like they were being transported back in time . . . to a place . . . to a moment in space . . . when no resentment lay between them . . . back to that tiny-ass apartment where he used to sit between her legs and let her grease his scalp with coconut oil. His chest ached as he hooked his fingers in the belt loops of her jeans and his lip quivered. Morgan Atkins could do no wrong. He was mad as hell at her—livid, in fact—for her moving on, for her choosing College Boy and for having the nerve to have a bit of Meek on the side. That tore him up inside, but he couldn't do shit but admire her from afar because losing her was his fault. He had done this, pushed her too far, cut her too deep, and now she was lost. Now she was searching for something she used to find in him. The thought hollowed him out like someone had cut away at him with a knife.

Morgan placed her hands on his chest and then moved flat palms up and around his neck, massaging the nape of him. People didn't put hands on Messiah. He was like a temperamental dog—an aggressive breed that might bite—but Morgan didn't care. She was his owner, and the silk of her fingertips against his skin made Messiah weak. A tear slipped from her eyes, and Messiah's tongue was on it before it could reach her chin. He showed emotion in the oddest of ways. The licking of tears and such. Morgan loved it. She opened her eyes as the wetness he left behind made her face cold.

"I hate that you cut your hair," she whispered. "I loved it. I loved you, and you changed up on me. You left me."

"I've done a lot of shit, Mo, but leaving you is the worst. It's the fucking worst," he whispered. "You hear me? I thought about you every day. Every fucking second. Even when it hurt too bad to think about anything, I always thought about you, shorty. For two years."

"But you didn't call me. You didn't trust me to choose you, Messiah. I would have. I was terrified of you after I found out who you were, but I still wanted you. You crushed me. I just wanted you."

"I know, shorty," he said. "I'm a sorry-ass nigga, but I couldn't stay, Mo, and I couldn't bring you. There was some shit I had to do alone," he whispered. He couldn't tell her about the cancer. It made him feel weak. It made him seem weak. He couldn't let her know that he had disintegrated to almost nothing . . . that he'd had to build up his strength to even come back. That he'd almost checked out. He just wanted her to always think of strength when she thought of him. He kissed her, filling her mouth with his entire tongue. Morgan swallowed him. Moaning. Weakened. Defeated. The deepest kiss she had ever received. He inhaled her, sucking on her whole face—chin, nose, both lips. She was sure he was imagining her pussy on his tongue because it was the exact way he used to devour those three meals and two snacks she would prepare him. They kissed for three minutes as the carousel spun, but it was Messiah that made her dizzy. When it stopped, he put his head in the groove of her neck, pulling that blanket around them tighter, then planted a feather kiss on her neck. Morgan trembled there.

"You're freezing. Come on, let's get you back. It's getting late."

He said it, but she didn't move. She knew that once he dropped her off, she would have to go back to fake smiling. She enjoyed what authenticity felt like. He stared down the bridge of his nose at her.

"I got something for you," he said. He pulled a piece of paper out of his back pocket. It was folded and wrinkled.

"What's this?"

"Your Christmas gift," Messiah said.

Morgan giggled. "But it's not Christmas," she answered.

"Yeah, I missed a couple," Messiah said. "I bought it last year." Morgan looked up from the paper and into his eyes, stunned. If only he had come back then.

"The last time I gave you a Christmas gift, you said it didn't feel like a gift. I hope this is better. It ain't really nothing a nigga can wrap, but it's yours," he said.

Morgan unfolded the paper and read the words on it.

"You named a star after me," she gasped. It was the most

thoughtful thing anyone had ever done. It was sweet, and Messiah didn't do sweet, so she knew the effort it had taken.

"It's corny. You can tell me if you don't like it. You're just so far from me, Mo. You're living with another nigga, wearing his ring, having his kids. I can't see you when I want. When I look up, I can see that. It'll always be there."

He pointed to the sky, and Morgan looked up. They had been out all day, and the night sky sparkling above them was proof of that. "It's that one right there. You've always been a star, shorty," he said. "It's dumb, right?"

Morgan shook her head as large droplets of emotion fell from her eyes. "It's not," she whispered. "I love it, Messiah."

"Come on, let's get you home before I smack fire from that corny-ass nigga for blowing up your line," Messiah said.

Morgan chuckled, and Messiah pulled her under his arm as they headed toward the car. The drive home was silent, but no discomfort existed between them. It had been a long time since Morgan had been in his presence without being angry, and it felt good. Her hand in his, her pointer finger drawing a circle in his palm . . . the rhythm it kept making him calm. When they pulled in Ethic's driveway, Morgan's stomach plummeted. It signified the end. Morgan could get out of this car and go back to her life, or she could follow her heart. In this moment, her heart didn't want this night to end. Her heart was open to the possibility of what life could be like with Messiah. The house was still. The only light that glowed from the inside came from the family room. Morgan knew that her kids were asleep inside. Ethic and Alani hadn't even called to see where she had disappeared to; they had just stepped up because no matter what, they would always have her back. She waited for Messiah to exit and open her door.

She stepped out, and he walked her to the front door.

"Do you want to come in?" she asked.

He shook his head. "Nah, I'ma break out," he declined.

"I would have done anything for you," she said as they stood face to face. It was the saddest he had ever heard her sound. "I just wanted you to want me like I wanted you. You have no idea what I've been through. What you put me through. Thinking you didn't love me. I'm still not sure if you ever did . . ."

She saw a streak of hurt corrupt his face.

"I'ma love you until the last breath leaves me, shorty. I don't give a fuck about nobody else. Just you. That's all I fucking care about, and I know I fucked shit up, but I'm never fucking with nobody else the way I fucked with you. You've got your family, and I get that. You got your doubts in me, and I placed them there, so I understand that too, but I'm just letting you know. In case you see me out, in case you think I'm trying to replace you. It will never happen, Mo. If at any time you want to let a nigga come home, I'll come running. I'll take care of another nigga kids and all, so if that's the issue—" He paused, and a sob broke through her quivering lips. "I'll take whatever is a part of you, Mo. Let me come home, baby. You promised I could come home. That you were home, and that home would always be there."

He had tears in his eyes, and Morgan lifted hands to his face. Morgan was in the worst predicament. She had a fiancé, one who was forcing her to stay. One who held deadly secrets over her head, and two men on the side whom she loved dearly. Messiah and Ahmeek. Somehow in this moment, none of that mattered, however. He was tapping into the part of her heart where only M&M existed. No one else dwelled in that part of her. Just Messiah. He was and would always be the one who'd loved her first. He gripped her wrist and kissed the inside of it, where that moth was tattooed.

"I'm sorry, Mo. I'm trying to be patient, but I need you. You're my Shorty Doo Wop. What I'm supposed to do without you? I'm dying, Mo. I thought it would get better, but if I got to die, I want you to be the last face I see. I can't live without you, Morgan. It's driving me crazy, shorty. Just let me come home," he said as he lifted her left hand. The ring she wore sent fire through his entire body. "Fuck this nigga, shorty. Fuck Meek too. I don't even give a damn about none of that no more. I just want you. Let's go grab your kids and break out."

Morgan's stomach tightened. She felt sick as she stood there, crying as the snow fell around them. She couldn't hide from him. She couldn't continue lying to him. She was terrified to admit the truth, but she knew that dying feeling he was describing. She was dying. Her twins were dying. They were half living because Daddy wasn't home. Their daddy . . . Messiah . . . her daddy . . . Messiah. A part of their unit was missing in their lives, and it was a slow death. She knew. At least she thought she knew what he was going through, and she couldn't bear it any longer.

"They're yours, Messiah," she said. "I tried to tell you. I tried to call you a thousand times, but you just left. The twins. Messari and Yara. They're yours. They're ours."

The revelation crashed over him like waves, drowning him . . . the weight of her words was an anchor around his feet, pulling him under. He wrapped his large hands around her wrists and pulled her into him hard, jerking her. "Don' t say that to me, Morgan . . . don't . . ."

"They're yours, Messiah!" she cried.

He took a step back, pushing her off him as balled fists went to his temples in anguish. "And you kept that shit from me?" The words were spoken in disbelief.

Morgan took a step toward him and reached for him, but

Messiah slapped her hand off him, like she were infected, like she were contagious. His brow furrowed in distress. He was enraged. "Keep yo' scan'lous ass the fuck over there before I slap the shit out of you, Mo."

Morgan's heart sank, and her eyes widened. "You weren't here, Messiah! You left me!"

"They think that nigga is their daddy!" Messiah barked the words at her, screamed them so loudly that Morgan recoiled.

The porch light came on, and Ethic pushed open the screen door, carrying Yara in his arms.

"Mo, come inside," he said.

Messiah froze when he saw his daughter, and tears came to her eyes.

"Ethic, I just need a minute with him—"

"Fuck you, Mo," Messiah scoffed. "Time's up, shorty. I ain't got shit for you. I'm done. You got another man raising my kids. They call him Daddy." Messiah's fists wrapped around the railing of the porch, and he lowered his head as he tightened his grip. He was breaking. He was falling apart. His fight to live, to come back for her, had destroyed his ability to have children. The chemo had killed his manhood, made him sterile, and here Morgan was with two living, breathing, mini versions of him right in her possession. He sobbed, and Morgan reached for his shoulder.

"Ssiah . . ."

"Don't touch me!" he said. "Don't fucking touch me!"

Morgan's heart was shattered.

"Morgan, inside," Ethic stated. Morgan rushed inside, crying, and Ethic opened the door wider for Messiah. "You too."

"I'ma need a minute," Messiah said, his chest quaking. He clenched his jaw so tight that his teeth hurt. *My kids. She had my babies.* Spittle flew from his mouth as his cries broke through his stubborn lips. He bent his head, chin to chest, as his grip on the wrought iron porch bars tightened. He was trying to gain control of himself, but he couldn't. He sobbed uncontrollably.

Ethic placed Yara down inside the house and stepped out into the cold, placing a hand on Messiah's shoulder. Messiah pushed Ethic, and Ethic grasped his wrists, arresting Messiah with his strength before wrapping a hand around the back of Messiah's head and pulling him into his body. Ethic gritted his teeth as he embraced Messiah, sniffing away his own emotion as Messiah broke. The young gunner, the menace, the beast, that Messiah Williams had cracked. A pretty little butterfly named Morgan Atkins had broken him, and pain was spilling out. Oh, the mess she had made.

Messiah fought Ethic, uncomfortable with affection, because physical contact with another man in his past had been abuse . . . unspeakable acts committed against him that had made him afraid to trust another.

"Trust me Messiah. I ain't here to hurt you. Nobody's going to hurt you," Ethic said through gritted teeth, reminding Messiah that with him, he was safe. He fought Ethic until finally giving in, wrapping his arms around his mentor and sobbing. He had to scream it hurt so bad. Two years had passed, and he had almost died, had fought to get back to her. He had been back for *weeks,* and she hadn't said one word. He had missed so much time. He had kids. Twins. A boy and a motherfucking girl to bring him karma.

Messiah pulled back from Ethic and lowered his head, pinching the bridge of his nose and sniffling uncontrollably. "She had my kids, man. I got kids." The words struggled their way out of his mouth because he couldn't stop crying. "I missed two years. Two fucking years . . . they don't even know me."

"It's never too late to be a father, Messiah. It's time to put away childish things. That rage you keep in your heart is dangerous. It's no good for you, and it's a danger to Mo, but this isn't about either of you. It's about these two babies in here. You got to be willing to do anything for them. Anything. Even put the aggression away. If you're going to be here, you got to man the fuck up. Man up. You missed two years. What are you going to do with the rest of them? You can't misstep with them. I gave you one pass. One. There won't be another. You don't pass down none of the pain Bookie caused you. I know what he did."

Messiah's eyes widened in horror at the discovery that his deepest secret was being spoken. That it was tangible and audible and released into the night air. It made him feel see-through. "Mo doesn't know. I'm the only person breathing who knows. Anybody else who knew is no longer breathing." Messiah's chin quaked as he met eyes with Ethic. Bookie was gone. Ethic had made sure of it. For Messiah. Ethic had killed the man that had molested him as a young boy. Messiah knew that had taken some effort, some discerning, because Ethic had changed his life. Ethic was on a journey to be a better man for the woman he loved. For Alani. His wife. He had taken a detour to avenge the trespass that had been done against Messiah, and everyone knew that Ethic only killed for the people he loved. For his family. Messiah was family, and if he hadn't known it before . . . felt it before, he felt it now. Messiah nodded in understanding, and Ethic placed a hand around Messiah's shoulders. "Come hold your babies."

Messiah nodded and stepped over the threshold to Ethic's palace. Morgan stood anxiously waiting, tears wetting her cheeks, as she held their daughter in her arms.

"Messari's asleep," Mo said. "Messiah, this is Yara Rae Atkins."

Messiah froze. He had seen the little girl before, but standing there in front of her as her father was different. It was humbling, it was terrifying, and Messiah felt gutted, exposed, like all his insides were being pulled out and put on display for the room to see. He didn't know what to say. What to do.

Ethic removed Yara from Morgan's arms and carried her over to Messiah.

"Say hi, Yolly Pop," Ethic signed with one hand as the pretty little girl with the feather-soft hair and the deep-set brow sat comfortably in his arms.

Yara waved.

Messiah scoffed in disbelief. "She's mine?"

"She's yours," Ethic confirmed.

"This is your daddy," Ethic signed.

Yara's brow furrowed deeper. Confusion.

"That's not my daddy," Yara signed. Messiah's stomach plummeted. Nothing could have hurt him more. His daughter, his deaf daughter, didn't even know who he was. He had left her for two years. The grief was overwhelming.

"She don't know me, man," Messiah said, chin quaking violently.

"That's okay. She will. She's yours," Ethic coached. Morgan went to take a step toward them, and Messiah backpedaled. He retreated as if Morgan were someone who had abused him, someone whose touch would injure. As if he were afraid of her.

"Yo, Ethic, keep her away from me. I can't even look at her. I'm just here for my kids. I just want to know my kids, man." Every word out his throat broke apart. His voice was vulnerable.

Morgan had hurt this man. The strongest and most callous man she knew was devastated at the discovery of seeds he had planted. Morgan had grown them inside her body, and he hadn't gotten to touch her bulging belly one time, hadn't even gotten to see it . . . he was nowhere to be found because he hadn't known. It was the one thing that would have brought him back to town, and she hadn't said one word. She had allowed him to miss it, and then she gave his kids to another man.

"Messiah—"

"We're done, Mo. Shit's unforgivable. I'm done. I just want to see my kids."

"Messiah, don't say that . . . Don't do this . . . You can't do this to me again . . ."

"You did it, Mo," he said as he pulled Yara from Ethic's arms. He placed his lips to the side of her head and lost it as just her scent invaded his space. Instinct made him press her tightly to his body. He squeezed his eyes shut and sobbed into her. He couldn't believe she was his. Blood of their blood, flesh made from their flesh. She was proof that his life had been worth something. The twins were the things in life he had gotten right, no matter how badly he had fucked everything else up.

Ethic walked to Morgan and placed two hands on her face. He could see her unraveling as she looked at Messiah holding their daughter. "Give him time with her. Give him time, Mo. Just let him get to know them. The rest can be worked out later, but that part can't wait any longer. A man and his kids. That can't wait. You got to let him have this. Go upstairs."

"I'm going to lose him again!" Morgan cried.

"Maybe, but they won't, Mo. You got to step outside yourself, baby girl. I know that's hard for you. This is about the twins right now," Ethic said.

He kissed her forehead, and Morgan closed her eyes, sending tears cascading down her face. Everything was so fucked up. She didn't know how it had gotten so far out of control, but somehow she was on the outside of her family looking in.

Messiah was home, but not for her, for them, their kids, and Morgan was now the bad guy. The tables had turned, and she was sick. She clung to the banister at the bottom of the stair-case, watching Messiah place kisses on Yara's face as he pressed his forehead to hers. He was sick. Crying as their daughter's small hands wiped the tears. It was heartbreaking, and Morgan just wanted to run to him, but she couldn't. She couldn't take this moment away from Yara or Messiah, so she allowed her weak legs to carry her up the stairs. Before she was completely out of sight, she heard his voice.

"Morgan."

Her heart fell into her stomach. *Morgan.* Not *Mo.* Not *shorty.* Not *Shorty Doo Wop* but *Morgan.* He may as well have called her *ma'am.* It was a formality coming off his tongue because he never called her that. He said it like he would rather be saying any other word, calling any other name besides hers.

She looked down at him.

"Bring me my fucking son," he said.

She shot desperate eyes to Ethic, who only nodded, urging her to do so.

Morgan rushed up the rest of the stairs and into the master bedroom, flicking on the light.

"Alani, please, please, you have to wake up!" she cried, blubbering, rushing to the bedside and stirring Ethic's sleeping wife.

"Mo?" Alani called out, confused, stuck between her dreams and her frantic stepdaughter. When the urgency in Mo's voice resonated with Alani, she swept the covers off her in-stantly, sitting up. "What's wrong? My God, Mo, what's going on?" Alani asked.

"Help me, please, Alani!" Mo cried. "He knows. Messiah

knows about the twins, and he wants nothing to do with me. He's going to leave me again. Alani, please, you have to help me."

Alani's eyes misted, her hormones from pregnancy not allowing anything other than for her to share this heartbreak with Mo. She stood and wrapped her arms around Mo. "Oh, baby girl," she said, consoling her. "Shhh. Shhh."

Ethic appeared in the doorway carrying Messari.

Alani placed concerned eyes on him.

"Keep her here. I'll be downstairs with Messiah and the twins," Ethic said before closing the door.

Morgan collapsed into Alani, so hurt, so broken. "He left me. He left. How can he hate me when he left me?! He told me he loved me, and he walked away."

Alani sat on the bed, and Morgan sat beside her before leaning over to place her head in her lap. Morgan tucked her hands between her thighs, bent her legs back, and cried. Alani's strokes to her hair were little comfort to the torment she felt in her soul. Messiah hated her. She saw it in his eyes, could hear it in his tone. Even during their worst fight, she hadn't heard this type of disdain in his voice. He wanted nothing to do with her. What she had done was unforgivable, and having him be a part of the twins but disconnected from her was killing her. She would never be okay with that, but she had no choice. It was the life she had chosen; now she had to be a big girl and live with the decisions she had made.

Morgan heard the front door slam, and she rushed to the window. The sight broke her down. Messiah was stuffing her kids into the back seat of Isa's car.

"He's taking them?" Morgan asked. She turned on her heels, rushing out of the room. "He can't take them! Where is he taking them?" she shouted as she rushed down the stairs.

Ethic caught her in his arms. "Ethic! He can't take my kids! Why would you let him take them?! How could he take them and leave me!" she shouted hysterically. She broke down, panicking, crying as Ethic wrapped her in his arms. Alani stood at the top of the stairs with one hand over her mouth. Morgan unraveled right before their eyes. The secret was out, the fallout was monumental, and Morgan could feel the agony of it in her bones.

17

Messiah blew out a sharp breath as he paced his living room floor. "Fuck!" he exclaimed.

"That's a bad word!" Messari shouted.

Messiah put both hands on top of his head as he stared down at the twins. They sat on the futon couch in his sparsely appointed apartment. He hadn't slept there much, so he hadn't found the need to furnish it properly. Now he wished he had.

The hurt in the center of his chest ached so badly that his eyes burned. He couldn't stop them from prickling, and he kept squeezing the bridge of his nose to try to calm the emotion inside him. A tear slid down his nose, and he sniffed while thumbing the wetness away. He cleared his throat.

"Messari, I want Mommy," Yara signed as she whimpered.

The sight of her little hands expressing words gutted him. He had to turn away because another fucking tear snuck out of his eye. Messiah couldn't breathe. Couldn't think. Could barely see as he choked on this discovery. He balled a fist and placed it against the wall, then rested his forehead on top of that. His sobs made a bitch of him, and he pulled his bottom lip into his mouth and bit down hard to stop himself from losing it. He cleared his throat again and took a deep breath before standing upright. *Shorty gave me kids,* he thought. It was unbelievable and overwhelming all at the same time. He felt a tug on his leg, and he looked down to see a glowering, khaki-colored Messari looking up at him.

Messari pointed to Yara. "Her want Mommy!"

Messiah focused on Yara. Her little eyes were so heavy with tears, and her bottom lip poked so far out that Messiah's heart exploded.

"Fuck yo' mommy," Messiah muttered.

"Hey!" Messari contested. He lifted his little leg and kicked Messiah's shin. Messiah looked down in shock before a snicker left his lips. "Yo' little badass is definitely mine," Messiah chuckled, scooping him up.

"You not nice!" Messari shouted.

"You not nice either," Messiah shot back. He carried Messari back to the futon and sat next to Yara. He reached for her, but she scrambled away from him, all the way to the opposite end.

"Her don't like you," Messari said.

It hurt Messiah's feelings beyond measure because he feared that it just might be true. His daughter didn't like him. Hell, his son had put hands on him twice. Messiah ached to know them. He prayed that the two years that had passed weren't irreversible.

Yara's inevitable tears started, and her cries were so loud that Messiah's stomach knotted with anxiety.

"Sit down right here for a minute, man," Messiah said as he put Messari down. He tried to pick Yara up, but she kicked and screamed, pushing his hands off her body every time he reached for her.

"Okay! Okay!" Messiah shouted. He stood up and swiped a hand down his head. "What the fuck, man?"

Yara was on her back, having a full-blown tantrum, flailing her little body all over the futon so hard that the mattress was sliding off.

Messiah looked down at Messari. "You stay right here with her. Stay here. I'll be right back," he said. He stepped into his bedroom, hoping it helped quiet the noise. It didn't. He pulled out his phone and dialed Bleu's number. He could barely hear her answer over the sounds of Yara's persistent wails.

"Messiah?" Bleu answered. "I can barely hear you. Who is that crying in the background?"

"B, I need you. I need you to come over here right fucking now."

Messiah was frantic. He had never been this unnerved. The crying hadn't stopped. Messari followed him everywhere asking a million questions, and he just couldn't think straight. He tried to hold Yara, but it only intensified her anguish, and Messiah was beginning to wonder if something was seriously wrong.

"Hey, you want this? I'll give you this if you stop crying," he signed, offering her his phone. He wasn't above bribery. He would do anything to stop this incessant crying. Yara snatched the phone and threw it, and Messiah grimaced.

"Her want Mommy!" Messari said as he ran around the futon.

Messiah was in over his head and didn't know what to do. The one thing he refused to do was answer Morgan's phone calls or reach out to her for help.

"Mommy had time with y'all for two years. It's my turn. I got to catch up," Messiah said.

"How come?" Messari asked.

"Because I'm your daddy, boy," Messiah said, his words coming out so whimsically, because he was still in shock.

"My daddy?" Messari asked, his mouth dropping open in an O of surprise.

"Your daddy," Messiah confirmed. "I know, kid. It's news to me too."

A knock at the door brought Messiah instant relief as he stood and hurried over to answer. He looked out the peephole before pulling open the door.

Bleu stood in front of him. She frowned as she looked around him to locate the source of the cries. "Messiah, why are Morgan's babies here?" she asked, confused. "What did you do?"

"More like what did she do?" he answered. "They're my kids, B. They're mine, and they don't fuck with me, and I can't get Yara to stop crying. I got kids."

The news was like a punch to the gut. Bleu placed a hand on her stomach. Her mouth fell open, but nothing came out. She was speechless. Her eyes prickled. "Wow." Bleu couldn't offer much more than that. It felt like he had pulled the rug from beneath her.

"Can you help me, B? I don't really know what I'm doing here, and she's screaming like something is wrong," Messiah said.

Bleu's eyes were pools of sadness as she stepped inside.

"Messari, come here, man," Messiah urged.

Bleu looked at the twins. She had seen them before in pictures. Never had she put the pieces together.

"This is daddy's best friend. Her name is Bleu," Messiah

introduced. He picked Yara up. She had been crying so long she was exhausted, wiping her eyes with tiny balled fists as she blubbered.

"Hi, Messari," Bleu whispered as she lowered onto her knees. "Nice to meet you."

Messari scurried to Messiah and climbed between the space between his arm and his body, then behind his back.

"And this is . . ."

"Yara," Messiah introduced. "She's deaf, B," he said. "My daughter's deaf."

Bleu's eyes met his for a beat before rolling down to Yara. "Hi, precious."

"This is Daddy's friend Bleu," Messiah signed.

Bleu picked Yara up, despite her protests, ignoring her dangling legs and her arms that were extended straight above her head. Bleu stood and pressed Yara's head onto her shoulder as she bounced while walking the length of Messiah's apartment.

"For one, Messiah, she's soaking wet," Bleu said. She pulled Yara's leggings back, revealing a pull-up. "She's wearing a pull-up. Do you have any here?"

"No," Messiah answered.

"Where are their bags? I'm sure Mo packed some," Bleu said.

"They don't have bags, B. I just took 'em. She told me they were mine, and I just flipped. I snapped and just took 'em," Messiah answered. "And now she won't stop crying."

"Messiah, you can't just take them without permission," Bleu said.

"They're mine, B. She kept them from me for two years. Fuck Mo and her permission," he barked. "Just get her to stop crying!"

"She's scared, Messiah. She doesn't know you. You have to take something like this slowly," Bleu argued. "You're breaking their routine. They're in an unfamiliar place. You don't have their clothes or pull-ups. Your house smells different, looks different. You're new to them. Of course she's crying." Bleu was trying to get him to calm down. He was just as traumatized as the twins. Bleu's mind was blown. The calmest person in the room was two-year-old Messari, who sat on the floor looking back and forth between the adults.

"I can't do this shit, B. What am I supposed to do with this?" He motioned to the twins with open palms and shrugged. "How I'm supposed to love shorty after she pulled some shit like this?" Messiah was forlorn, and Bleu looked at him sympathetically.

"Shhh," she whispered in Yara's ear, trying to console her. Nothing was working, and Bleu sighed. "It's okay, sweet girl," Bleu whispered as she bounced Yara. She could tell the little girl was tired. Yara kept rubbing her eyes as she fussed. She was fighting sleep because she was uncomfortable with this sudden change.

"I don't know, Messiah," she answered. "You and Morgan exchange a lot of hurt back and forth. That's not what these babies require. Somehow the two of you have to get all that pain out of the way. They'll feel it." Bleu paused to take it all in. "Wow. She gave you two babies." Bleu couldn't help the tear that slid down her face. She blew out a breath. "How did I miss this? How did we all miss this?" Bleu's mind went to the child she had lost. Messiah's son. He would have been close in age to his twins, and the thought of that was breaking her down.

Messiah bent down to pick up Messari.

"Are you mine?" Messari asked.

Messiah's glower matched Messari's. They were both skeptical of each other. Matching temperaments.

"Yeah, man. I'm yours, kid. And you're mine. Nobody's going to get it mixed up ever again. Daddy promise you that."

"He's not answering!" Morgan cried. "Ethic, please call him. Please." She didn't even know where her panic was coming from. She didn't think Messiah would hurt the twins necessarily, but she hated that he was so irrational, so enraged. She had seen him that way before, and she didn't want her babies around him when he was in that state of mind. She just wanted them home. She wanted them with her, and she was becoming undone because she knew Messiah didn't know the first thing about taking care of children.

"You got to let him calm down and wrap his mind around this, Mo. He just found out something that changes everything for him. Give him time to process it. You can't back him into a corner just because you need to be pacified," Ethic said. Morgan sat with her legs crossed in the middle of the king-size bed as Alani sat beside her, rubbing her hair gently as Morgan rested her head on Alani's shoulder. It was as if she were a little girl, sitting in the middle of her parents' bed because the boogeyman had scared her. In a way, he had. Messiah had blown up so quickly. He was like a ticking time bomb, and Morgan never knew when he would detonate.

"He won't even answer my calls," Morgan whispered. She shook her head in despair as she dialed him for the fourth time. It had only been two hours since he had stormed out with the twins, but it felt like forever. "They don't know him. What if they're scared or crying? Messiah doesn't know that Yolly is allergic to peanuts, he doesn't know that Messari likes to sleep at the foot of the bed. They sleep with their ladybug night-light; he doesn't have that. They need me, and he won't even answer."

Morgan's panic was that of a true mother. Nobody was capable of loving her babies like she was. No one knew them like she did. The only person she ever felt 100 percent at ease with to care for them was Alani. Anyone else always left her with a twinge of worry on her heart. Messiah left her with a canyonsize hole of concern.

"Messiah won't hurt the twins. They're safer with him than with anyone else on this earth. They're fine, Mo. He may not know what he's doing, but he knows what he's feeling. There's this moment when you see your kid for the first time, you recognize the miracle of your DNA inside someone so good, and it just changes you. In that moment, you vow never to let anybody hurt that child. You know that you'll die for your flesh and blood. It's a split-second change that happens instantly. He's missed a lot, but tonight he's discovering that feeling. He's falling in love with his kids right now, and you have to give him space while he does it. He got hit with a lot tonight. Just give him some time."

"He's Mizan's brother, Ethic," Morgan whispered. "Mizan's brother has my babies."

Ethic was surprised that Messiah hadn't told her otherwise yet. Ethic's brow lifted, and he sucked in a deep breath. "He's not," he revealed. He had known the information for a while. Now seemed like the appropriate time to share it. Morgan had been so unstable over the years that even mentioning Messiah would cause her to pull away.

"What?" she asked. She sucked in air. She knew she had to be hearing him wrong.

"You had a hard time after we thought he died. I thought I would lose you too. You moved across the world to get away from his memory. I wanted to tell you before, but you weren't ready. You weren't strong, Mo, and anytime I even mentioned his name, you shut me out more. Shut everyone out, and all we wanted you to do was let us in." He paused and rubbed his beard. "Let me in, Mo. I'm sorry I didn't tell you this before, but it's true. I verified it time and time again. He's not related to Mizan. He believed he was for a long time, but he's not. He's not anything like the man who hurt Raven, and I know he mishandled you, Mo, but I don't think he's capable of ever intentionally harming you. When I look at him, and I look at you, I see what could have been. I see me with your sister. I see a chance for the world to witness what Raven and I could have been. He loves you. He's not perfect. Niggas ain't perfect, but he does love you. I discounted that before, when he asked me for permission with you all those years ago. I should have given the green light. I regret that, Mo."

"Things happened for a reason," she said sadly. "We could have been so good, you know? Like I think back, and I miss that feeling, that feeling of loving him without fearing him. I used to trust him so much. I used to wrap my arms around him on the back of his bike going a hundred down the highway in the rain and not have one worry, Ethic, because I knew he'd never let anything happen to me. And then *he* happened to me. He didn't let anybody hurt me, but he hurt me. He was so close I never saw it coming, and the way I've held my breath since then, the way I haven't really had a moment without aching inside since then—" Morgan paused. "I just want a love that doesn't hurt."

"You don't always get to choose," Alani said soothingly. She spoke so softly that Morgan wondered how she had ever found it in her heart to hate this woman.

"But I've felt it. I've felt a love that didn't hurt at all, and it was lovely. It was healing. It's the feeling I wish he could give me. Ahmeek loved me without effort."

She closed her eyes again, and her face contorted just at the thought of Ahmeek Harris. How she had ended up here, without him, without Messiah, she didn't even know.

"If he loved you that well, you would have chosen him," Ethic said. "You never did. So he might love you. In fact, I believe that he does. I've seen him with you, with your kids. A man who loves on kids like that when they aren't his can only have infinite love for their mother. So yeah, the nigga loves you, Mo, but how about you? You love him the same? Or you shortchanging that man so you can keep a little saved up for Messiah, cuz if that's the case, you ain't all the way right either."

"What do you feel for Messiah, Mo?" Alani asked.

"Today, I loved him," Morgan answered. "Today, I remembered what it was like to love him freely." Morgan closed her eyes, and his face was there. "I hate him too, though. For hating me right now because even when I said I hated him, I never meant it. He never gives me the same. He never loves me the right way. So I hate him, and I mean it this time."

"Same as love. You can't hate a man without loving him first. Hate is just disappointed love, Mo," Alani said.

"How do I forgive him?" Morgan asked.

"You just do," Alani said. She looked up at Ethic as she spoke. "You reach down in your soul and choose to love him regardless of his flaws and of the mistakes he's made."

"Only Messiah didn't make mistakes. He made choices. He made clear choices, and that choice was never me. He never picks me." Morgan stood to her feet and pushed out a deep breath of angst. "I just need to clear my head for a bit. I'm going to call Aria. Go dance."

"It's late, Mo," Ethic said.

"I just need to get some of this out of my heart. It helps. Dancing makes my heart beat and makes me want to let it keep beating," she said.

Ethic's eyes widened, and he pulled Morgan in for a hug. Alani stood and placed a hand to Morgan's hair, smoothing it out as she wrapped her arms around her too. "It's hard today, Mo. Not every day. Just today. It was only a bad day. Tomorrow will be better. Go dance. We'll call you if Messiah calls."

Morgan pulled away from them and walked out. She was so flustered that she dropped her handbag, sending the contents of the huge tote bag spilling out onto the front porch. She could barely see through her tears as she bent down to pick up her belongings. She threw everything back inside one by one, but her hands froze when she saw the small box in front of her. It was the gift from her graduation dinner. The one Ethic had slid to her. She hadn't used this bag since then.

How did I forget to open this?

She took a seat on the porch steps, quickly put the rest of her things back in her junky bag, and then removed the pretty bow. Her fingers peeled off the wrapping paper. A black velvet box was inside. She had gotten so many diamonds and jewels in her lifetime that they didn't even excite her anymore. She flipped open the lid and frowned. A piece of paper was folded inside. Morgan opened the paper and held her breath as she discovered a key taped to a note.

Congratulations, love.

There was an address written at the bottom of the paper, and Morgan's heart pounded as she pulled out her phone. She typed the address into her GPS and then hurried to her car. She sped through the city streets until she sat in front of the address. She stepped out of her car and was breathless as she looked up at the commercial building in the middle of downtown Flint.

She gripped the key tightly in her hand and then approached the glass front door. It fit, and she turned the lock and pushed into the building.

She started crying as soon as she flipped the light switch. A dance studio, her dance studio, from Ahmeek Harris to Morgan Atkins. Weeks had passed, and she hadn't even opened the gift. The deflated balloons that spelled her name now lay on the floor.

Her heels against the wooden floor echoed as she crossed the room and touched the mirror in front of her.

Don't let anybody stop your dream, Morgan Atkins
Ahmeek

He had written in black marker right on the glass, and Morgan sobbed as she placed one hand to his name.

Her life was in shambles. She had mishandled so many things. Messiah hated her. After discovering this gift, she was sure Ahmeek hated her as well. Bash was going to make her life a living hell. Her babies weren't around to make it better. Morgan felt herself going dark. She could feel herself giving up. A girl who was so addicted to love possessed none. Morgan pulled out her phone and dialed Aria's number as she sat on the floor, resting her head against the mirror in despair.

"Morgan? It's two in the morning." Aria's sleepy voice came through the phone.

"Messiah knows about the twins." Morgan couldn't waste time apologizing for the late hour. She didn't even have time for a greeting.

"Bitch, I know you fucking lying!" Aria exclaimed. All hints of exhaustion were gone.

"I wish I were," Morgan answered. "He took them. He was so mad. Then I found this key to this dance studio. Ahmeek bought me a dance studio for graduation, and I didn't even say thank you. I didn't even know it was here. So I've lost not one man but two. I fucked up. I fucked all this up, Aria. How did I end up being the one to hurt people? They hate me, Aria. I love them, and they both hate me." Morgan sobbed as she gripped the phone and clenched her eyes tightly. "Messiah couldn't even look at me."

"Where are you, Mo? Are you still at the dance studio? I'm going to come," Aria said.

Morgan sniffed and wiped her nose with the back of her hand. "No, you don't have to. I just . . . I don't know. I just feel like I have no one. I'm fine. I'll talk to you later."

Morgan hung up the phone and stood. She snatched off her jacket and looked around the room until she located the speaker system. She rushed to it like her life depended on it and connected her phone. Play. Repeat. She would be here for a while.

When you sayyy,
You understand, you with the plan, you done with him
You better mean it

Repeat.
Repeat.
Repeat.
Repeat.

Morgan poured her soul into the song, dancing and crying like her life depended on it. Face turned up in disgust, she didn't miss a count. She had to purge the turmoil she felt. Dancing was like therapy. It allowed her to get it all out. Her mind wasn't even present. It was on Messiah and Ahmeek and her twins and Bash and Ethic. Everyone except herself. She danced to rid her mind of the burdens of everyone else. She felt an unbelievable guilt pressing on her. She knew Messiah was aching. Confused. He wouldn't even answer her calls to receive an explanation, and she feared that he'd meant what he had said. He was done, done with her forever, and that destroyed her because even when she had thought he was dead, she had never been done. Their chapter was historic, one she relived in her mind often. A part of her was relieved. It unburdened her that the truth was out. She knew her twins were safe with Messiah, but she could only imagine how confused they must be.

She spun in alarm when the front door was pulled open and her vision blurred when she saw him. Ahmeek Harris. Skin like onyx. Waves on swim. Denim and a black sweater with tan boots. No jewelry besides the earrings sparkling in his ear, real diamonds, and the timepiece on his wrist.

Her heart fluttered at the unexpected sight of him. "You bought me a dance studio," she said in disbelief while shaking her head. "I didn't know. I just found the box. I would have called . . . I would have . . ."

"You would have done exactly what you did, Mo. I'm learning that about you. You do a lot of fucked-up shit," Ahmeek stated.

"I don't mean to," she answered, her voice small. "I love this. I absolutely love you. I'm so sorry. For everything, Ahmeek."

"Yeah, well, I ain't here for apologies, Mo. It's not necessary." Ahmeek winced, scratching his temple with one finger.

"Why are you here? How did you know where to find me?"

"Aria," he answered.

He kept his distance, taking a seat on the edge of the windowsill as he swiped a hand down his head and then ran both hands down his face. He didn't hug her. Didn't kiss her. Didn't even come near her, and the hair on the back of her neck stood and her stomach plummeted.

He knows.

She could tell by his temperament. Space wasn't something they ever craved when in each other's presence. The fact that he was still all the way across the room spoke volumes.

"I'm trying real hard to figure out what I want to say to you, Mo."

Morgan's stomach tensed. *Mo,* she repeated it in her head like it wasn't her name. *He keeps calling me that.* He was angry.

"Ahmeek—"

"I heard some shit about you, Mo, and I was like, nah," he said, struggling to get it out as he shook his head. "Nah, she wouldn't do no shit like that. I need you to tell me something different, because the girl I love wouldn't do no foul shit like what I heard."

"I can explain," she answered. Morgan stood before him. It was judgment day. Time to answer for decisions she had made when Messiah had disappeared from her life. She hadn't known they would come back to haunt her. She hadn't anticipated that at all.

Ahmeek leaned forward and rubbed his hands together, then looked beyond his furrowed brow. "Are the twins Messiah's?" he asked. His voice was sterner than it had ever been with her.

Why was this admission just as hard as it had been with Messiah? Morgan couldn't even look him in the eyes. Her silence was shame-filled.

"They're his," she admitted.

Ahmeek scoffed, shaking his head as he stood.

"Ahmeek!" she called. She didn't want to follow him, but her heart always marched to the beat of its own drum around him. Not even her pride could defy it. "Give me a chance to explain."

She pulled his arm, and he spun on her so swiftly she startled. His hand gripped the bottom half of her face, pushing her pretty cheeks in firmly. She gasped. Murder Meek was in the building. Fire lived in his eyes.

"They're his fucking kids, Morgan!" His voice echoed off the walls.

"I thought he was dead!" she cried.

"What about the rest of us? Huh? We were here! You had his kids and acted like nobody else gave a fuck! Got that ho-ass nigga taking the credit! Fuck is wrong with you? You let me fall in love with Messiah's kids! Fucking with you was already enough to burn that man! Now he got to think about me loving on kids he don't even know? You dirty as fuck, Mo. This is fucking the lowest shit, man." Ahmeek was sick to his stomach at the revelation. "We would have taken care of his kids. We thought he was dead, and you didn't even let us see his seeds. You didn't give us a chance. He been back and you ain't gave him a chance to know his kids. What the fuck is wrong with you? Are you that selfish?"

"He put me in an impossible position, Ahmeek. I didn't do it to hurt anybody. I was trying to protect my babies. Bash was there for me, for them too. He's not perfect, but he helped."

"Because you didn't give nobody else a fucking chance. Messiah been back for months, and yo' ass didn't say one word. That should have been the first thing out yo' mouth!" He removed his hands and took a step away from her, looking down at her in disbelief.

"It wasn't like that. He tried to kill Ethic! He hurt me!

What was I supposed to tell my kids when they grew up and asked me about their daddy? Huh? He didn't leave me with good memories to share with them, Ahmeek. He was a snake. He was a liar," Morgan argued. She was hysterical. Her chest ached because the look in Ahmeek's eyes was familiar. It was the same look she had given Messiah all those years ago on Bleu's lawn. A look of confusion because she hadn't recognized him. Meek didn't know who he was staring at, and it tore Morgan up that he judged her. "I don't owe him shit."

"You owe them! You owe them enough to let them know their real fucking father!" He took another step back from Morgan. Despair saturated her.

"Ahmeek, how can I make you understand?"

"I don't think you can, Mo," he said, finally lowering his voice. She reached for him, and he dodged her; for the first time ever, he denied her access. He frowned and scratched the tip of his eyebrow. "You looking real different to a nigga right now. Shit's foul as fuck," he said.

"So you're taking his side?" Morgan shouted.

"Ain't no sides, Mo! When it come to them kids, it's just right and wrong, and this is wrong. You dead-ass wrong," he said. "You ain't no little-ass girl nursing a broken heart. You're a mother, and you on some spiteful-ass shit to hurt Messiah got you looking crazy to me. I don't even know who the fuck I'm looking at right now." Ahmeek pushed out of the dance studio and walked out into the night.

Morgan didn't move. Fuck it. If he wanted to leave, he could leave. She was tired of crying, tired of the finger being pointed at her when she hadn't been the one to cause this. Everything that was came from what had been. This was the butterfly effect of Messiah's treachery, the consequence of his actions and the mistrust that had been birthed from his abandonment. Morgan walked over to her bag and snatched it up. She had never felt so misunderstood. There wasn't a malicious bone in her body. She hadn't kept this secret to spite Messiah. She had done it because she didn't know him. His actions never backed up his words, so how could she be sure that he wouldn't hurt her again—or worse, hurt her twins? Morgan couldn't take chances with them. She had made a decision to give them a boring life. She wished she could undo it, but she couldn't get time back, and no matter how hard Messiah tried, neither could he. She wasn't naïve to the position Ahmeek was in. They had walked into the gray together, willingly, but when they had made the decision, Messiah hadn't been a factor. They had taken a leap of faith to trust love, but she knew that if they had known Messiah was alive, neither of them would have ever chosen this path. Now that they had, it was too intoxicating to forget. Drunk off lust, high on love, the addiction was uncontrollable. Was she sorry? It was an absolute truth that she was. She remembered what she'd shared with Messiah. She'd fought the ghosts of those emotions every single day, but those memories were built on lies, and Morgan would do anything to stop herself from falling down the rabbit hole with Messiah again.

She turned out the lights to the dance studio, flung the duffel bag over her shoulder, and walked out. Her heels against concrete and her shadow against the brick wall escorted her across the parking lot.

The red taillights that greeted her when she rounded the corner made her stop walking. Ahmeek leaned against the car.

Her breath hit the air in frosty clouds as she stood there. He didn't speak. She could see his anger. He was bothered. He hated everything about the situation. He was so angry, but he was still there.

"He almost killed me. Ahmeek. He sucks the air from my

lungs and leaves me to die. And you wanted me to hand my babies off to him like it never happened. I couldn't do that. I just couldn't. I gave him my heart once before, and the way he tore it apart—" Morgan stopped and shook her head. "Yara and Ssari are living, breathing pieces of me. Of my heart. They are my heart. He doesn't have a good track record of protecting my heart."

The compassion she spoke with cracked through his discontent. Ahmeek crossed the parking lot, and Morgan met him halfway, dropping her bag along the way as she met him with urgency.

"Don't be mad at me," she pleaded as she threw her arms around his waist. He kissed the top of her head, fisting her hair as he pressed her into his chest. They stood there letting the seconds of their discontent wear away, unsure of what to say but knowing exactly what they felt.

"I'm real fucking mad at you, love, I can't lie," he answered. She expected him to let her go, to walk away because she was no longer the perfect girl he had imagined her to be. This was the moment where he gave up on her, but instead, his hold tightened. "You can't play with that man's kids, Mo. The girl I love is better than this. You got to do better."

"I know," she whispered. It had been so long since she had been in his arms. It was freezing outside, but she didn't feel it. The warmth he filled her with was all she recognized. She pulled back and then looked down at her feet. "I was going to give it a try. A family with Messiah. I don't want to lie to you again, so I got to tell you everything. How it happened. How he found out. I saw him at Ethic's, and for the first time since he's been back, we were able to spend time together without fighting, without me being angry."

Ahmeek pulled away, brow denting. He nodded. "That's

what it is, then, Mo," he said. He dug in his pockets and pulled out his car keys. He took a step back.

"Ahmeek—"

"What you want me to say, Morgan? Huh? Y'all got kids. That changes shit. I can't fault you for wanting to work that out. That's what you felt like you needed to do earlier? So do that, Mo. Do what's best for you."

"You're what's best for me," she said.

"And earlier when you were telling Messiah about his kids and wanting to give it a try? It was him then, right? You tell him this same shit? You cry these same tears for him?"

Meek was beyond fed up. Morgan was exhausting. Loving her was painful, and he thought he was insane because a large part of him wanted to do it anyway. Ahmeek hated that he was this attached. He had always been able to remove himself from any situation, but this one was getting the best of him. He was in too deep here. He loved this girl, loved her kids. It was excruciating to be away from them.

"Shit ain't that difficult, Mo. You say you with it. You running down when you even think I'm with somebody else, but you bullshitting where it counts. First it was the nigga Bash, now it's Messiah. You got every excuse in the world not to commit," he said.

"You don't understand," she replied. She wanted to tell him everything—about the threats, the risk she took if she left for good, but she couldn't. It would only expose Ethic's sins to one more person.

"You be easy, Mo," he said. Every step he took away from her obliterated her.

"Ahmeek!" Morgan called out as he unlocked his car. He climbed inside without acknowledging her. Morgan's vision blurred. Her hands shook as she cleared the emotion from her face. This was it. Their epic love affair was shattering before her very eyes. She couldn't help that she loved him. She couldn't help that she loved Messiah too. There was no one occupant of her heart. She loved them both, and nobody seemed to understand.

He put the car in reverse and drove right by her without even looking her way. It seemed like everyone was giving up on her, but Morgan knew she couldn't fold. She had already been through too much to give up. She'd just have to figure out how to love herself a little extra now that neither Meek nor Messiah seemed to love her at all.

18

Only Morgan Atkins could unnerve Ahmeek Harris. It was something about her that burrowed beneath every guard he had in place and made him weak. The night's revelations were heavy on his mind as he drove through the city streets. He had always had his reservations about loving Morgan. He had known if he got too close to her the result would be all encompassing. He had admired her from afar. He hadn't missed a single detail. The curve of her smile made his chest ache long before he'd ever had the privilege to experience her love. The slant in her eyes when she laughed had always caused goose bumps to form on his arms. The fucking scent of her. Her skin. Even just when she used to greet him with a friendly hug had made his stomach hollow. Before Messiah ever mentioned one word about the pampered Morgan Atkins, Ahmeek had thought she was lovely. Whenever she would come around the way, Ahmeek's day would take a turn for the better. She was a symbol of light, of warmth. No matter how dismal and small his world seemed, whenever he laid eyes on her, he was reassured that beautiful things did exist despite the ugliness around him.

She would wave at him, rings sparkling on each of her dainty fingers as she drove down the block. She had been young, too young, and Ahmeek knew Ethic was sending trespassers to early graves behind Morgan Atkins, so he kept it respectful because he knew hood niggas weren't fitting for the likes of her. She was a goddess, and Ahmeek was merely a mortal, so he never made his move. Never took his shot. Then he watched Messiah sweep Morgan off her feet. He witnessed him give the least to earn the most of her, and he couldn't do anything but suffer through it because Messiah had approached her first. When he had seen the intensity that they shared, Ahmeek knew that Messiah needed Morgan in his life. Whatever he had felt no longer mattered. Everything he saw in her, the things he admired, the ways she made him feel were null and void once Messiah claimed her for himself.

Then tragedy transformed all of their lives. Death—or what they had thought had been such—made them appreciate the borrowed breaths that God had given them. When Morgan and Ahmeek had crossed paths again, this time, he couldn't let her pass him by. This time, he allowed her to sneak past his stoic nature, she peeled back all his layers, and now he was exposed, and it hurt like a motherfucker. Morgan gave love like a river flowed. Strong and loud. Snaking through the caverns of his soul, pouring into his heart, submerging him in a feeling so good that he couldn't let go. Even when they weren't speaking, she spoke to him. Her face was always in his head. Mind occupied. Heart occupied. Taken. A girl who no one possessed somehow had established residency in his life. He couldn't be mad at Morgan for wanting her family to work. He loved her enough to know she deserved whatever her heart desired.

He wanted her happy, even if it meant he didn't come out of their experience the same. He didn't realize where he was until he parked the car. Messiah's place. The place he thought was low-key, but Ahmeek had known where to find him all along. He and Messiah had been many things to each other over the years—at the moment, they were enemies—but beyond it all they were brothers. Despite the rift in their bond, Ahmeek felt obligated to pull up on Messiah. He knew the emotional challenges that Messiah had. Knowing he now had two children had to be taking an emotional toll on him. Ahmeek was aware that he was the last person Messiah would want to see, yet still, he stepped out of the car.

He made his way to the building and defied his heavy heart as he placed knuckles to the space next to the metal 3 on the door. The number pulled a sentiment from him that was rooted in friendship. Three. Three hardheaded boys who had come up from the sandbox with nothing but ambition and pride to carry them to the top. Three friends. Three brothers. A bond so solid that they had survived war after war on concrete battle grounds. Messiah. Isa. Ahmeek. MIA because opposition knew that's what would occur if there was ever static. The Crew would leave niggas MIA for anything less than respect. Messiah's disappearance had demolished them all; his reappearance had torn down the frame that was left standing within Ahmeek. He knew they could never go back to being the same. Their love for the same girl had changed them. Still, he knocked because behind every inch of disagreement in his heart, he had just found out his brother had two kids. He had just found out that the brother who felt nothing was feeling everything right now, and he wasn't sure if he could handle the flood of emotions.

He could hear Yara's cries all the way through the door,

and his heart pulled inside his chest. He wasn't sure the twins could handle the sudden change either.

Surprise greeted him when Bleu pulled open the door.

"Ahmeek," she greeted, a bit of relief in her tone. "Did you know?" she asked.

"Nah, B. I didn't know this," Ahmeek answered solemnly.

She stepped aside and motioned for Meek to enter.

"Yara, baby girl, you're killing me. What's wrong? What do you want, huh? What Daddy got to do to make you stop crying?" Messiah rounded the corner and reentered the living room, and when he saw Ahmeek, he stilled. "Fuck you doing here?"

"I heard, man," Ahmeek replied.

"You trying to say you ain't know?" Messiah barked. "Fuck you too, nigga. You knew that shit."

"I don't condone bullshit. You know that ain't my vibe, G. I thought they belonged to Bash," Meek answered. "She made it seem like—"

"She was hoeing with that nigga while I was around. Shorty would rather let me think she a ho than be attached to me," Messiah said, face broken in disbelief and anguish. Yara wailed in his arms and reached for Ahmeek, opening her fists and closing them repeatedly in desperation. Ahmeek could see the brokenness in Messiah as Yara practically lunged for him.

"Just take her, man," Messiah said. "She don't want me."

Ahmeek reached for Yara, and like magic, those cries calmed. She was so worked up she hyperventilated a bit, lip trembling, chest heaving as she laid her head on Ahmeek's chest. Another shirt ruined. It was insult on top of Messiah's injured heart.

Meek saw Messari peek out of the bedroom.

"Meek!" He ran across the living room, and Meek reached down to scoop him too. "Her want to go home Meek. Me too!"

Messiah lost his legs, sitting on the futon as Bleu sat with him. Ahmeek's heart felt like an anchor were chained to it. These were his little people. These were babies he had planned to raise. He wondered if he had connected with them because of their bloodline to Messiah. Had it felt natural because their true heritage belonged to his brother? It was heartbreaking to think he may not be in their lives after this day. It prickled his eyes and tore out his gut. Morgan's lies, Messiah's lies, had turned their lives upside down. Or had he done that to himself by getting involved with her in the first place? He had known all along even before Messiah's return that Morgan was a guilty pleasure.

"It's a lot of change for them, Messiah," Bleu said.

"Just take 'em, man. Take 'em back to Mo," Messiah said. "They don't want to be here. Fuck it." The rejection of these two-year-old twins was the worst he had ever felt.

The sight before him tore Ahmeek right down the middle. Mo was pulling on one side, and Messiah was pulling on the other. This triangle of emotion was excruciating. He didn't even know how he had become the man in the middle. He hadn't wanted this. Hadn't asked for this. A complicated love for a complicated girl had led him to this moment.

"If you were any other nigga, I would do exactly that, bruh. But you my brother, and I'd be an ain't-shit nigga to let you miss out on them, man. They're kinda dope as fuck," Ahmeek said. "You just got to slow-walk this shit. You got to get to know your kids, and they got to get to know you. My nigga, you got kids. Can you believe that shit?" He scoffed. "This what the late nights was for. What the grind was for. They yours, man. The love they got to give—" He paused and shook his head. "You don't want to miss out on that, man. I ain't gon' let you." Ahmeek held a calm Yara and a sleepy Messari. "Yo, homie?"

Meek directed that last one to Messari, and his head popped up. "I want you to be nice to my man. He loves you. Very much, Ssari. He's your dad."

"No, him not. You trick me," Messari protested.

"Why would I do that? You my potna, right?" Meek asked.

Messiah didn't even look up. He couldn't. He just sat there leaned onto his knees in despair as Meek reassured Messari.

"Wight!" Messari agreed.

"So I would never lie to my potna, right?" Ahmeek asked.

Messari glanced down at Messiah and then back at Meek. His little brow furrowed more.

Meek chuckled. "Quit frowning, homie. That's your daddy."

"You like him? Him your friend?" Messari asked.

Ahmeek looked at Messiah, who glanced up in amazement as he awaited the answer. They both knew the answer would make or break Messari's opinion.

"He's my best friend, and I love him, homie," Ahmeek stated, eyes burning so fucking badly because it took his all to admit it aloud. "Why don't you free up my arms a little bit and sit with him. How that sound?"

"But I want to stay with you!" Messari cried.

Ahmeek kneeled. "I ain't going nowhere, homie. That's my word. Let's just give it a try, okay? I'm strong, but your daddy? The strongest man I know." Meek looked at Messiah. "Get your son, man."

Messiah took him off Meek's hands, and Messari frowned hard.

"You big, man," Messiah said in amazement. It was like now that he knew he was his father, the kid's presence hit him in the gut. He looked to Bleu, who smiled with so much emotion in her eyes that Messiah felt a drop of wetness grace his cheek as a tear fell. Bleu wiped it away. "You think you want to give me a chance?"

Messari looked back at Ahmeek, and Ahmeek gave a nod. Messari turned to Messiah and nodded too. "Yolly mean. Her not gon' try like me, right, Meek?" Messari said.

"She'll try," Meek said. "B, take Ssari. Come get your daughter, Messiah."

Messiah stood, swiping hands down his face. His overwhelm wore him down.

"So she feels everything, man. She can't hear, but she can feel exactly what you feel. You can't be on no bullshit with Yolly. She a straight shooter. Kinda like you. If you got some ill on your soul, she gon' see the stain," Ahmeek said, rubbing Yara's back. "She kind of fussy at night. She likes to be rocked to sleep, and she ain't taking no less than a hundred back rubs before her eyes start lowering. You want to try? She don't bite, nigga. Fix your face."

Messiah snickered. "Nigga, you sure? Cuz her little ass was on a nigga head with the crying," Messiah said skeptically.

Ahmeek passed Yara, and she immediately lunged for him.

"Put her face to your chest. She likes to feel your heartbeat," Ahmeek said.

Messiah did as he was told, and Yara fought him a bit.

"Nigga, you know how to tame pits. Tame your seed," Ahmeek said.

"Nah, her bite a little worse than any dog I've ever handled," Messiah said.

Ahmeek snickered because little Yara Rae had her daddy shook. "Nah, Yolly's good money, bruh. She gives the best hugs and kisses. Little girl knows how to turn your whole day around. Come on, bruh. She's yours. She gon' follow your lead. Your heart can't be racing, or she's going to feel like she ain't safe. Like you don't got her, bro. Put your hand on the back of her head and show her it's okay," Ahmeek said.

Messiah swayed back and forth and followed instructions to an exact science.

"Yo, she stopped crying," Messiah whispered. He kissed the top of Yara's head, and he felt her little chest lifting, then falling as she breathed. Her little heart was thumping in her chest, and she was tense, but the more he rubbed those circles on her back, the more she relaxed. He turned to Bleu.

"She stopped, B," Messiah said in disbelief.

Bleu's face was wet in emotion. "It's a shame that anyone came between y'all. When you're on the same team, it's beautiful," she whispered, wiping her tears. She stood. "I'm going to go."

"Nah, B. You stay," Ahmeek stated. "I'ma slide. Congrats, bro." The shit tore him up because he loved these twins. He loved their mother. He wanted parts. He'd take on every role they'd needed filled, but he felt unneeded. Messiah was their father, and Ahmeek finally realized why taking them off Bash's hands had felt natural, because Bash was unnatural to them. Now that he was in the presence of their real father, he felt the connection despite the twins' hesitation; he could sense the innate ownership that only nature could nurture. The twins had been unsettled for hours and were already giving in to the exhaustion of the eventful day. "At least call her and let her know they're all right."

Ahmeek walked to the door and pulled it open.

"Yo, Meek," Messiah called.

Ahmeek paused and turned.

Messiah couldn't speak. Didn't speak. He was too stubborn to say thank you but too indebted to hate him. He threw up that three-finger salute. A finger for him. A finger for Isa.

A finger for Ahmeek. Crew shit. Hood shit. Ahmeek returned the gesture. So much reluctance between two men who loved each other dearly. This unspoken sign was all they had to extend to each other, and it was a tragedy.

As Meek went to close the door, he heard Messari's sleepy voice as his head popped up off Bleu's shoulder.

"Meek! You didn't tuck us in!" Messari shouted. He scrambled from Bleu's hold and raced across the apartment. Meek bent down so that he was eye level with Messari.

"Your daddy got it covered, homie," Meek said.

"Noooo, youuuu, pweasseee," Messari said as he pulled Meek's hand.

"Just get him settled, man," Messiah said. Meek looked up, and he could see the distress in Messiah's face.

"Nah, you got it," Ahmeek said. He kissed the top of Messari's head. "Ya' daddy gon' take real good care of you. I'ma see you around, homie. Love your mama for me, a'ight?" He hated that his eyes burned. This felt a lot like letting go. An excruciating goodbye. He stood and walked out the door. For the first time, he wished he had never gone to London to see Morgan. It was the first time he weighed what had been lost, and it pressed on his soul tremendously.

Morgan sat in the car, gripping her steering wheel, squeezing it repeatedly as she lingered in the parking lot of her building. She glanced over at the car she was parked next to. A navy-blue Jaguar. Bash's car. He was inside. He was waiting, and Morgan didn't realize how intimidated she was by him until now. Messiah had stolen her shields. The twins stopped Bash from being able to take things too far. There had been threats and tension, but she knew he tempered his reactions because of the twins. He hadn't touched her in a while, and it made her think that the few times he had hit her had been a mistake he regretted. Now that she had to face him alone, Morgan was afraid. She had been trying to work up enough nerve to enter her own apartment.

"This is crazy," she said to herself. She opened her car door and made her way up. She called Messiah one more time along the way. Voice mail. The phone wasn't even ringing on his end anymore, and she was sure he had turned it off to avoid her calls. She wasn't getting Yara and Messari back until he felt like returning them. She prayed it wouldn't be too long. She wanted them home, not because she wanted to keep him from them longer but because she needed them. She needed to talk to him about what being their parents meant. His anger was so great that she was certain any chance they had to make their relationship work was gone. Just the way that he was ready to condemn for one mistake turned Morgan off. Messiah had done so many things to hurt her. He had crushed her time and time again, but the expectation was always forgiveness. Messiah wanted her to look past all his ill deeds, wanted her to love him like nothing had ever happened, and Morgan would have tried. She would have because he wanted her to, but this one sin of hers was judged heavily. This one mistake. This one thing that she had done to him, he judged harshly. Morgan could never forgive the hypocrisy of it all. The expectation that she could be hurt time and time again, yet she was cut off for hurting him once. *He didn't even try to hear me out. Didn't even give me a chance to explain.*

Messiah's judgment didn't feel good.

Morgan placed the key into her door and pushed into her apartment. Her breath hitched when she saw the candles and flower petals that decorated her living room. Bash sat hunched over on the couch, and upon hearing her enter, he looked up.

She had expected anger, but she saw nothing but worry on Bash's face.

"You're going to leave me, aren't you?" Bash asked.

Morgan didn't know how she was supposed to answer that question. If she was honest, he would get angry. If she lied, she would add another chain that kept her enslaved to him . . . indebted to him. Her eyes misted. It was never supposed to be this way with Bash. She had let things get so far out of hand.

"If I say yes, what's going to happen to me and my family, Bash?" she asked.

Bash placed praying hands over his nose, blowing air into them as his eyes focused on the blank space in front of him.

"I don't want to hurt you, Mo. I've never wanted to hurt you, but it seems like that's the only thing you respond to . . . pain. It's like you don't appreciate any other thing I have to give. You run back to your past because its full of pain, so I keep asking myself if that's what I have to give you for you to act right," Bash said, his tone low.

"I don't love you, Bash." Morgan was so afraid to say those words, but she was more afraid not to. "If you're honest with yourself, you can say you already know that, though. You knew when I came to London with you two and a half years ago that love was the furthest thing from my mind."

"Who said anything about love?" Bash asked. "This is possession. I own you. There was an unspoken agreement. You get the respectability and legitimacy that comes with being a part of my family. I get you."

"That would have been good enough for me before."

"Before what?" Bash asked, chuckling.

"Before Ahmeek," she said. "And before I knew that Messiah was alive. He's their father, Bash."

"I'm their father!" Bash debated.

"He knows, Bash!" Morgan shouted. "I told him about the twins."

"Where are my kids, Mo?" he asked. His tone was intolerant, and he stood.

Morgan took a step back. "I couldn't keep hiding them, Bash. He's their father. He has a right to know."

"Where are my kids?" Bash's voice boomed off the walls, and he was across the room in seconds. Morgan didn't have time to run. He gripped her face so tightly Morgan winced.

"They're not your kids!" she shouted, pushing him off. "You can't make someone love you! What's wrong with you?!"

Bash jerked her so hard that Morgan felt dizzy. She grabbed the back of her head and staggered as he released her. He turned, rubbing the nape of his neck and raging as he placed balled fists to the sides of his head before pointing at her.

"What was I supposed to do?" Morgan screamed, hysterical as she threw her hands up. "I can't keep him from his kids!"

"I can," Bash said devilishly, maliciously, like he would make it his mission to keep Messiah away.

"What does that mean?" Morgan shouted, eyes flooding with tears. "You can't do that!"

Bash pulled out his cell phone and pressed one button before placing it to his ear as Morgan watched in horror. She fought him for that phone, but one hand pushed her away. She fought harder. Reaching for it.

"Bash, stop. Don't do this," she pleaded. "You can't do this." She was over his shoulder, trying to walk around him to get to that phone because she knew whoever was on the other end had the power to blow up her life. Bash spun around suddenly, and the blow he delivered to her midsection pushed all the air from her lungs. Morgan folded into him, grabbing his forearm as he caught her. He rubbed her head as she gasped for air. Her fingers dug into his skin. Her face crushed in destruction. No one had ever put so much malicious intent behind touch that was meant for her. An aching spread through her as he stepped back, letting her fall to the ground.

"Bash, please!" she gasped, holding her side. Her ribs. She could barely pull in a breath. She was sure her ribs were broken. She was curled in a fetal position, and even the notion of standing up straight sent waves of pain through her body. Morgan tasted metal, and she lifted a shaky hand to her mouth, pulling back a bloody hand. He had hit her so hard she was spitting up blood.

"Ezra Okafor and Messiah Williams. Take care of it," he said. There was a pause, and then an afterthought forced more out of Bash's mouth. "Oh, and Ahmeek Harris. Let's attempt to make something stick there too." Morgan's heart plummeted. He paused and looked back at Morgan smugly. "Yeah, I owe you one, Bill." Bill Lance, commissioner of the Michigan State Police, and a friend of the Fredrick family. Bash had called in a favor.

"What did you do?" Morgan cried as he backed her against the wall.

Bash gripped her chin, and Morgan snatched her face away. He gripped harder. He pressed his lips to hers, and when he pulled back, her blood was on his lips. He fingered his lips and smirked triumphantly like he had won, like her pain meant victory for him.

"What you made me do," Bash answered.

"Even if I stay," she said as she staggered to her feet, using the back of the couch to add strength to legs that didn't work. She was trembling, but she was determined to get up from the floor. "If you trap me here, I will never stop trying to get to them. They don't even have to love me back, but I'll always love them. It'll never be you."

Bash scoffed and then brought his face close to hers, so close the smell of his breath made her stomach turn. "Love them from the other side of a glass wall, Morgan, because by the time I'm done, they'll never be free again," Bash stated. "In the meantime, get your act together. There is no out. It can be a very good life if you let it."

Morgan's chest heaved, as just the thought tore her in half. He walked away, headed to her bedroom as Morgan slid down the wall. The hard realization that she would never be able to leave Bash caused her to break down. He had caught a butterfly, one that was so beautiful he would rather watch it die than set it free.

19

"They're finally down," Messiah said as he looked down at the little bodies that occupied his bed. He had never been so exhausted. Putting the twins down for bed had taken hours. He didn't know how Morgan managed to do it every night. He had only had them for a short time, and they had been more work than he had ever done. Realizing Morgan had been raising them for two years, carrying the burden without him, put guilt on his soul. Maybe she was justified for moving on, for finding a man who could help, because Messiah definitely needed help. He needed Bleu there just for the moral support alone. He and Bleu sat on the edge, afraid to move, afraid to breathe too loudly because waking the twins would be a disaster. "He knows them like a mu'fucka, B," Messiah said, voice clipping in emotion. He sniffed it away, clearing his throat. "How do I get to know them like that? That type of shit ain't in me. I'm too cold." Messiah's woe weighed down the room as a tear slid down the bridge of his nose. "Shorty killed me, man. She's killing me with this shit."

Bleu placed a hand on his back as he leaned forward. It was like she was could feel his pain beneath the pads of her fingers. "You don't have to love them like him, Messiah. You love them like you. You're their father. No one can know them like you. You don't have to get to know them, because they are of you. You are them. You already know everything there is to know about them," Bleu said.

Messiah stood abruptly and walked out of the room, disappearing into the bathroom in the hall. Bleu rose, and her gut flipped as she heard him fighting himself from behind the closed door. He was resisting sobs so badly that her eyes watered, then her tears fell. She covered her mouth with one hand and closed her eyes. He was hurt, and Bleu felt it. She had never judged Morgan, never felt ill will toward her. She thought Mo was a beautiful girl with a spirit so kind that she emitted light, but in this moment, as she witnessed the peeling of Messiah's soul, Bleu hated her. There was a line that people who loved each other should respect, and Morgan had crossed it by hiding Messiah's children. Then again, she also acknowledged the fact that Messiah had blurred the lines long ago when he had left town so unremorsefully. Bleu's heart was cut open for everyone involved. For herself. For Messiah. For Morgan. For Meek. Most importantly, for the children who were caught in the middle. The twins were beautiful and around the same age as the son she'd lost would have been. Just seeing them cut her deeply. Messiah pulled open the door, and the only evidence of his undoing were his red eyes. She looked up at him, and the stare between them was weighted. A broken man stood before her. He surprised her when he reached for her, pulling her into him and then losing his resolve as he bent into her, melting, imploding as he pulled her to the floor.

"Shh."

Bleu sat, leaning against the wall, and Messiah lay in her lap, on his back as he trained his stare onto the ceiling. She had no idea how much he needed her in this moment.

"I'm fucked up, B," he admitted.

"Anybody would be, Messiah. It's a lot," she answered. "So much has happened, but you're a father. You're somebody's daddy, and they're sooo cute. Oh my God, they have her whole face and your whole attitude. They're beautiful." Bleu laughed.

"They gang like a mu'fucka," Messiah said, smirking. "Bad little mu'fuckas, man. Just looking at them light-skinned mu'fuckas, you wouldn't think a nigga had nothing to do with it. Ol' R&B-singing-looking-ass kids." He snickered as he shook his head. He could hardly believe they belonged to him. "How they get so mean, yo? They some lil' thugs."

Bleu laughed. "And who you think they get that from?" she asked, smiling.

She looked down at him, and they both grew silent.

"My shit tore open, B. Like my shits ain't even inside my chest no more," Messiah said.

"I'll keep it for you," she said. "Keep it beating, remember?"

Messiah's hand found hers, and he interlaced his fingers with hers, tattoos locked. Picture complete. He brought her knuckles to his lips, and the kiss awoke Bleu's entire body. She held her breath as he kissed her hand again, then her wrist. She couldn't even breathe.

Messiah reached up with one hand and gripped her hair and pulled her face toward his.

Bleu pulled back. "Messiah, no."

He paused.

"I can't do this again," Bleu said. "The only time you want this is when you're mad at her. I don't want it like this."

Messiah's brow furrowed, and he rolled up, turning to her as he opened wide legs around her. He pulled her thighs, sliding her across the floor, drawing her in. Bleu let him. Moths and flames.

"But you do want it?" Messiah asked. His face revealed shock, as if it were a wonder that she could possibly love him.

"What do *you* want, Messiah?" Bleu shot back.

He couldn't answer that. He was a selfish-ass nigga. He wanted it all. What good was cake if you couldn't eat it? Cake-and-eat-it-too-ass nigga. Messiah was selfish, and Bleu was giving. It was a deadly combination, one where reciprocity would be uneven. In this moment when Morgan had shown him unbelievable deceit, he didn't care enough to stop himself.

"Don't matter what I want. I ain't shit. I can't afford to break you, B," he answered.

"You have no idea how good you are. You're too busy believing the bad," Bleu whispered.

"That ain't the only time I want it, B," he admitted. Bleu's eyes lifted in shock, and she held her breath.

He leaned into her, trapping her, no running because his hand was behind her neck, bringing her forward. A tear slid down her cheek, and Messiah slid it away with his thumb.

Just as he was about to kiss her . . .

Boom!

The sound of the front door being kicked in pulled him back.

"Police! Let me see your hands!" A full team in SWAT gear poured into his apartment, forcing them apart. The police swarmed in so swiftly, all Bleu could do was scream as they put knees to her back and forced them onto their stomachs, placing them in cuffs.

"Stop fucking touching her!" Messiah barked.

"Ow!" Bleu screamed. "You're too heavy! Please stop!"

Messiah was enraged as he fought against the officers. "My kids are in here, man!"

"Who else is here?!" one of them yelled.

"Just my kids, man! They're two years old!" Messiah barked. "She ain't got shit to do with this, man! Get the fuck off her!"

Messari came out of the room, and he stood, eyes wide, staring at the chaos as the officers turned to him, guns drawn.

"Get that gun off my son! I'll fucking murder you, man! Don't fucking touch my kid!" Messiah shouted.

"Cut her loose and let her get to the boy," one of the men ordered.

The cop on top of Bleu relieved her of the cuffs, and she quickly rushed to Messari, picking him up and pushing his head over her shoulder. The cops forced Messiah to his feet.

"Where are you taking him?" Bleu demanded as she followed behind them frantically. The rest of the unit was tearing the apartment apart, searching, hunting.

"Get my kids, Bleu!" Messiah shouted.

His voice carried into the night as they walked him to the awaiting squad car and pulled away.

Bella sat in the driveway, shotgun in Henny's old school.

"My daddy's going to kill you if he catches you here this late," Bella said, smiling because she loved the fact that he was willing to take the risk.

"I'm in and out. I just wanted to see you, smart girl, before I called it a night," Hendrix stated.

Bella smiled and looked out her window, up at her house. "Well, you saw me," she said as she rolled pretty brown eyes back over to Hendrix.

"You took that test you was telling me about? The ACT and shit?" Hendrix asked.

"It was just a practice test," Bella answered.

"How you do?" Hendrix asked.

"I did okay," she said. "It was hella hard, and I was super nervous. I need at least a 23 to get into Clark."

"You got it," Henny stated.

"I heard you were around the way with Isa. They said you helped him shoot up a house," Bella said.

"Man," Henny said as he rolled his gaze out the side window. "Tell whoever the fuck 'they' is to keep my name out they mouth."

"Did you?" Bella asked.

"I got to put in work when it's my turn. I'm getting money with the Crew. I can't bitch up when it's time to get my hands dirty," Henny said.

"You promised, Henny," Bella reminded, voice dipped in sadness. The expectation that Hendrix just may self-destruct broke her heart. Ethic's daughter had been bitten by the love bug. She had been close friends with Hendrix for two years. She admired his resilience. She respected the things he had survived. Hendrix made her feel as if she were the therapy that eased his traumatized heart. He was her best friend, and they had a plan. He had made promises to stay out of trouble so that when she went away to college, he could leave too. He was deviating from the plan. He was taking risks that would derail things altogether, and Bella's heart ached. He had a job at Ethic's shop. She didn't understand why he was determined to mess that up. "Does my dad know you're still in the game? You don't need to do that stuff. He will help you with money and everything."

"He's your daddy, Boog, not mine," Hendrix shot back,

calling her by the nickname he had given her. Girls around the way called her *bougie*. They meant it as an insult, one they could joke about and pretend it was love when really it was a bit of hate laced in the undertone. Henny peeped game and instantly shortened it, calling her *Boog,* making it cool. The most popular boy on the block, giving her clout because hood niggas wanted bougie girls anyway. It didn't take long for the name to stick and others to follow suit.

"He gave you a job. I don't understand why you still want to be out there with the Crew," Bella stated.

"Ethic look out for me. Keep me in the books, helped me get my GED and all that, showing me about managing money and investing and shit. I got to have something to invest, though, smart girl. Them eighteen dollars an hour on some part-time shit ain't going to get me nothing close to what your daddy got you used to. I got to make my own way on the block, earn my respect, so when it's time for the real world your pops teaching me about, I'm ready. I got to make it out the hood first, though, before I can think about the shit Ethic's teaching me. It ain't forever, but I got to stack right now. Real paper, not no nine-to-five shit."

"If something happens to you—"

"Nothing's gonna happen, Bella. Come on. I didn't come all the way out here for no speeches."

"Well, stop doing dumb stuff, and I can stop giving them," Bella said. Her body language was everything as she leaned closer to the door and crossed her arms across her chest.

"You know I hate when you mad, Boog," Henny said, smirking. "You get real mean, and your nostrils start flaring." Henny teased Bella, sticking his finger up her nose. She slapped his hand away.

"Stooop, Hendrix!" she cried out. "You play too much!"

She swatted his hand, and he kept bypassing her protests, aiming for her nose until she fell into laughter. She grabbed his finger tightly. "I'm going to break it."

"Pretty girl love breaking shit. Hearts and all," he said. He leaned across the armrest and planted a kiss to her cheek. Bella turned suddenly to give him her lips. He pulled back in surprise, and Bella blushed as she lowered her head.

"You got to stay focused, Hendrix," Bella said. "You're more than a dope boy. I wouldn't love a dope boy like this."

His eyes widened. He was taken aback by her candor. "I luh you too. More than everybody."

A true teenage love affair.

She kissed him again, this time on his forehead. "You're too smart to act stupid. You're not like those other guys," she said. "I've got to go. Text me when you make it home, okay?"

"Yes, ma'am," Hendrix said, smiling charmingly as he bit his bottom lip.

Hendrix exited and walked around the hood of the car before opening Bella's passenger door. She stepped out.

"I'ma make you happy one day, Boog," Hendrix said.

The stars in Bella's eyes shone brighter than the ones in the night sky. He wrapped his arms around Bella's waist as hers fastened around his neck.

"I hate when you have to leave," she said, resting her head on his chest. "I hate every single second between the time you leave and the time you come back."

"Quit counting the seconds, Boog. Sometimes I might have to be gone. Sometimes you might have to be gone. We gon' get back, though. Every time," Hendrix reassured.

"How do you know?" Bella asked.

"Cuz what we got is real, Boog. Ain't no faking about it. No matter how much time pass, no matter how far you go with school or traveling the world or whatever. I know I might not always be able to keep up, cuz your shot ain't gon' always be my shot, but whenever you slow down, whenever you come back, we gon' get right back," Henny promised.

"What if we lose touch one day?" Bella asked.

Henny didn't answer right away because the idea pained him. "We got to make a promise. If we ever go more than two years without talking, we got to meet on New Year's Eve."

"Two years!" Bella protested, yelling as she pulled her head back. "Why would we go two years without speaking, Henny?"

"I'm just saying shit happens," Henny explained.

"Not to us. I can't see that," Bella whispered.

"But if it does, Boog. On New Year's Eve, we got to meet. On the football field at your high school. That's my word; I'ma show up for you every year until you feel like showing up too."

He held up his pinkie, a ritual he had gotten from her, an action she had been taught by her father . . . a symbol more binding than any contract.

"I pinkie swear," she said.

"A'ight, let me bounce before yo' daddy wake up," Henny said, smirking.

Bella reluctantly let go, and her heart ached as she watched him get in his car. He had never turned his car off. He didn't want the sound of an engine starting to alert Ethic or Alani of his presence. She waved as she watched him pull around the circular driveway. Bella typed the code to the gate into her phone to let him out. Dismay filled her when she saw the red-and-blue lights pull in front of him and block him in.

"Get out the car! Get out the car now!"

Guns. Bella saw guns and heard the screeching of tires as Hendrix came to a stop.

"Daddy!"

She screamed for Ethic, and before she knew it, her feet were pounding pavement as they carried her down the driveway in Hendrix's direction.

"Don't shoot!" Bella screamed as she panted, fear coursing through her body as she ran as fast as she could. "Help! *Daddy!*"

"Bella!" That was Alani's voice. Behind her. At the front door. "Ezra!"

Bella couldn't even take the chance of looking back, terrified of the possibility of looking away only to hear gunshots ring out next. She saw the driver door pop open.

"Show us your hands!" She might as well have been running in slow motion.

"Bella!"

Thank God. Her daddy's voice. Ethic was behind her. She heard him. He would fix this. He could fix this.

"Wait!" she shouted as she plowed into Hendrix, who stood wide-eyed, fear-filled, as he raised his hands. She wrapped herself around him, holding on tightly. He couldn't even hug her back because they knew that if his hands disappeared, bullets would fly. They'd have to cut through two bodies because Bella was glued to him. She could feel Hendrix's entire body shaking.

"Bella!"

She turned, blocking Hendrix's body with her own. "Don't shoot!"

Ethic was down the driveway and headed in their direction. Bella counted the men. Ten. There were ten of them. Semiautomatic rifles in their hands. Bodies covered in assault armor, helmets on their heads. Lights shining from the beams of their guns.

"Get down!"

Half of them were aiming at Ethic, the other half at her and Hendrix now.

His hands were up and visible. "That's my daughter and her friend. They're minors. This is my property, and they're unarmed. I'ma need the guns lowered."

Alani approached, hair wild, silk robe wrapped around her swollen belly as she stepped in front of Ethic.

"You're going to have to kill four people out here today," she said, voice trembling as she pulled out her cell phone. "I'm live on Facebook right now. I'm a *New York Times* bestselling writer with over a million followers, and they're watching. The Michigan State Police is at my home in SWAT gear with guns pointed at my teenage daughter and her friend and my husband."

"Put down the phone!" one of the men yelled.

"Put down your guns! It's not illegal to have a cell phone. I'm recording every single second, so if one bullet flies, I have proof." Alani looked at her screen. "A thousand witnesses and growing. Nobody is armed here but all of you! Y'all see this shit? This abuse of power? This invasion on our personal property!" Alani shouted. She was so terrified; she couldn't steady her tone.

Ethic pushed her behind him. Tension cut through the chill in the air.

"Lower those guns off my goddamned daughter!" Alani screamed.

"We're just here for Ezra Okafor."

"That's me. Whatever this is about, it doesn't involve them. They're kids. It's in everybody's best interest if you and your men put those guns away. It doesn't take ten officers and riot gear to approach me. The longer this lasts, the worse it's going to be in the end, remember that," Ethic stated.

The lead officer approached him and apprehended one wrist and then twisted it behind Ethic's back before handcuffing the other.

"No! Wait!" Alani shouted.

"Go in the house, baby. Get them inside. Don't worry. I'ma be home soon. It's nothing for you to worry about, I promise. Get everybody in the house," Ethic instructed. He was calm. Unbothered. He kissed her lips as Bella cried as she watched the police walk Ethic to the back of a police car.

"You got some ID?" an officer asked.

"No! Get off my property. He's a kid! He doesn't have to give you anything. You have no cause to ask him for anything!" Alani shouted as she shifted her focus to Hendrix and Bella. She aimed the camera at his shield. "This is harassment— Officer Bennett, is it?"

The officer snatched the phone. "I said put the phone down!" he yelled.

"Aye, man!" Hendrix protested as he and Bella watched the officer rough Alani up a bit. "Get your fucking hands off her, man! She's pregnant! You ain't got to handle her like that!"

Another officer accosted Hendrix, gripping him by his collar and then slamming him hard onto the hood of his car.

Hendrix grimaced as the hand to the side of his face pressed him harder into the steel frame. His legs were kicked open.

"You got anything on you that can injure my officers, boy?" the cop asked.

Hendrix didn't respond. He just locked in on Bella, who was standing just yards away. He saw her lips moving, but he couldn't hear her. He was trying to prepare himself for what would happen next.

"What do we have here?" the officer asked, finding Hendrix's pistol. "Felony possession of a firearm and a controlled substance."

Bella looked on in horror as Hendrix was placed in handcuffs. He heard her protests as Bella's face dipped in panic. She was crying, and he had to close his eyes because he hated it. He detested the sight of her tears.

Bella ran into Alani's arms, sobbing as the police took her father and Hendrix away. "What's going to happen to them?!" she asked frantically.

"I don't know," Alani answered. She feared the worst. She knew Ethic's pedigree. She knew there were no small crimes with him, and she prayed that he wasn't harboring secrets that were now threatening to ruin them.

20

You good, Mo?

Aria kept staring at the text message. She had sent it hours ago and then dozed off. Morgan had never responded, and Aria was unsettled. The only thing that made her feel better was the fact that she had called Ahmeek. She was sure he would take care of things, so instead of anticipating a response, she finally clicked out of the thread. Her worry about Mo had distracted her from the fact that Isa wasn't home. She looked over at the empty spot beside her and then swung her short legs over the side of the bed. She threw on a Michigan State hoodie and didn't bother with pants as she walked out of the room. The house was silent. Aria's fingertips graced the red walls in the hallway as she made her way toward the living room.

"Isa?"

She heard the faint sound of his voice and followed it to the living room. The front door was wide open, and Aria frowned.

Her heart fell when she saw him leaned over onto the roof of a car. A girl was parked curbside. The car window was down, and both his hands were on the roof as he leaned into her. Aria felt like she would be sick.

"You got me?" The sound of Isa's voice made tears come to her eyes.

"Yeah, I got you. You know how I get down." The girl's response ripped through Aria. The disrespect was high, and Aria's tolerance was low.

"I'm so stupid," she whispered. She wasn't even disappointed in Isa. She had failed herself. She knew what type of man she was dealing with. She had chosen him against her brother's wishes, fighting her better judgment, and she felt like a fool. Determination filled Aria as she took heavy steps back to their bedroom. She grabbed her Chanel bag and then grabbed Isa's keys and phone, dropping them into the toilet on her way to his safe. She emptied it inside her oversize tote. There was a price for pain and a tax for wasting her time. He was lucky she wasn't headed toward his storage unit. If she were dirty, she would leave his ass on empty, but Aria loved fair and fought fair. A man would never be able to burn her name after she left a relationship. The money she'd taken was what she was owed plus a little more for pain and suffering. It wouldn't break Isa. Just bruise his ego and stroke hers. Aria slipped into ripped jeans and Valentino boots before heading to the front door. Isa was waltzing in as she rounded the corner. He froze.

"Fuck you doing with bags?" Isa asked.

"Leaving," she answered curtly.

"Man, stop playing, yo," Isa said. "Fuck you got bags for?"

She went to walk around him, and Isa grabbed her wrist. Aria dropped the bag to free one of her hands, and before she could stop herself, she swung. "Don't touch me!" she shouted.

Isa jumped hard from the blow to the side of his head.

Then he touched his ear in shock. "What the fuck wrong with yo' crazy ass?" he shouted.

"You!" Aria screamed. "I'm done!"

"You done?" Isa asked.

"That's what the fuck I said, nigga. Done with all this shit," Aria said.

Isa scooped her, picking her up.

"Put me down before I beat your ass, Isa!" she screamed. "You just dumb disrespectful. It doesn't get no more disrespectful than you. You bringing bitches to our house while I'm asleep? You that fucking dirty, I can't even close my eyes without worrying about you and some ho!"

Aria was flung over his shoulder as he turned the corner to their room, knocking her head against the wall from the change of direction.

"Ow!" Aria shouted as she hit him again, this time aiming for his back as she kicked her feet. "Put me down, Isa!"

They were back in the bedroom, and Isa flung her onto the bed before yanking one ankle and then quickly restraining her with a cuff. Ankle to bed frame, she was trapped.

Aria kicked at the bed. "Give me the key, Isa! I'm not playing."

Isa stood in front of her, playing in his chin hair with one hand as the other arm crossed his chest. "You're a fucking nut, you know that?" he stated. He winced as he scratched the top of his head.

"Did you or did you not have a bitch pull up to this house while I was asleep? I'm not this girl, Isa. I'm not the one to forgive bullshit time and time again. I'm Left Eye, nigga. I'm going to geek out on you, and one of us will end up hurt behind you fucking these random-ass, dusty-ass, put-five-dollars-in-my-tank-ass hoes!" Aria shouted as she kicked the bed frame again in frustration. "So before that happens, I'm just going to let this go."

"I'm not fucking nobody, man," he stated. "You stay tripping."

"I heard her, Isa!"

"You ain't hear shit. You assuming. Making an ass out ya'self," he shot back. "I told you I was gon' be straight up with you, Ali. If I ain't got my word, what I got?"

"You're just like a nigga. You want me to trust your word over my eyes, over my ears. My intuition has never lied to me; I'ma trust that," Aria snapped. She kicked the bed frame again, and the cuffs rattled. "Now let me go!"

"That bitch ain't shit, Ali," Isa said. He took a seat across the room, ass to carpet, back to wall as he reached into the square pocket on his shirt.

"What is it this time? She takes pain better? Cuz that's the game you sold me last time. What is she doing for you that I don't?" Aria snapped. "Cuz I been doing a hell of a whole lot for your light-skinned ass." Her heart was racing. Adrenaline and heartbreak were a deadly combination. If only looks could kill.

Isa pulled out a blunt. He kept them rolled—actually *she* kept them rolled for him, and the fact that she had been so accommodating pissed her off in this moment. "Why aren't I enough, Isa?" she asked.

"You're the whole damn pie, Ali," he said. The lighter was next. It was like he borrowed the fire in her heart to light the weed, because her anger turned to sadness.

"What she doing for a nigga, you can't do, Ali. It's business, and I don't mix business and pleasure," Isa said. "I don't even want to bring that type of energy to you. I come home after that to escape. I don't want you wrapped up in my bullshit. I'd have to hurt somebody, man. My mind won't be where it's supposed to be if you're involved."

"What is she doing, Isa? A bitch shouldn't be in your business, period. A woman shouldn't know something about you that I don't," Aria snapped. "I'm not going for that."

"I'm not fucking her. She setting a nigga up for me, Ali. Damn!" Isa barked.

Aria jerked her neck back in shock. "What?"

"A nigga riding me and Meek for some paper. We into a nigga for a lot of money from a job that went bad a few months ago. He's a square. A suit-and-tie-wearing-ass mu'fucka. I'ma rob him. She's my way in," Isa stated.

"Why would she do this for you if you're not fucking her?" Aria asked.

"You ain't never did nothing for a nigga without fucking him?" Isa asked, smirking as he lifted the smoke to his mouth. He blew it out, then moved over so that he was sitting against the bed. He lifted the blunt to her mouth. "Feisty ass need to chill."

"I don't know where your mouth been," Aria said.

"On you, with your funky ass," Isa shot back.

"You fucked that girl, didn't you?" Aria asked, refusing the blunt.

"Before you, I fucked a lot of girls," Isa stated. "I don't fuck with them no more, though, and that's all you got to worry about."

"And you're sitting here telling me that this girl was before me and that you don't mess with her no more, yet she's willing to hit a lick for you? Make that make sense," Aria stated.

"She getting compensated, baby girl, ain't doing it for free, but it's straight business, Ali. Ain't no nothing with me and her. She just a pretty face. The type of face I need to pull this off."

"Why can't you just leave this shit alone? Maybe Nahvid was right. You're not ready for this. I'm going to ruin my whole life fucking with you," Aria stated.

He gripped her face. Her words had struck a nerve. "Your brother don't know shit about me, Ali. You want that nigga to keep breathing, you might want to stop while you ahead."

"*You* want to keep breathing, you might want to stop while you're ahead," Aria snapped back.

"You swear that D.C. nigga so tough," Isa stated.

"And you swear he ain't," Aria replied. "You swear you the toughest nigga alive. Like it's not a possibility that somebody can hurt you. Like you can't be touched, Isa. We're supposed to be getting married. You think I want a life of worrying about you? You think it's cool to be a husband and take these types of risks every night? You're going to die on these streets, and I'm going to be alone. If that happens, I'll never be the same. It isn't worth it. I want this forever, but forever can be over in a flash if you don't get out."

"If this play goes down smooth, I won't have to do shit but spend this money and fuck my bitch for the rest of my life," Isa replied. "This nigga Hak got it coming, yo. It's fair play. All a part of the game."

"Ain't no manipulating some girl's affection when you with me, Isa. I don't play those types of games. You won't be making promises, putting money in a bitch pocket, none of that. I don't care if you not having sex with that girl. You won't be fucking with these bitches mentally either. These hoes shouldn't even have your number. So it's not happening. That's dead, or I'm gone," Aria stated. "What if I told you I was going to do the same shit for a man I used to deal with?"

"You can't tell me shit like that. Every nigga you used to deal with is dead," Isa stated. "Niggas are memories already."

Aria's heart galloped because she knew Isa wasn't playing. It both terrified and excited her. "Your ass is a hypocrite."

"What am I'm supposed to do, Ali?" Isa asked.

"Use me. I'll do it. One time and then you're done. Then we plan this wedding, and you put this Crew shit behind us. You go legit."

Isa stood and unlocked the cuff, then went right back down to his knees as he lingered between her thighs as she sat on the edge of the bed. She put her hands on his face, and Isa tried once more to offer her the blunt. She took it in this time, eyes lowering a bit before she exhaled it in his face.

"Absolutely not," Isa protested. "Fuck I look like using my girl on a lick? You use bitches that are expendable. Bitches who you willing to toss in the fire."

"Then it's not happening, because you bring any other woman around for the sake of"—Aria put her fingers up in air quotes—"*business* and I'm done. I'm not having it."

Isa blew out a breath of frustration and massaged his forehead as his eyes closed.

"This is exactly what I feel every time you walk out the door," Aria explained. "We take the risks together from now on. It's me and you. I'll be fine, Isa. Just tell me what you need me to do."

Ethic and Hendrix occupied the small space of the holding cell. They didn't speak as they faced off. Ethic dragged a slow hand down his beard before rolling forward, leaning onto his knees as he shook his head. He had been filtering his words for the past hour. He was trying his hardest to withhold the buildup of anger that he was feeling in this moment. Hendrix was the second young boy he had given a chance. Somehow they always disappointed him. He cuffed his knuckles, keeping his hands busy to avoid wringing Hendrix's neck. This second time was supposed to be different. This mentoring of sorts was supposed to work. He had tried to do things differently this time around, yet things had still ended in disaster. He had to stop getting his heart involved with these young boys. They didn't value what he tried to teach them enough to put action behind the lesson. When Ethic saw the silver bracelets close around Hendrix's wrists, his heart broke. His own arrest, he could handle that. He could beat that case like Ike beat Tina. His lawyer was on speed dial. He had no worries about that, but Hendrix . . . the loyal, witty, smart, and finessing-ass little nigga Henny had gotten caught red-handed with product and a loaded, unregistered weapon on him. He knew there was no walking away from that unscathed. Another good one lost to a cold world with a fucked-up system, and Ethic's soul was crying.

"What you have on you?" he finally asked, voice low, but the disappointment was loud.

"A quarter," Hendrix answered, head leaned against the wall.

Two hundred and fifty fentanyl pills.

Ethic blew out a breath and pulled up, back aligning as his face bent in turmoil. The opioid crisis that Michigan was fighting would make Hendrix's case high profile. Any judge he landed in front of would be eager to punish him hard.

"What did I tell you?" Ethic asked. "I told you to come to me. If you needed anything. I told you to—"

"I just wanted to earn my respect," Hendrix admitted.

Ethic's heart clenched because he knew respect was a currency on the streets of Flint. He had been there. He knew what it was like. He pinched the bridge of his nose and cleared his throat. "Niggas who don't respect themselves can't ever respect you, Henny. You don't even respect yourself selling that shit.

Not when you have access to better, to more. I've given you access. You should have utilized it."

"They gon' lock me up, ain't they?" Hendrix asked.

"I'ma do everything I can," Ethic stated. "But every day you not free, I'ma walk 'em down with you. I'ma be there. I didn't want to have to be there, though, Hendrix. You're hard-headed. Too fucking smart for your own good."

Hendrix lifted his chin and lowered his eyes because they were burning. He was terrified, and Ethic could see him fighting it.

"You'll tell Bella I'm sorry?" Hendrix asked.

It was like someone had hit Rewind. Déjà vu, only these words about his daughter were coming from Hendrix, not Messiah. Messiah had asked him to deliver a similar message to Morgan once before. He was always the courier of goodbyes when it came to his girls, and those messages were heavy.

Ethic nodded.

"We're not there yet. When we're there, I'll make sure you have a moment with her to say what you need to say. I'ma put the best lawyers around you."

"Don't waste your bread, man. I know what they about to hit me with," Hendrix said. "I came over your crib to kiss my girl tonight, man," Hendrix said, shaking his head.

"Lil' nigga, don't get brave," Ethic snickered.

A solemn Hendrix laughed as he shook his head. "They gonna throw me away, man," he said, eyes filling with emotion as he lowered his head. "I know niggas that went in for trying to feed they families who ain't never getting out. They won't ever even breathe free air again. They gon' do that to me. Put me in there, then forget about me."

"I'm not," Ethic said. "Every single day, you hear me? We gon' walk 'em down one at a time together. Get your mind right so they can't capture that. Your freedom is up here." Ethic tapped his temple. "I'ma do everything I can to make sure that don't happen, but if it comes down to it, you need to be strong. Your mental always got to be sharp. Hold your head up."

Hendrix squared his shoulders and stared Ethic in the eyes, clearing his throat to rid his overwhelm. The sound of the locks being buzzed open pulled his attention to the door of the cell, and Ethic stood as he saw Messiah's face. He was guided inside.

Ethic frowned.

"I'm assuming you the reason I'm in here," Ethic said. He had no idea that this was Morgan's doing. Messiah was the likely suspect. This had to be his doing. Something that had blown back on Ethic as a result of Messiah's carelessness. The assumption was fair. Messiah knew it, so he didn't take offense. He sat across from Henny.

"I don't really know what the fuck this is about, OG." Messiah looked over at Henny. "What you doing in here, lil' Henny?"

"I was at Ethic's when it went down. Fucking SWAT or something flew through there. Searched me. I was carrying," Henny stated.

"Carrying for who?" Messiah asked.

"Crew shit. You know the deal," Henny stated. "I'm deaf, blind, and dumb to that shit, though. I know how to stand on my own two."

"That's real shit," Messiah stated. "Look like we all gon' have to strap up our boots. Somebody want us out the way. Somebody close."

"Somebody too close," Ethic stated.

Ahmeek lay in bed, arms bent behind his head as he stared up at the ceiling of his loft. Her loft. Their loft. It had never felt lonelier. He couldn't predict where his life was going next, and it was torture. The thought of the unknown. The fallout behind the secret Morgan had kept was catastrophic. He had never felt an ache so deep. He felt the buzz of his phone, and he rose a bit to fish it out of his back pocket.

The Sun.

The name he stored Morgan's number under was exactly how he felt about her. She just melted shit inside him . . . warmed him. Today, she had burned him. In fact, she had burned them all. Morgan Atkins's truth had shone down on them like a one-hundred-degree day, showing no mercy. It took everything in him to hit the red button on her.

He powered off his phone and placed his eyes back on the ceiling. It would be a long night. A long life. Without Morgan. A knock at the door pulled him to his feet, and his brow bent, heart stalling a bit because not many people knew about the location of the loft. He knew it had to be Mo. She had called from outside his door, and now she was knocking. She was there to apologize. To tell him she loved him. To figure out how to work it out with Messiah as the twins' father and still keep Ahmeek in her life. They would fix the shit. They could because they loved each other too much to let the shit rot and die. That was the story he'd pieced together in his head before he even pulled open the door.

"Hi . . ."

The reality that greeted him on the other side threw him off. Livi stood before him, and Ahmeek felt like his insides were spilling out. He hated this shit. This feeling. Feeling anything, in fact. The lack of control he had over this entire situation made him uneasy. No one had ever manipulated his emotions before. Morgan Atkins was the first, and he promised himself she would be the last.

Ahmeek wasn't particularly happy to see her, but she was the perfect stroke for a bruised ego.

"I don't mean to pop up—"

"Yet here you are," he interrupted.

His crass response shocked her. "I just can't stop thinking about you," she admitted.

"It's four in the morning," Ahmeek said, frown so deep that it made Livi nervous. "You drove an hour . . ."

Livi loosened the belt to her tan trench coat, revealing neon-yellow lingerie, a full set because Livi wasn't a halfway bitch. If she did something, she did it correctly. Thong, lace bra, and the garter belt to match. See-through stiletto heels revealed white paint on her pretty toes. "I mean I really, really, missed you," she said. "I got niggas on my line all day and all night, but never you. When all I really want is you."

Somebody wanted him. Somebody needed him. He wondered if she felt the rejection Morgan made him feel. Had he put the same feeling of unimportance on her soul? If he did, he regretted that.

"That's how you feel?" he asked.

She nodded and stepped across his threshold, tracing the front of his jeans with her stiletto nail. She reached for his neck and leaned into his lips. Ahmeek moved his head slightly. Livi paused and stared at him. "One day, you're going to let me in, and everything you thought mattered won't even be a thought anymore."

He loomed over her like a gray cloud as storms of indecision took over his body. Livi placed the softest lips on his neck.

"I would be so good to you, Ahmeek," she whispered. "Just let me . . ."

TO BE CONTINUED IN
Butterfly 4
COMING SOON

DON'T FORGET TO CHECK OUT THE ETHIC SERIES.
BOOKS 1–5 ARE AVAILABLE NOW ON AMAZON.

Ash Army, make sure you head to
www.thebooklovers.co
to receive a sneak peek of *Butterfly 4* now!

-xoxo-
Ashley Antoinette

Oddball Dsgns

ASHLEY ANTOINETTE is one of the most successful female writers of her time. The feminine half of the popular married duo Ashley and JaQuavis, she has cowritten more than forty novels. Several of her titles have hit the *New York Times* bestseller list, but she is most widely regarded for her racy series The Prada Plan. Born in Flint, Michigan, she was bred with an innate street sense that she uses as motivation in her crime-filled writings.

f /authorashleyantoinette

𝕏 @Novelista

◎ @AshleyAntoinette

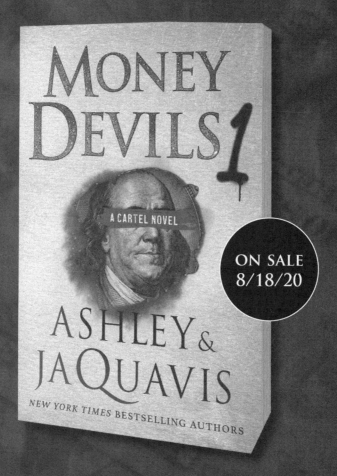